A Scan

In the past, when Lloyd had returned from a business trip, Olivia had raced into his arms and told him how much she'd missed him. She had pampered him and pandered to his every need. Not this time, though. She had given him a vague greeting without leaving her computer. This was a new Olivia; an Olivia who no longer needed him. She could see that her aloof attitude was worrying him; making him eager to please her. She would bide her time until he was desperate. And she was determined that day would come.

A Scandalous Affair

HOLLY GRAHAM

BLACK
lace

Black Lace novels contain sexual fantasies.
In real life, make sure you practise safe sex.

First published in 2000 by
Black Lace
Thames Wharf Studios,
Rainville Road, London W6 9HA

Reprinted 2000

Typeset by SetSystems Ltd, Saffron Walden, Essex
Printed and bound by Mackays of Chatham PLC

ISBN 0 352 33523 8

*All characters in this publication are fictitious and any
resemblance to real persons, living or dead, is purely
coincidental.*

Chapter One

'**W**arm and sensuous . . .'

The words weren't in upper case, but Olivia's gaze was drawn straight to them.

Sensuous. The choice of word pleased her.

Every morning, she switched on her computer to check her e-mail and every morning, there was a letter from Steve waiting for her.

If I don't meet you soon, he had written, *I shall be starving in a garret. All I can think about is you – and your warm and sensuous personality . . .*

Olivia corresponded with lots of people via e-mail but only Steve had the power to stir her emotions. She didn't really know why that was. He had a quick sense of humour which she liked. He was also perceptive to her moods. None of that explained the tingle that raced down her spine, though, or the way her heart began to beat a little faster when she saw his name in her mailbox. Nor did it explain the nights she lay in bed, wide awake, wondering about him, fantasising about having his body next to hers.

They had never met so she had no idea what he looked like. She knew from his letters that he was married with two young sons, and that he lived in Brighton. She knew he was thirty-two, four years older than her. And, like her, he was a writer.

It was their writing that had brought them together. Olivia was currently being hassled by her editor to finish her overdue biography on Chamberlain. Steve, a novelist, used political settings for his books, and they had first started to correspond when they found themselves researching the same Act of Parliament on the same Internet list. At first, they had argued good-naturedly about politics. It was only later that their mail had become more personal. At least, Steve's had. Olivia gave little away. Steve knew she was married and lived in London, but she guessed that his idea of her 'flat' bore no relation to her fashionable Kensington home. She used her pen-name, Jane Marshall, for her correspondence, so he couldn't know that she was Olivia Standish, wife of Lloyd Standish MP.

Steve's four novels were published under his Ronan King pen-name and, shortly after they began to correspond, Olivia bought them all. Finding them hadn't been easy; Ronan King wasn't on speaking terms with the best-seller list. She had hoped to see his picture on the covers, but he was only published in paperback. Each book followed a formula that combined mystery, intrigue and sex.

She read his letter again and lingered thoughtfully at the final paragraph.

I would love to be with you right now . . .

The mail they exchanged was innocent enough perhaps and yet there was an undercurrent of something deeper, or so it seemed to Olivia. Surely he was aware of it too. Was he sitting at his computer right now and thinking about her? Was he fantasising about touching her? He was more likely to be working, she decided. She should be working too. She had promised her editor the penultimate chapter by Friday and she was fast running out of relatives to bury. She tried to work, and spent long hours in front of her computer each day, but she simply couldn't concentrate for more than a few minutes at a stretch. It wasn't only Steve; it was Lloyd and the sheer frustration of life.

The phone on her desk rang, startling her.

She picked it up, half-expecting to hear the dreaded sound of her editor's voice.

'Hi, gorgeous!'

'Lloyd!' It was an unexpected pleasure to hear his voice.

'Listen, there's been a change of plan. I'll be back this evening after all.'

'Really? Oh, that's wonderful. I've missed you.'

He laughed softly. 'I've missed you, too.'

'We'll go out to dinner, shall we?'

'That would have been great, but I'll have Monty with me.'

'Oh, no.'

Monty – Sir Montague Aubrey – was another of Olivia's father's cronies, another that Lloyd had to suck up to if he wanted that place in the Cabinet.

'Sorry. He's a pain, I know, but he's a pain I happen to need at the moment. See if you can get Dorothy to rustle something up for us, will you?'

'Yes. Yes, of course.' She tried to hide her disappointment. At least he would be home.

'Thanks. I'd better go. See you later.'

The connection was cut before she could reply.

She kept the phone to her ear for long moments and listened to the insistent burr of the dial tone. All it did was increase the longing that never left her these days.

Unable to even think about her work now, she padded barefoot to their bedroom.

Warm and sensuous. Would Lloyd agree with that? There was no need to ask; she knew he wouldn't.

She opened the wardrobe doors and ran long, slim

fingers down the sleeves and across the lapels of his suits. Expensive, well-cut suits. She lifted a sleeve and held it against her warm cheek. If she breathed deeply, she could just detect the lingering trace of his cologne.

She dropped the sleeve and moved to sit on the stool in front of the mirror. The face gazing back at her was too familiar for objectivity. Her skin was pale, almost translucent, giving her an appearance of fragility. Her face was heart-shaped, almost elfin, dominated by blue eyes. Her blonde hair was cut short, curling around a long, slender neck. She looked like a coy goody-two-shoes – whereas nothing could have been further from the truth.

She stood up to survey her figure, adopting different poses in front of the mirror. Overall, she was satisfied. She was slim, and had always had a boyish appearance in her youth but, much to her relief, her full, perfectly rounded breasts had soon spoiled that illusion. Her waist and hips were slim, her legs long and slender. The simple blue dress she wore was fitted around her waist but was loose on her hips and breasts. She showed no cleavage but the material accentuated the shape of her breasts as she moved. She had a good figure and was attractive enough. She had been described as beautiful many times. She wasn't sexy, though. Men loved to have her dangling off their arms like a piece of expensive jewellery they could show off, but they didn't go wild with desire for her.

She ran a finger over her breast, outlining the shape, and her nipple stiffened at her touch. With a sigh, she moved away from the mirror and threw herself face down on their bed. The ache in her body started in her stomach and travelled down past her navel. She longed for the touch of a man. She longed for Lloyd's touch.

He would be home soon. She would feel him inside her that night.

Unfortunately, the thought did nothing to lessen the ache.

They had been married for three months, and every day Olivia's craving for fulfilment had increased. It was becoming unbearable.

She reminded herself that she should be doing some work but all she could think about was Lloyd. She remembered the first time she spoke to him.

As a huge fan of her father's, an outspoken member of the House, Lloyd was a frequent visitor to their home. Oddly, though, his visits always seemed to coincide with Olivia's absences. She'd almost missed him this time too. She'd been on her way out but had stopped on hearing her father's voice raised in anger.

'This could end your career, Lloyd! How could you be such a bloody fool? The slightest excuse, the slightest hint of sleaze, and they'll come down on you like a ton of bricks. To be caught on video like this –' Lost for words, he gave his desk a furious thump.

'They're amateurs.' Lloyd spoke more calmly. 'And they've been paid off. I'm sure that's the last we'll hear of it.'

'You're sure?' her father echoed furiously. 'How in hell's name can you be sure? You don't even know who's behind it.'

'I have to believe we've heard the end of this. There's nothing we can do about it now.'

'God, Lloyd, you're a bloody fool. A damn good career carved out for yourself and you throw it all away with this – this smut!'

Olivia was intrigued.

'You need to marry again.' Her father's voice was resigned now, but there was a note of steel in it that Olivia knew well. 'You have to be squeaky clean, Lloyd.'

'Well, yes, but a wife? Damn it all, James, you can't go out and find a wife to order.'

5

'It wouldn't be the first time it's been done,' James said dryly. 'And as for this bloody video –' His chair squeaked, as if he was spinning round to look out of the window. 'There's providence. Margaret's having a bonfire. The best thing we can do is burn this video and pray to whatever god we know that there aren't more of the same. Meanwhile, you need to live the life of a monk. Got that?'

Olivia was burning with curiosity. Normally she knocked on her father's study door and waited to be invited, but today she simply knocked and stepped inside.

'Oh, I'm terribly sorry. I didn't realise you were busy.' She turned a bright smile on Lloyd. 'It's Lloyd Standish, isn't it? I've seen you on TV.'

She put out her hand and it was immediately swamped by his. His hand was large and strong, the fingers firm. It was tanned, too.

Confused by the effect his touch had on her, she turned to her father.

'I was looking for Mother.'

'In the garden, sweetheart.' The endearment and the forced smile were for the benefit of their visitor.

There was little love lost between Olivia and her father. As the only child of disinterested parents, Olivia had always felt the need to rebel, if only to gain some attention. The night she was arrested on a drugs charge and hauled off to spend the night in a stinking cell, she knew she had gone too far. That was almost ten years ago, but he had never forgiven her.

'Here,' he added grimly, 'you can tell her to burn this old thing. And make sure she does!'

'Of course.' She took the video from him and turned her smile on Lloyd again. 'Good to meet you, Mr Standish.'

She left her father's study, raced up the stairs to her

6

room, swapped the video for one of her own, and went outside.

It never failed to amaze Olivia that her mother could take no interest in her husband, daughter, friends, or life in general for that matter, and yet could be so passionate about her garden. It flourished beneath her tender, loving care and even Olivia had to admit to a grudging admiration. She doubted if any weed would dare to show its face.

'Father wants you to burn this,' Olivia explained.

The video was thrown on to the bonfire and was soon a melting mass amid the leaves. No questions were asked. Olivia supposed Margaret knew better than to get involved in her husband's affairs. Or – and she suspected this was more likely – Margaret simply wasn't interested.

Olivia watched the video burn. It was a folk festival that she had recorded from the television. As all it had shown was a bunch of drunken, fiddle-playing females that she had never heard of, it was no loss.

It was late that night before she had a chance to inspect the video her father had given her.

A whole gamut of emotions raged within her as she watched it; she was shocked, thrilled, scandalised, excited –

She watched it over and over, all through the night. By morning, she had one aim in life. Lloyd Standish wanted – or needed – a wife and Olivia was determined to be that woman.

Looking back, it had been easy to seduce him. Olivia did her research well, 'bumped' into him a few times and put him in the position where he either had to buy her lunch or appear very rude. Lloyd, the perfect gentleman, or simply eager to win her father's approval, had opted for the former. They discussed politics and Olivia thanked her lucky stars she was so knowledgeable on the subject. They even fell in love. That was a totally unexpected bonus.

Now, she had exactly what she wanted. She had been married to Lloyd for three months. It wasn't a new feeling as Olivia was used to getting what she wanted, but it wasn't a particularly good feeling. She should have been somewhere up on cloud nine, not feeling lonely and frustrated, and aching for his body.

She got off the bed and went to her jewellery box. There was a secret compartment at the bottom that was just large enough to hold a video. She took it out and ran her hands over the case.

Before their wedding, she had watched the film many times, but she hadn't seen it since. It might be interesting to watch it now.

She put it in the machine, sat back on her bed and hit the remote control.

The interference, she knew from experience, lasted four minutes and fourteen seconds. Even the dark screen, bursting with specks of white light, excited her. Her skin grew warm.

Oxford Street appeared on the screen; an innocent enough scene. Shoppers and sightseers pushed and shoved their way along the crowded street for a full minute and twenty-six seconds.

Olivia was already breathing fast. She brought her knees up to her chin and held her ankles tight. The screen went black momentarily, then she let out a sigh when Lloyd's face suddenly filled her television screen.

When she thought about it, which wasn't often, Olivia was always shocked to remember that he was sixteen years older than her. He didn't look it. He had a handsome face that was all angles and planes, a firm, determined chin, beautiful dark eyebrows, searching eyes, and an air of self-confidence. It was the face of a man who knew exactly where life was taking him.

The camera pulled away and Olivia saw the girl

lying on the bed. She was naked. Her long legs writhed so that the crimson sheet hid parts of her body at times. Her hips were quite large, and her waist narrow by comparison. Her skin had the golden glow that only an exotic sun can provide. Her hair – God, her hair was amazing. A tumbling cascade of dark auburn curls. Her breasts were full and heavy, the nipples rosy and hard. Eyes, dark green and catlike, danced with mischief and promise.

The camera flicked back to Lloyd's face for a brief moment – just long enough to see the hunger in his eyes. Who could blame him? This girl was incredible.

The first time Olivia watched the video, she had expected him to go to the girl, and had been surprised when he hadn't. Why didn't he? How could he resist?

Now, Olivia's feelings were different. Jealousy formed a tight knot in her stomach. She was jealous of this tantalising stranger. Even more surprising, she was jealous of Lloyd, too. She wished she could touch the girl, caress the smooth, tanned skin, lose her fingers in those thick auburn curls, and touch the springy auburn hair that hid the woman's secret place. Olivia had never known a woman's touch, had never wanted to, and her longing for this stranger shocked her. She watched, mesmerised, as the camera captured the girl's hand moving slowly to her breast. The stranger caressed her breast as if showing its perfection to an audience. Olivia felt her own breasts tingle in response. She let her thumb briefly stroke them through the thin fabric of her dress, and her nipples hardened with desire. The girl ran her finger along her lips, then sucked on it. Laughter danced in her eyes as she, very slowly, circled her rosy nipples with her moist finger. Olivia watched enviously and fought the desire to touch her own tingling breasts again.

The camera angle changed abruptly to spotlight

another girl. A blonde, this time, slimmer than her companion, with pale skin and smaller breasts.

Olivia hit the button to freeze the frame. She wanted to savour the moment before this new beauty moved with a catlike elegance that Olivia had watched so many times before to join her companion on that huge bed.

Unable to wait, she let the video run.

The blonde moved with the slender suppleness of an athlete. Smiling at her friend, she kneeled on the bed in an almost childlike pose. The curve of her spine was delicious. Her bottom was perfectly rounded.

The two girls couldn't have been more different, yet both were stunningly sexy. Their bodies – one deeply tanned, the other milky white – could have been moulded for the other. The blonde girl leaned forward and they kissed, causing a shudder of excitement to run down Olivia's spine. One long kiss, then brief, pecking kisses on the lower lip.

'Touch me.' This whispered plea came from the red-haired girl. Apart from the rustling of the satin sheet, this was the first sound on the video. Not the last, though, Olivia thought. Oh no, certainly not the last.

Impatient now, Olivia hit the fast-forward button. She knew exactly where to stop the film.

The screen flickered momentarily, then she saw the girls caressing themselves. There was a deep reverence in their touch. Their pleasure was obvious.

Olivia envied them. Her own body ached for a similar touch. How would it feel, she wondered, to be caressed by those soft hands? Her own feminine skin caressed by the same soft touch . . .

The urge to pleasure herself was almost overwhelming but Olivia resisted. She wanted to save herself and take her pleasure from Lloyd.

She concentrated on the television screen, waiting. Her breathing quickened.

A deep groan – the sound she had come to dream of – provoked a sharp cry. If only Lloyd would give voice to his longing for her. Every night she hoped to hear a similar sound from him and every night she was disappointed. With Olivia, he was a silent, almost uninterested lover.

The camera turned on him, capturing the intense longing etched across his face. Hunger burned in his eyes as he watched the girls pleasure themselves. For a brief moment, his eyes closed, as if he could bear the torment no longer. Then he flicked them open again. Olivia guessed he couldn't bear to miss a single touch.

'Oh –' That deep, guttural groan again. 'Oh, please – enough!'

Olivia held her breath.

Of their own volition, her hands touched her aching breasts. She rubbed a thumb across her already hard nipple, the material of her dress providing the only barrier. Oh, how she longed for him. How she yearned to see such desire in his eyes when he looked at her. How she craved to hear him voice his hunger for her body.

She sighed, suffering as he suffered.

The camera pulled back, revealing his strong neck and broad shoulders. Then lower, so that his chest, smooth and free from hair, was on view.

'Lloyd –' His name escaped her lips as she finally saw the chains that held him captive.

A thick, heavy chain held his wrists firmly behind his back and wrapped around his waist. The chain was padlocked to a huge link in the wall behind him.

Olivia was aware of the warm dampness spreading between her thighs.

'Oh, please! Come on, girls. I'm begging you!' His pleading increased.

The camera pulled back further, showing him in his naked splendour.

Olivia's eyes, as always, were drawn to the longest, hardest, most beautiful cock she had ever seen. As if it possessed a will of its own, it jerked spasmodically, trying to reach the objects of its desire. Moisture glistened on the purple tip.

Olivia's gaze travelled down his well-muscled thighs. His legs were apart, fastened at the ankles by those same heavy chains. His groans, his cries, his pleading became more urgent and more angry. Sweat glistened all over his beautiful body.

'Mercy!' he snapped out suddenly.

Olivia felt a delicious sensation hit her navel at the command. It was obviously a pre-arranged signal because both girls immediately jumped off the bed and crossed the room to him. The blonde-haired girl quickly released the chains while the red-haired girl kissed the marks made on his skin.

'You horny little bitches!' he cursed them, laughing as he pushed the red-haired girl on to her knees.

Freedom had brought him relief. Olivia knew there would be no pleading now. Lloyd was in command.

'Suck it,' he ordered, his hands in the girl's hair as he guided his engorged penis to the perfect 'O' her lips had formed.

Olivia squirmed in her own dampness. It was like watching a stranger. She couldn't imagine him speaking or acting in such a way.

'All of it,' he growled. 'Take all of it. Oh, yes, you like that, don't you? You like a big fat cock to suck.'

The girl nodded. Her mouth was too busy to allow an answer.

'Feeling left out, Julie?' he teased the blonde-haired girl.

Her wistful expression answered for her and he laughed.

'You shall have your fill. Meanwhile –' he grabbed her hand '– cup my balls. Oh yes –'

His breathing quickened and he grabbed her by the hair.

'Lick them. Lick my balls.'

Olivia could feel her own moisture soaking into her panties. Her breathing was more rapid, her skin warm. It was foolish to torture herself in this way, but she couldn't drag her gaze from the screen.

The girls' heads bobbed vigorously as they licked and sucked. Lloyd offered words of encouragement, and gave them a mix of compliments and orders in short, ragged bursts of breath. It was the expressions flitting across his face that fascinated Olivia, though, a tantalising mixture of pleasure and agony.

She hit the fast-forward button again.

Now, the three lovers were lying on the bed. Lloyd's skin was dark when compared to the milky whiteness of Julie's, and the golden tan of the red-haired girl. The girls – Olivia swallowed hard – the girls were worshipping every inch of Lloyd's body as if it were a holy shrine. They caressed it with their fingers, their lips, and their greedy tongues. Occasionally, the girls kissed each other. It was obvious that the sight excited Lloyd.

Olivia wound the video forwards. Her arousal was making her skin burn. Jealousy, anger and resentment warred for supremacy, but really, it was the emptiness that hurt.

Lloyd was using his lips and tongue to drive Julie wild with excitement.

Olivia hit fast-forward.

Lloyd was guiding his penis into the red-haired girl's secret place – the pleasure he was giving the girls tore at Olivia's heart. It should have been her!

Olivia slid her hands up her thighs. With one finger, she moved her white panties aside and touched herself. It was the lightest of touches but the heat coursed through her veins.

'No!'

13

Angry with herself, she hit the remote control and the television screen went black.

It was Lloyd's touch she hungered for, not her own. And she would damn well have it.

Dinner was a long, tedious affair.

Dorothy, who Olivia suspected was as eager for Lloyd's body as she was, had, as usual, done her best to impress. She had succeeded, too.

Shortly after they were married, they had contacted an agency to employ a cleaner and Dorothy, who looked nothing like a cleaner, whatever they were supposed to look like, had come to them. When, in an emergency, she had been persuaded to cook for them, Lloyd insisted they take her on full-time. She was efficiency personified, impossible to fault, but Olivia disliked her intensely. With Lloyd, Dorothy maintained a polite but warm friendliness. With Olivia, she was distant to the point of rudeness. She was in her late thirties, quite a plain-looking thing with her scrubbed face and gleaming, unpolished fingernails. Olivia doubted if Dorothy had ever been called beautiful in her life. She had that certain something, though. That certain something that men found sexy. That certain something that Olivia knew she lacked.

Sir Montague claimed he had an early start in the morning but, despite this, he wasn't going to be rushed. He enjoyed every mouthful of pâté, chatted his way through the beef, drooled over Dorothy's sorbet, then attacked the cheeseboard as if he hadn't been fed for a month.

'I don't suppose you need to watch your figure, Olivia. I'm sure Lloyd does that for you.' He slapped his thigh at the joke, then added in a stage whisper to Lloyd, 'You're a lucky sod!'

'Indeed I am, Monty.' To prove the point, Lloyd leaned across the table and kissed Olivia.

'I'm the lucky one,' Olivia responded dutifully, exchanging a knowing glance with Lloyd.

They chatted over coffee, then Lloyd and Monty withdrew to Lloyd's study.

'I won't be late,' Lloyd said in an aside.

Olivia hoped not. She was so hungry for his touch, it was driving her crazy. Throughout the evening she had been watching him; the way he ate, the way he spoke and how he emphasised points with his hands. His every movement had excited her. She longed for his touch, and she longed to feel him hard and insistent inside her. Her whole body was tense with longing.

Having said goodnight to Monty, Olivia went upstairs to their bedroom. It pleased her to see the signs of Lloyd's presence. There was a pile of loose change on the dressing table that he had taken from his pockets when he changed for dinner. With this were two tickets for a concert given last night. She wondered briefly who he had taken.

Olivia undressed quickly, wrapped a large white towel around herself and went to run her bath. She poured a large dollop of camomile extract in and watched the water foam.

Letting the towel fall to the floor, she turned off the taps and stepped into the bath. The sudden warmth brought goose-bumps to her skin, making her shiver. She lay back, resting her head on a small air-filled pillow, and enjoyed the unexpected tickling sensation caused by the sudden heat to her vulva. The bubbles foamed to tease her nipples. Her skin felt soft and smooth from the moisturising foam, and she slid her hands over the curve of her breasts. Dipping her hands beneath the water, she stroked her abdomen, and down to the hair of her mound. Her breathing quickened in anticipation. Soon it would be Lloyd's turn to marvel at her soft, smooth skin . . .

When she finally stepped out of the water, her body

felt heavy and tired. She wrapped her towel around herself, shivering slightly as droplets of water trickled down her spine and legs. Once dry, she put on her scarlet satin robe – a gift from Lloyd – and padded barefoot down the stairs. There would be a bottle of wine chilling in the fridge. It would wake her up. Besides, Lloyd always enjoyed a glass of wine as he unwound after a long day.

As soon as she reached the bottom of the stairs, she heard his voice. It was difficult not to hear it. Curious, she walked towards his study.

'What more can I do?' he demanded furiously. It sounded to Olivia that he banged his fist on the desk. 'It was – suggested –' his voice was heavy with sarcasm '– that I find myself a wife. I've done that.'

'A very beautiful wife,' Monty pointed out mildly.

'Beautiful? Oh, yes. She's beautiful all right. She's also bloody demanding.' His voice hardened. 'And no, I don't mean in the bedroom. She wants and expects my undivided attention. For me, this is a bloody inconvenient marriage of convenience. For Olivia, it's everything. She's suffocating me, Monty.'

Olivia leaned against the wall for support. Her knees began to buckle, and she had to fight off waves of nausea.

'If I hadn't been pushed into marriage,' Lloyd went on, 'I could have chosen someone older, someone more mature, someone with a life of their own –'

Olivia didn't stop to hear more.

The bottle of wine forgotten, she fled to her bedroom – their bedroom.

She climbed into bed and switched off the light. *A bloody inconvenient marriage of convenience.* She felt sick. She lay still, curled up in the foetal position. Everything was a sham. Her life was nothing more than a lie. *A bloody inconvenient marriage of convenience.*

When Lloyd came into their bedroom, Olivia couldn't

16

move. She felt the bed sag as he got into bed beside her and, within minutes, the regular pattern of his breathing told her that he was asleep.

It was almost dawn before Olivia fell into a restless sleep.

Chapter Two

There were a few e-mails waiting when Olivia went online to check. Nothing important or, more accurately, nothing from Steve.

She brought some of his recent mail on to the screen and read it again.

It would be wonderful if we could meet – just for coffee or something.

Wonderful.

Would it be wonderful? Pointless was probably a more apt description, Olivia suspected. She was curious about him, but nothing more. Curious about him in an unusual sort of way, though, she had to confess. She often wondered what he looked like – probably bald and fat – and sometimes, when she couldn't sleep, she found herself wondering what sort of lover he was.

She could easily arrange to meet him. She could take the train to Brighton. There was no point, though. She wasn't that curious. She was simply restless. At one time, her work had been everything. Not now. Lloyd was everything. Or had been. A week had passed since she had overheard him describe their marriage as one of convenience and the pain had subsided. She was more angry than anything else now.

She stabbed at her keyboard and brought more of Steve's mail on to the screen. His letters, and she had kept every one, were in a separate folder. She read each one and tried to decide at which point their correspondence had become more personal. It was impossible; the shift had been too gradual. A month ago, he had given her his telephone number – 'in case your Internet server's down again'. Olivia hadn't returned the favour.

Seconds later his number was memorised. She had no intention of calling him . . .

It might be fun, though. It would satisfy her curiosity. She couldn't work, so it would pass a few minutes. Feeling reckless, she tapped in 141 to withhold her own number, then called his. It was answered almost immediately, taking her by surprise.

'Steve?'

'Yes?'

'It's – er, Jane.' Just in time she remembered to use her pen-name, the name by which Steve knew her. 'I'm suffering from writer's block,' she said with a tinkling laugh, 'and I wondered if a chat with a fellow writer would help.'

'What a lovely surprise!' His voice was deeper than she had imagined, and it had a vaguely disturbing, sleepy quality to it.

'Any tips for writer's block?' she asked, and he laughed.

The deep, undeniably attractive sound sent a shiver down Olivia's spine.

'Take the day off,' he said immediately. 'When I can't settle to work, I like to do something – stimulating. Physically stimulating,' he qualified that.

Olivia felt the heat fly to her cheeks.

'Like what?' she asked.

'Any physical activity that you enjoy. What do you enjoy, Jane?'

'Like jogging round the park?' she asked, side-stepping his question.

'A bit too physical for my tastes,' he said, laughing softly.

There was a long pause which should have been uncomfortable but wasn't.

'I have to visit Brighton on business – next Monday.'

The lie came from nowhere, prompted by goodness knew what.

'Really? Hey, that's great. I'll buy you lunch. Will you have time?'

She hesitated only briefly.

'I don't think I'll have time for lunch.' If he was awful, she would never cope with lunch. 'A quick drink would be good though.'

'I'll look forward to it. We can finalise the arrangements by e-mail.' Another pause. 'I've been longing to meet you,' he added quietly.

'Why?'

'I don't know.' He sounded genuinely baffled. 'There's something about you. I know we've never met, but I feel as if I've known you for years. Your letters fascinate me. They make me laugh, they make me think, they inspire me.'

His letters affected her, too. They often made her laugh.

'My current heroine is based on you,' he told her.

Olivia didn't know what to make of that. Having read his novels, and given that he seemed to have a penchant for the whore, she knew exactly what his heroines spent most of their time doing.

'What's she like?'

'Wonderful, of course. I'm crazy about her.' He laughed. 'She's strong, caring, witty, passionate and sexy. God, is she sexy!'

'Perhaps we shouldn't meet then,' Olivia remarked coolly. 'I'd hate your illusions to be shattered.'

'If they're shattered,' Steve said seriously, 'I might stand a chance of getting some work done. I'm doing precious little at the moment. I can't get you off my mind for a second.'

'I have to go, Steve.' His frankness made her panic. She, too, was struggling not to think about him. 'E-mail me about meeting. OK?'

She hung up.

It was absurd. She had never laid eyes on him, but so often in the past she had wished he would make love to her.

But it wasn't only Steve. Yesterday, while out shopping, she had stepped into a lift with her mind on the shoes she intended to buy. She had taken one look at the lift attendant and – wallop. He had looked about ten years older than her, and had a strong, powerful body. His hair had been thinning slightly, and he'd been nothing to write home about, but she had been close enough to smell his highly arousing male scent. She had wished he would stop the lift between floors, to take her by force.

'What is wrong with me?' she murmured, but all was silent.

What had prompted her to arrange a meeting with Steve? What did she want from him? Was she looking for love? But she loved Lloyd. Didn't she? She had loved Lloyd, and love didn't die overnight. Was she looking for someone to love her? But she had believed Lloyd loved her. She certainly wasn't looking for romance. She didn't trust romance. Revenge? Was this a pathetic attempt at getting back at Lloyd? Sex? But she wasn't going to have sex with a perfect stranger. Or was she?

* * *

Lloyd cursed as he failed to miss a clump of nettles growing across the towpath. Dusk was falling – he didn't want to risk being seen around the marina in daylight – and it was getting difficult to see. He had taken a taxi and had thought, wrongly, that it would be pleasant to walk the last mile of the journey.

The *Sheba* was moored in its usual spot which did nothing to improve his mood. To get to it, he had to clamber across the *Lucinda May*, a huge narrow boat that belonged to Ivan, the owner of the marina.

Like the *Lucinda May*, the *Sheba*'s paintwork gleamed, even in the failing light.

He was stepping on to the *Lucinda May* when the smiling, fresh-faced Ivan appeared.

'Oh, hi, Lloyd.'

'Hi,' Lloyd responded somewhat irritably. Ivan had a habit of recounting his business deals to anyone fool enough to listen and Lloyd wasn't in the mood for small talk.

'Linda's in. And cooking by the smell of it.'

'Thanks.' Lloyd jumped on to the *Sheba*'s deck and, sure enough, the strong smell of curry wafted up to him.

Ivan had disappeared and Lloyd stepped down into the *Sheba*'s galley. He remembered to duck; he just didn't duck low enough.

'Shit!' He put a hand to his head, checked to make sure he hadn't drawn blood, and cursed again. 'Shit, shit and shit! Christ albloodymighty, Linda! Why you have to live on this death-trap of a boat is beyond me!'

'I'm always telling you to duck.' Laughing, she reached up and kissed his forehead. 'Sit down – before you really hurt yourself.'

'I have damn well hurt myself!' Still rubbing his head, Lloyd dropped down on to the couch that doubled as Linda's bed.

How people lived on these things was a mystery to

him, but he wasn't going to risk saying so again. Linda was passionate about her home and once she started on her favourite subject, there was no stopping her.

'I haven't seen you for ages,' she said, turning away from him to stir whatever was in the saucepan – a hotchpotch of leftovers mixed with curry powder, he suspected.

'I've been busy.'

'And how does married life suit you?'

'It doesn't!'

She laughed.

'No, I don't suppose it does. Hungry?'

He wasn't, but he knew that, despite the somewhat off-putting smell, her curries were delicious.

'I'll have a spoonful. Thanks.'

Linda found her two cleanest plates and split the curry fifty-fifty. After searching for two clean forks, she gave up and handed Lloyd his plate and a spoon.

'You really know how to live, don't you?' he said dryly.

'It all tastes the same,' she answered with a careless shrug.

It was like old times. As university students, they had often sat tucking into curries and drinking cold beer. They had been an item for three years and had remained good friends. Intimate friends. On leaving university, they gave each other up to do their own thing: Lloyd to work his way into politics, Linda to concentrate on her painting.

She hadn't changed much since those days. Half a dozen grey hairs had appeared in the midst of the dark, and there were a few tiny lines around her eyes, but she still had that 'student' look about her. She wore clothes that she rescued from Oxfam shops and jewellery that she made herself.

'I've got problems,' Lloyd told her, getting straight to

the point of his visit. 'There was some trouble with a video. I paid them off, but –'

'Blackmail? Oh, I'm intrigued.'

'An occupational hazard,' he muttered. 'Anyway, they now want more money, of course. They're threatening to approach Olivia.'

'Ah!'

'I couldn't give a toss about that,' he said, 'but I refuse to watch my career go down the can for the sake of five minutes spent with a couple of whores.'

'And? What does this have to do with me?'

'I don't know who the hell I'm dealing with,' he explained. 'They're amateurs, that much is obvious, but apart from that, I don't have a clue. In my position, it's difficult to get outside help, but I was thinking about your brother – the private detective. He's trustworthy, isn't he?'

'Peter? Well, yes. But I'm not sure he's much good. He does a lot of divorce stuff – you know, snapping away with his Nikon to prove adultery – and he does a cracking Philip Marlowe impression. But he's not what you'd call successful.'

'Yes, well, beggars can't be choosers. Of course, I can't use my usual legal people on this one, you understand. Would you give me his address?'

'Of course.' She took his empty plate from him and dumped everything in the sink before tearing off the corner of an old newspaper, grabbing a pen and scribbling down an address and phone number. 'Here. He'll be glad of the business.'

She stuck the scrap of paper in his pocket.

'Are you staying?'

He hadn't intended to, but – well, what the hell.

'For an hour or so.' He nodded.

'Good.' She eased off his jacket. 'I've been having to make do with Ivan.' She jerked her head in the direction

24

of the *Lucinda May*. 'He spoils me to death and I love him to bits, but he doesn't have your staying power.'

Lloyd was helping her take off his tie when her mobile phone rang.

'Ignore it,' he murmured.

'Can't. It might be business.'

She jumped away from him and found her phone beneath a pile of clothes.

The call went on and on, and she smiled apologetically at Lloyd as she tried, without success, to end it.

Lloyd began to wish he was back in the warmth and comfort of his hotel. One of the guests, a petite redhead, had given him an inviting smile. On the other hand, Linda was a known quantity. What you saw was what you got, and what you got was good, uncomplicated sex. She was worth the wait.

'Sorry,' she said, when she finally finished her call. 'That was a woman who commissioned a portrait of her dog – yes, I know, but it pays the mooring fees. Anyway, she tends to gush a bit.'

'I wish you'd gush all over me.' Lloyd grabbed her round the waist and she laughed knowingly.

'That will depend on whether or not you're very, very good to me.'

'Oh, I will be.'

What he liked about Linda was that she knew what he enjoyed and, unlike some women, was more than happy to indulge him. It worked both ways though. He knew what she liked, too. He knew that, initially, she liked to be kissed. He knew it excited her to feel his tongue probing deep inside her mouth.

As he kissed her, she fumbled with his trousers, finally lowering the zip. She tasted of hot, spicy curry. Lloyd supposed he did, too.

He offered no resistance as she pushed him down on to the couch then lifted her dress. No matter how cold it got on this Godforsaken boat, she never wore any underwear. Lloyd wondered briefly if she possessed any, but he forgot about it as she took off her dress. Her body was familiar to him but it always came as a pleasant surprise. She had large hips and breasts, strong thighs, and the tiniest waist he had ever seen. His cock stiffened with anticipation.

The boat was cluttered with junk, but Linda carefully hung his jacket, shirt, trousers and tie on a rail. Shoes, socks and boxer shorts, however, were hurled to the floor to land on top of her dress.

'God, it's good to see you, Lloyd!' Beneath her appreciative gaze, his dick stiffened still more. 'I should be painting you instead of screwing you.'

For a moment, Lloyd thought she was seriously considering this. With her back to him though, she straddled his chest and ran her tongue along his hot shaft.

'You always taste so damn good,' she murmured, taking more and more of him into her mouth.

Delicious shudders ran through his body as he felt her teeth. He gripped her waist to prevent her moving, and closed his eyes to enjoy the exquisite sensations caused by her mouth, teeth and tongue.

'Olivia's a lucky cow, having this at her disposal,' Linda said.

He knew her well enough to know she spoke with no trace of jealousy. There was no need, he thought grimly. Olivia had never tasted him. Olivia had never fastened her lips around his cock and taken the full length of him into her mouth as Linda was doing.

Lloyd gripped her waist tighter and lifted his hips off the coach to thrust deep into her throat. She lowered herself on to his chest so that Lloyd could feel her hot, wet flesh against him. He parted her buttocks and traced circles around her anus with his fingers, making her gasp. He began to probe her gently and she went wild. She sucked and licked on his prick while pushing

26

back and wriggling on his finger. He probed more deeply and she cried out with pleasure.

'I need to feel you inside me,' she gasped.

She swung round to face him and, holding his penis, she sank down on to it.

'Oh, Lloyd –'

'Has it been a long time?'

'Last night, but only Ivan.'

Lloyd acknowledged a childish sense of satisfaction on hearing that Ivan – the man with the Midas touch – was no good in the sack. He was getting far more satisfaction from Linda's body, though.

She rode him slowly, then teased him by remaining perfectly still, her head thrown back and her eyes closed. Lloyd's cock jerked inside her and her movements became more urgent. She rode him vigorously. He could feel her muscles contracting around his cock until her orgasm had her crying out his name over and over again. With a grateful gasp that he found touching, she collapsed on top of him.

'God, I needed that!'

'Mmm. And you know what I need.'

'Patience is a virtue, Lloyd,' she teased.

'I know. Unfortunately, I possess neither patience nor virtues. Come here. Let me taste you.'

Knees bent, she straddled herself across his face and lowered herself gently, sighing when his warm tongue probed her opening.

Lloyd's tongue darted in and out, pushing, probing. Linda inserted a finger and he could feel her long nail scraping along his tongue. He loved the taste of her, revelled in her warm, sweet wetness on his lips. The way she used her hands – one working with his tongue, the other caressing her breasts – was so erotic. The ache in his cock was becoming unbearable and he reached down to rub it. It was hard and throbbing. He was torn between the thrill of watching her caress herself, and the strong desire to feel her lips around his cock again. From the way she writhed with pleasure, pushing down harder on to his tongue, he knew she was close to orgasm again and the knowledge thrilled him.

'Thirsty work?' she asked, her voice husky with excitement.

'Very! Oh, God – Linda, yes –'

She lifted herself so that his tongue was inches away from her throbbing sex. Lloyd felt the deep shudder that shook her body as she parted her labia, exposing herself to him.

'Now, Linda! Oh –'

Her urine was hot on his face. It spilled down his chin, and on to his neck and chest – hot, slightly sticky, and so improper. When the spurt slowed to a trickle and then to nothing, Lloyd lifted his head to smear his chin on her thighs. He licked her clean.

Feeling as if his body would explode, he lifted her off him so that she was on her knees with her back to him. He plunged a finger into her anus while rubbing his throbbing cock. The tip glistened and he smeared the moisture around her anus. With his hand as guide, he nudged her forbidden entry with his cock, and then pushed, very slowly, but he was far too excited to hold back for long. He plunged deep inside her, making her cry out. He withdrew, almost to the tip, plunged again, felt her muscles tight around him, and groaned with a heady mixture of pleasure and pain. He withdrew. He plunged.

'Faster, Lloyd,' she pleaded.

He held her hips and obeyed. He was so, so close.

There was nothing passive about Linda; there never had been. While he pounded into her, her fingers sought her clitoris and she caressed herself. While she pushed back hard on his cock, he could sense her fingers working at a frenzied speed. All the while his thrusting kept pace. . . .

When she reached orgasm, the wave after wave of shudders that shook her body brought Lloyd to a hot, burning climax of his own.

Spent, sweating and exhausted, they collapsed on the couch.

'God, I've missed you, Lloyd!'

Their breathing was slowing to a more normal pace when the door opened and someone stepped down to the galley.

'It's only – Oh!' Ivan's face flushed with embarrassment. He looked at his feet, saw their abandoned clothes, and fixed his gaze on the stove. 'Sorry. I heard someone stepping off the *Lucinda* and assumed you'd left, Lloyd. Er – sorry.'

'If you've finished apologising, make yourself useful and get us a drink.' Linda sat up and brushed her damp hair away from her face. 'There should be a bottle of wine at the back of the cupboard.'

Ivan looked grateful to be given something to do and Lloyd thought he spent far longer than necessary finding the bottle.

Having inspected it, he said in a voice that was slightly higher than normal, 'I think we can do better than this.'

He left them alone and Lloyd wondered if he was giving them time alone – to get dressed, perhaps. If he was, it didn't work. They were too exhausted to move.

Ivan returned, brandishing a bottle of champagne and three glasses.

The pop of the cork brought Lloyd slowly back to reality. Linda too, it seemed. As if waking from a dream, she stretched luxuriously.

'You heard someone stepping off the *Lucinda*?' she said with a sudden frown. 'Who was that? We haven't had visitors.'

'I don't know,' Ivan answered. 'I assumed it was Lloyd leaving. That's why I came.'

'Really?' Linda smiled knowingly. 'Feeling horny, Ivan?'

Lloyd suspected Ivan was having too many problems pouring their drinks, and handing them over without actually looking at their nakedness to feel horny. While he sympathised slightly, at least Ivan could take comfort from the fact that he was wearing clothes. Linda didn't seem in the least bothered. Why should she? It seemed that she and Ivan got together regularly. Lloyd felt uncomfortable, though. If he could have reached his clothes without having to squeeze past Ivan in the narrow confines of the boat, he would have been dressed and walking along the towpath by now.

Linda sat on the edge of the couch, Ivan sat cross-legged on the floor, and Lloyd stayed where he was – lying on the couch and feeling like an unwilling artist's model.

The champagne was welcome, though, and he was more than ready to have his glass refilled.

Linda suddenly spluttered with laughter.

'You look ridiculous with your clothes on, Ivan.'

Lloyd would have told her in no uncertain terms that they looked ridiculous with their clothes off. Ivan didn't, though. He gave her an embarrassed smile, then slowly, almost reluctantly, peeled off the cashmere sweater he was wearing. His narrow chest was tanned a deep golden colour.

'Ivan's just returned from the Med,' Linda said, as if she too was admiring his tan.

'You could have come with me,' Ivan reminded her.

'But it was business.'

'Not all the time.'

Very meticulously, he untied the laces on his shoes and removed them. Socks next. Standing up, as much as the boat would allow, he quickly took off his jeans and a pair of white boxer shorts.

Lloyd wondered what he would do next but he

simply sat down on the floor again in the same cross-legged pose. His legs were thin and his knees bony, but every inch of his body boasted that golden tan.

Given the space, or lack of it, Ivan had no choice but to sit cross-legged, and it gave Lloyd a full view of his cock. Lloyd tried not to stare, but the sight intrigued him. Ivan's penis was an enviable length, but thinner than his own.

'More champagne,' Linda said, thrusting her glass at Ivan.

Lloyd wanted to make his excuses and leave. The words were on the tip of his tongue but something stopped him, and he wasn't entirely convinced it was the thought of struggling to dress with any dignity. In any case, Ivan had filled their glasses again.

Linda sat on the floor beside Ivan in the same cross-legged position. Lloyd was shocked, thrilled and envious as he watched her dip her fingers in her champagne and then smear the liquid across the tip of Ivan's penis, making him inhale sharply. Laughing, she bent over and licked it off.

Lloyd's breathing quickened. He had always loved to play the role of voyeur. He relaxed a little, watched her take a large swallow of champagne before she coated her fingers once more and dripped the liquid on to Ivan's cock. While she licked it off, she offered her fingers to Ivan who held her hand to his mouth and licked as she licked. He finished his champagne, put the glass out of harm's way, then ran his fingers through her hair as she licked his cock. Ivan's eyes were closed. He seemed oblivious to Lloyd's presence, to their surroundings – to anything but the pleasure Linda gave. Lloyd knew that pleasure well. He rubbed his own stiffening cock as he watched Linda sucking on Ivan's.

'We need more room,' Linda murmured, lifting her head. 'Move over, Lloyd.'

Lloyd lay on his side with his back against the boards of the boat. Ivan lay beside him and Linda straddled Ivan to take his long, hard shaft into her greedy mouth. Lloyd felt his cock twitch against Ivan's thigh – not an unpleasant sensation – but both men's gazes were fixed on Linda's mouth as it worked its magic on Ivan's lucky prick.

'We still need more room.' Linda abandoned Ivan. 'Come on, you two. Help me pull this bed out.'

It took them a full five minutes and a lot of cursing to turn the couch into a bed. She was right, though; it offered more comfort and more space.

'I'm worn out after that.' Laughing, Linda threw herself down in the centre of the bed. 'What I want,' she said huskily, 'what I've always wanted, is to take two big, hard, throbbing dicks in my mouth at the same time.' She grabbed two pillows and pushed them under her head to give her extra height. 'Lloyd, come this side. Ivan, you kneel here.'

Lloyd climbed over her, only too willing to put his hard cock in her mouth. It seemed to Lloyd that Ivan hesitated slightly before he too offered himself to Linda.

On several occasions, Lloyd had experienced sex with two, three and four women, and he'd taken part in group sex activities, but never had he had such close contact with another man. Never had his cock shared the delights of a woman's mouth with another. Never had his cock hardened and jerked greedily against another. Never had the highly sensitive tip nudged another. He found the new, unexpected sensations extremely exciting.

Lloyd could tell that having the two of them in her mouth was exciting Linda, too. She was whimpering with pleasure and squirming on the bed.

Deciding she deserved all the pleasure she was giving, Lloyd withdrew from the tightness of her busy mouth and sought her sex. Her hips jerked off the bed as he covered her hot sex with kisses and slowly – oh, so slowly – pushed his tongue inside her. The more he probed with his tongue, the more vigorously she sucked on Ivan's cock. Lloyd wasn't jealous, far from it. He pushed his tongue as deep inside her as he could while watching the play of emotions on her face, the almost tortured expressions on Ivan's face, and the way Ivan's long prick thrust into her eager mouth.

'Fill me, Lloyd,' she pleaded.

'Greedy cow!' Lloyd laughed.

He kneeled astride her, took his swollen cock in his hand and teased her with its tip for a few moments before plunging inside her. His eyes were closed as he felt her muscles contract around him, but he enjoyed the role of voyeur far too much to keep it that way. He had no need to move; Linda thrust eagerly with her hips to take more and more of him.

Ivan, too, must have decided that she deserved her pleasure because to Lloyd's surprise he withdrew from her mouth, moved to bend over her, and sucked noisily on her hard nipples. He caressed her breasts and teased her nipples between his teeth, and kept sneaking what seemed to be envious glances at Lloyd's cock.

'Feel him, Ivan.' Linda's breath was coming in short, ragged gasps. 'Feel him entering me. Feel his balls banging against me.'

Much to Lloyd's surprise, Ivan didn't hesitate. He cupped Lloyd's balls in his hand. The thrill of his touch came as a huge surprise to Lloyd. It was the first time he had been caressed by a strong, male hand. He had been kneeling upright above Linda, but he dropped down, taking his weight on his elbows, thus giving Ivan easier access. He thrust harder as Ivan rolled his balls in his expert hand. He withdrew, right to the tip, to allow Ivan to feel the whole length of him. Burning shudders raced through his body as he experienced the exciting contrast of Linda's warm, wet softness and

Ivan's rough, strong hand. He withdrew his cock completely and slid it along Ivan's hand before sinking deep inside Linda again.

'I want you both inside me,' Linda exclaimed breathlessly. 'Ivan – here. Lie on your back.'

Ivan did as he was told and Lloyd couldn't help but admire his long, straight penis as it pointed at the ceiling.

Linda, it seemed, felt the same. She toyed with it, stroking the long length of it, before slowly straddling him and dropping down on it.

'Oh, that's good. Lloyd, can you – Oh! Lloyd, take me from behind. Can you?'

While she bounced up and down on Ivan's cock, she leaned forwards slightly, offering Lloyd easier access to her forbidden place.

Lloyd circled Linda's anus with his thumb, applying pressure now and again. His prick nudged the tightness of her secret place, giving her the promise of things to come. The very tip of his cock pushed a little way inside her back passage. He probed, a little deeper each time, then withdrew. Then finally, when he could stand it no longer, he plunged deep inside her.

Linda cried out with gratitude.

The harder he thrust into the forbidden delights of Linda's anus, the harder Ivan drove into her sex. Lloyd could feel Ivan's cock inside her and the double pleasure sent him wild. Half of him wanted the sensations to last for ever, and half of him knew that such intense pleasure could only be endured for a short time. The agony of the ecstasy. He was determined to savour each delicious moment.

Both men gained momentum until Lloyd could no longer tell where one body ended and the other began. Linda banged back against him, demanding all from his ever-thrusting cock. Beneath her, Ivan pounded into her sex. It was as if they had melded into one erotic whole.

A sea of exquisite pleasure engulfed the thrusting mass of their bodies until, in one final wave of ecstasy, they came. Sated and exhausted, they collapsed on the bed. No one spoke. There was no need for words as each tried to recapture and cling to the essence of their experience.

'What's that?' Linda broke the silence.

'Footsteps!' Ivan was on his feet in an instant. 'Someone's stepping off the *Lucinda*!'

Chapter Three

As the train gathered speed, Olivia stared at the passing scenery. Nothing registered, though.

She had lied to Lloyd, saying she was visiting an old schoolfriend in the city. It had been easy to lie; all it had taken was the memory of his chat with Monty. Lloyd had been leaving for Brussels so he hadn't really been interested anyway. His secretary, the efficient and coolly attractive Joanna, was accompanying him. Olivia had nothing on which to ground her suspicions but she couldn't help wondering if they would share a bed.

Twice Lloyd had made love to Olivia during the last week, and twice she had been disappointed.

She brushed an imaginary speck of dust from her skirt. How did she look? Like a happily married woman about to embark on a shopping binge? Like an author on her way to a business meeting? Or like the guilty wife of a well-respected Member of Parliament on her way to meet the man of her fantasies?

It had taken her a long time to decide what to wear. She hadn't wanted to look as if she was out to impress – and yet she wanted to impress Steve. Even choosing her underwear had taken a long time, and no one would see it. She wanted to feel good, though, and hadn't been able to decide between a sexy thong or loose satin briefs. In the end she chose a lacy bra, suspenders, and thong in a vibrant plum colour. Her suede skirt was navy – she loved the rough texture of suede – and she wore a pale blue shirt. Her long, navy coat almost reached her high-heeled navy shoes. She wore large, tinted spectacles, too. Apart from a couple of wedding photographs in the society pages, her face was unknown. Few people would have a clue what Mrs Lloyd Standish looked like so it was highly unlikely that she would be recognised. It was a risk she didn't want to take, though.

A few flurries of snow drifted down from a grey sky.

For one brief moment, she wished she was at home, surrounded by all that was safe, instead of heading towards a man she didn't know. Except nothing felt safe at home any more and she wasn't a child, for God's sake.

The train dragged itself slowly into the station.

Olivia had planned to look round the shops, but there was nothing she wanted so she went to a noisy, crowded coffee bar and sat at a table near the window.

Outside it had started snowing again. It showed no sign of settling; it simply vanished. People hurried along the street, many of them laden with bulging carrier bags. Several shoppers had rolls of brightly coloured wrapping paper sticking out of bags. The coffee bar's only concession to the forthcoming celebrations were a small, plastic Christmas tree on the counter, and strings of fairylights in the windows. It looked more festive from the outside.

Olivia's hands were trembling slightly as she picked up her coffee. It was strange really; she was normally at ease with strangers. There was something about Steve, though, or about her confused feelings for this unknown man, that made her nervous. It also excited her, she acknowledged.

She lingered in the coffee bar for as long as was decently possible, then stepped out into the street. There were another two hours to kill before she met him.

It had stopped snowing but it was bitterly cold so she sought the warmth of a department store. Nothing held her attention until she saw their display of lingerie. It was a new line, designed by someone called Rossi. The name meant nothing to Olivia but the display was eye-catching. Although the designs were understated, no woman could fail to feel sexy in such garments. Olivia couldn't resist touching the smooth satin, nor could she resist buying four pairs of French knickers and matching camisoles. She sighed as she carried them to the till. Feeling sexy was very different to looking sexy . . .

Having completed her purchase, she made her way to the wine bar Steve had suggested. She was over half an hour early but she wanted to be there first. She ordered a dry white wine and, as most of the tables were taken, sat on a stool at the bar to wait. To make sure that no one took the stool next to her, she put her handbag and carrier bag on it.

Her surroundings came as a pleasant surprise. The wine bar was crowded with noisy students. Olivia began to wish she'd dressed more casually, but it was the sort of place where no one could feel out of place. A Counting Crows CD was playing loudly. Olivia sipped her wine, but her mouth and throat remained dry. Each time the door opened, her stomach turned over. At least no one would hear the pounding of her heart over the loud music.

Steve was ten minutes early. Olivia instinctively knew it was him.

He walked straight up to her, dark eyebrows raised in question.

'Jane?'

The name caught her off-guard momentarily, but she quickly recovered. She smiled and nodded.

'Steve?'

He leaned forwards and dropped a swift kiss on her cheek.

Her first impression was that he looked far younger than thirty-two. Her second was that he was extremely good-looking. So much for bald and fat, she thought with amusement.

He ordered a red wine for himself and nodded at Olivia's glass. 'What's that?'

'Dry white, please.'

Olivia didn't miss the appreciative gleam in his eyes as he watched the girl get their drinks.

Olivia used the moment to study him unobserved. He was taller than Lloyd, well over the six feet mark. Light brown hair curled in all directions, looking as if he made little effort to tame it. Dark brown eyes had the same sleepy quality as his voice. His clothes were casual but smart: combats, crisp blue shirt, brown leather jacket.

He swung his gaze back to Olivia. 'I was expecting you to look completely different.'

'Disillusioned already?' she quipped.

'On the contrary,' he replied, regarding her steadily from velvety brown eyes. 'You're very beautiful.'

'I'm also very married.'

Steve laughed.

'It's rare, I grant you, but the two have been known to go together, you know.'

'I was merely saying that there's no need for you to flirt with me.' Nerves were making her sound petulant.

'That's a pity. I think I would enjoy flirting with you, Jane.'

This time, his use of her pen-name helped. It made everything more anonymous. And exciting. She could be Jane far more easily than she could be Olivia. Jane could be far less inhibited.

'Flirt away, then,' she said carelessly.

He paid for their drinks and put the change in his pocket.

'Let's find a table.'

She grabbed her bags and followed him to an empty table in the corner. Once they were seated, Steve studied the menu.

'Hungry?' he asked.

Olivia shook her head.

'Not even a sandwich?' Without giving her the chance to argue, he said, 'I'll order a selection of sandwiches.'

He returned to the bar and Olivia watched him laughing with the girl at the bar. So he was a flirt. She didn't care.

While they waited for the sandwiches, they chatted about politics but Olivia had little enthusiasm for the subject and she was pleased when the food arrived.

Steve polished off three beef sandwiches, eating with obvious enjoyment. His teeth were amazing; strong, white and perfectly even. She found herself examining every part of him, from the tiny network of lines surrounding his eyes to his strong-looking wrists. His fingers were long and straight. They were expressive fingers, sensitive fingers. Olivia felt herself grow warm as she imagined them caressing her soft skin. She nibbled on an egg and cress sandwich and wondered if, having seen her in the flesh, he still thought of her as warm and sensuous. She wished she could ask but even the less inhibited Jane couldn't ask that.

'Your husband's a lucky man,' Steve remarked suddenly.

'I'm not sure he'd agree with that!'

'Problems?' he asked.

'No, not really. We had a tiff,' she lied. 'You? Is your wife well? And the children?'

'They're well, yes.' He didn't seem inclined to talk about them, but then he changed his mind. 'You know, my marriage isn't all it should be, Jane. People change. I don't think I've changed, but perhaps I just can't see it. Donna has, though. Since becoming a mother, she's matured. She used to have fun. Now she's more – responsible.'

'I suppose most couples have to adapt when children come along,' she replied vaguely.

It was no use. She couldn't concentrate on anything except her growing desire. Would he be a quiet lover or an adventurous one? Would he be gentle or rough? Demanding or submissive?

The Counting Crows CD had finished and they were being subjected to a medley of Christmas songs. They laughed at the music, and chatted about films and books. It was very impersonal, but very friendly.

'I ought to be going,' Olivia said, hoping he would suggest another meeting.

'What time's your train?'

She told him and he glanced at his watch.

'There's plenty of time. Would you like me to get you a taxi or would you prefer to walk? It's not too far to the station.'

'I'll walk.' She needed to feel the cool, fresh air on her face.

When they got outside, he fell into step with her.

'There's no need to come with me,' she said.

'I'd like to.'

Olivia was pleased. She waited, but still he didn't suggest another meeting.

There was something very right about the rhythmic sound of their footsteps as they walked. Their steps were even; they both slowed down at the same time, both quickened their pace to dodge pedestrians at the same time.

A stray snowflake landed on her nose, catching her by surprise. Steve tried to brush it away but it had already melted, leaving her nose wet.

Neither of them spoke and they were soon standing on the station platform with a tense silence between them.

'This is my train,' she said, her lips suddenly dry.

'I'll come with you,' he said on an impulse. 'It doesn't leave for five minutes. Wait here and I'll get a ticket.'

Olivia watched him go. Five minutes. She didn't know whether to wait for him or board the train. She waited until the last minute and was about to get on the train when she saw him sprinting down the platform. He walked with an aloof lope, yet he ran like an athlete.

'Come on!' He grabbed her hand and pulled her to the first set of open doors.

He took a brief look inside the compartment and shook his head.

'It's packed. We'll have to stand.' He guided her towards the locked door opposite.

'But –' She stopped. There was no need to tell him her seat was reserved. They might not be able to sit together.

'Why are you coming with me?' she asked instead.

'Because I don't want to watch you leave yet,' he answered simply. 'I can easily catch the next train back to Brighton. It's only a couple of hours out of my day.'

The train jerked forwards, catching Olivia by surprise. She staggered slightly and Steve put out a hand to steady her. Her coat was made of thick wool but still his hand almost circled her arm. It really was a beautiful hand. She looked up at him, only to find him gazing at her. He seemed to be staring at her lips as if – what? Did he want to taste them? Without conscious thought, she moistened them with her tongue. Their gazes locked; his questioning, hers uncertain. He stroked her arm through her heavy coat, then lifted a hand to trace a finger around her throat. Her breathing quickened and she arched her neck like a contented feline.

She was still holding her handbag and the carrier bag, and Steve took them from her. He was about to put them on the floor in the corner when something made him stop.

'What did you buy?'

Olivia couldn't answer. He opened the carrier bag and looked inside, smiling when he saw the French knickers and camisoles.

'Did you buy these because you like to feel satin next to your skin?'

Olivia nodded, surprised at such perception.

'I would love to see you wearing them.' He put her bags on the floor. 'Perhaps next time?'

It was a question and, again, Olivia nodded.

'You like satin?' he murmured. 'You like to feel it caressing your skin like an attentive lover?'

Olivia bit her lip. 'Oh, yes.'

Her desire for this man was almost overwhelming.

'You're such a sensuous creature.' He leaned close as he spoke and Olivia felt his warm breath fanning her cheek.

'You're too warm,' he added, and he slowly – very slowly – unfastened the four large buttons on her coat.

His gaze fell on the outline of her breasts. Her breathing was rapid, and her shirt rustled slightly as it rose and fell.

'Is that better?' he asked softly.

'Much. Thank you.'

Her heart was racing. Her whole body was on fire. The train slowed slightly, jolting as it crossed the points, and the movement set her nerves tingling. Steve put his hand on her waist as if to steady her again and she could feel the outline of his hand through the thin fabric of her shirt. His thumb stroked her ribcage, his touch gentle yet firm. She gasped when his thumb slipped between the buttons and touched her warm skin.

'Such accommodating clothes,' he murmured.

He moved to stand directly in front of her. He was close – so close to her. The train's movement had them bumping arms. Occasionally his thigh would brush against hers. He unfastened one of the buttons on her blouse.

'Satin and lace,' he whispered huskily as his light touch found her bra.

Olivia squirmed with pleasure as his fingers outlined the swell of her breasts. His thumb sought and found her aching nipple and it hardened at his touch.

The automatic doors opened and a man carrying two plastic cups filled with coffee walked past them. He gave Olivia a polite nod. The knowledge that she was hidden, by Steve's body at the front, and by her own long coat at the side, excited Olivia still further if that were possible.

'Your whole body is aching, isn't it?' Steve murmured. 'You want an orgasm, don't you, Jane? That's all you can think about, isn't it?'

'Yes.' Olivia could never admit to such a thing, but Jane could. 'Sometimes I think I'll never be fully satisfied,' she confessed. 'My body is constantly craving pleasure.'

His thumb flicked her aching nipple and she had to put her hands on his hips to support herself.

When he lowered his hand, she felt bereft for a moment, but then he lifted her skirt and ran his hand up her thigh, pausing for a long, tantalising moment when he reached the top of her stocking.

'I bet you're wet already. Are you, Jane?'

'Yes.'

She squirmed in her dampness. His talk aroused her still further. How she wished she could speak so freely. She felt his hand at the top of her thigh and instinctively parted her legs a little. Somehow she had to maintain her control. They were on a train, a public place. She took several deep breaths to try and calm herself but it was too late to stop him. Not that she wanted to. She would like to abandon herself completely but that was out of the question. Steve's hand slipped between her thighs and pushed aside the carefully chosen thong with ease.

'So wet,' he remarked with pleasure.

She gasped as the first shock of his touch shuddered through her body. He smiled at her reaction. The large hand that she had so admired was flat against her, covering her vulva, and he brushed it up and down.

'Oh!'

His finger touched her bud and a moan of pleasure fell from her lips. As he applied more pressure, she closed her eyes. His middle finger penetrated her slowly and her muscles instinctively tightened around it. She sighed loudly as he pushed in still further. Such pleasure made her knees tremble. He moved his fingers as if he had been born to pleasure her; hard and fast one second, tantalisingly slow the next.

The man who had carried the coffee emerged from the automatic doors once more. Again, he treated Olivia to that polite nod. The sight of him, and the knowledge that all he would see was a couple in a close but innocent embrace, excited Olivia. Steve, sensing her heightened state of arousal, rubbed her clitoris hard and fast with his thumb.

The noise of the speeding train mingled with the blood pounding in her ears. Her thigh muscles contracted violently as she climaxed. Her hips jerked against his hand.

Steve's hand was perfectly still but he didn't remove it. The stranger had long gone.

'I thought you were going to cry out and attract his attention,' Steve whispered in her ear.

'I almost did,' she confessed, her words coming in ragged, breathless bursts.

'Did you want him to know what I was doing to you? Would you have liked him to watch you climax?'

She nodded but couldn't look at him.

His thumb started to caress her and she surprised herself by climaxing again almost immediately. Weak now, she dug her fingers into his shoulders to keep herself upright.

'We're about to pull into the station.' He spoke with regret, as if he wanted to continue. However, he moved his hand and straightened her skirt.

Olivia didn't know what to say. She was acutely embarrassed by her display of wantonness and relieved when the train slowed for the station. She picked up her bags, grateful to do something that might hide her embarrassment.

An icy blast of cold air hit her straight in the face when the doors opened, making her shiver and huddle deep inside her coat.

They parted on the platform in an absurdly formal way.

'Until the next time, Jane.'

'Yes. I must dash. Bye.'

'I'll e-mail you when I get home.'

She hurried away from him, realising too late that she was heading in the wrong direction. She doublebacked, gave him a sheepish smile, and strode off to the taxi rank.

Having given the driver her address, she sank back against the upholstery and began to relax. The traffic was light for a change so she was soon home.

Once inside, she took off her coat, went straight to

her bedroom to drop her bags, then wandered from room to room as she relived every second of that hour's train journey. If she closed her eyes, she could still hear the train's engine, and the wheels speeding along the track. She could almost feel Steve's touch. A sudden laugh escaped her and she wrapped her arms around herself, hugging her happiness to her. She felt wild and reckless, abandoned and free. Ever since she had been a curious teenager, she had known there was a world of pleasure waiting for her. What she hadn't known, and still couldn't quite believe, was that she would be twenty-eight before she had any proof of that.

The wasted years were her own fault, she supposed. Alan, a young history student, had taken her virginity when she was eighteen. It had been an easily forgotten experience. Olivia had been left feeling confused, unsatisfied and entirely to blame for the unsatisfactory experience. Her next lover, when she was twenty-two, was Darren. He had been gorgeous. He'd had a body that made her knees tremble every time she looked at him. They made love six times, and each time was a bitter disappointment. For them both, Olivia suspected. She could see them now, clutching the sheets around their naked bodies in acute embarrassment. Olivia had known she was to blame. She knew what she wanted but couldn't pluck up enough courage to voice her desires. Likewise, she knew, or thought she knew, how to give a man pleasure, but she couldn't bring herself to take the initiative. When, shortly afterwards, Darren took a new lover, a male lover, Olivia's self-esteem sank to new depths.

For six years, Olivia had buried her frustrations in her work. When it came to business, or dealing with people in general, she could be a hard-nosed bitch. When it came to anything intimate, however, she was totally at a loss. During long, lonely nights, her faithful fingers were her only friends.

Then she saw the video of Lloyd. She saw a man who knew exactly how to please a woman, or even two women, and who took his own pleasure as easily. He knew what he wanted, didn't hesitate to voice his desire, and expected his partners to do likewise. So why had the physical side of their relationship been such a huge disappointment? Because she couldn't take the initiative? She had asked herself that question countless times and still she didn't have an answer. But it was a disappointment. Lloyd would kiss her, fondle her breasts, then enter her. His soft murmurings would become more urgent with every thrust until he came inside her. He would flop on top of her for a few moments, kiss her again, and tell her he loved her – a lie, she knew now. Then he would roll away and sleep, leaving Olivia feeling used and very, very frustrated . . .

Her computer whirred into life as she hit the 'on' button. She sat in front of it and gasped at the stab of pain that shot up her spine. Frowning, she wondered – there had been a metal handrail on the train. She had leaned against it and it must have bruised her back. She wriggled in her chair now and the pain became a pleasant reminder.

She downloaded her e-mail messages and saw there was already one from Steve. She brought it to the screen. It was brief: *I can still taste you on my fingers. S.*

Olivia shuddered at the memory of his skilful fingers on her wanton flesh. She closed her eyes and remembered every pleasure-filled second of that train journey. Steve's face swam before her, then Lloyd's face, such a handsome face. Lloyd's face, Steve's hands –

One day, she vowed, she would have Lloyd on his knees, begging for her!

When Carmen arrived at the flat, Steve was staring thoughtfully at his computer.

'Are you working?' she asked.

'Nope.' The typist's chair creaked as he swivelled round to look at her. 'I've only just got home. I caught the train to London with her.'

'And?'

'She's very different to how I imagined her. The Olivia you know and the one I met today are totally different people.'

'Knew,' Carmen corrected him.

It was a long time since Olivia had looked down her long, sophisticated nose at Carmen. Carmen hadn't forgotten those days, though; she hadn't forgotten a thing about the snooty pupils who had shared her schooldays.

'Knew,' he agreed. 'I thought she was OK, really.'

'Men always think she's OK,' Carmen muttered. 'When I started at that bloody awful school, she was the first girl I saw. She was instructed to show me round and – how did the headmistress put it? – make sure I settled in. God, that was a laugh!'

'How come you went to the same school?'

'My dad.' Carmen didn't blame her father for walking out on them when she was five. Years spent living with her mother had taught her that it would have taken a saint to put up with such erratic behaviour. 'I suppose it was guilt on his part,' she went on. 'If he gave money to Mum, she either poured it down her throat or put it on the backs of three-legged dogs or tired old nags.'

Having lived in near poverty with her mother, Carmen supposed it should have been bliss to find herself at the exclusive boarding school in Buckinghamshire. It wasn't, though.

'I was never likely to make friends,' she went on. 'I didn't have the plummy accent, the wealthy family members driving up in their flash cars to take me out to tea, or the hampers arriving on a daily basis.'

'But why Olivia?' Steve asked. 'What did she do that was so awful?'

Carmen perched on the edge of his desk.

'She had some money stolen – or said she did. She and her friends automatically pointed the finger at me. The money was never found, but I was branded a thief from that moment on. A few months later, she had some jewellery stolen.'

'And you were accused again?' Steve guessed.

'Accused and found guilty,' Carmen replied grimly. 'She insisted on my belongings being searched. Lo and behold, there was her jewellery, in my locker.'

'Ouch!'

'Indeed. I always vowed I'd get my revenge on that lying, toffee-nosed bitch.'

'You don't know for sure that Olivia put it there,' Steve pointed out.

'Who the hell else could it have been?'

Steve didn't answer that.

'She seemed almost shy to me,' he said instead.

'Ha! Shy? You have been screwing the right woman?'

'It was the right woman, but I haven't been screwing her. I couldn't make up my mind if she was inexperienced, frigid as hell, a tease, or what.'

'You didn't screw her?' Carmen knew Steve too well to believe that.

'I didn't even get a hard-on.' He turned back to his computer, hit a few keys and brought a selection of tiny photographs to the screen. 'I think she's probably a devoted wife, though. Yes, I'm sure she'll pay handsomely to save hubby's career.'

'I hope so. Barry risked his neck clambering all over that boat.'

Barry, Carmen's disreputable half-brother, was responsible for a high-quality video showing Lloyd Standish in action. That Lloyd subsequently married Olivia came as a pleasant surprise to Carmen. She had nothing against Lloyd, or nothing more than she had against any other politician who went into holier-than-thou mode just before finding a couple of whores to fuck. She disliked Olivia intensely, though, and would dearly love to see her face when Barry's photographs landed on her doormat.

'Barry wants to send all the photos at once,' Steve said, 'but I think we'll send them one at time. We'll save the best till last.'

He hit a key and one of the photographs filled the screen.

'And that has to be the best!' Carmen said with a chuckle.

The female owner of the narrow boat was sitting on some guy's prick while Lloyd took her from behind.

'I bet that gives you a hard-on,' she added, grinning.

Steve unzipped his jeans, letting the object of her desire answer for itself.

'Mmm.'

She licked her lips as she hitched up her short skirt. She pulled down her panties, tossed them aside, hitched her skirt still higher, and swung her leg over him.

'Mmm.' Her appreciation was even greater as she lowered herself on to his prick. It slipped in easily, going deeper and deeper. She tightened around it, her hands on his shoulders.

Steve was grinning happily as he unfastened the half dozen buttons on her blouse. With a well-practised movement, he snaked round the back and unfastened her bra, then pushed it up towards her neck.

As she rose and fell on his ample length, her breasts jiggled in his face. Like a man bobbing for apples, he caught a nipple in his mouth and sucked noisily. Carmen was enjoying herself immensely. Up, down, up, down, she withdrew to the tip, cupped his balls, circled the base of his ecstasy-giver, sank down hard. Still with his mouth around her nipple, Steve pushed down on her thighs as he began to jerk her up and down. He was deliciously hard. She started to come, squirming on him, tightening around him, digging her fingers into his shoulders, crying out.

Steve was close to orgasm, too. He began to lick the small butterfly tattoo on her neck, then bit hard as he started to come. She could feel him jerking inside her, then he was lifting them off the chair as he pounded into her.

Carmen flopped against him. It was several minutes before she felt strong enough to climb off him.

'Let's get started, then.' She nodded at the screen. 'We'll send Miss High and Mighty a taster . . .'

Chapter Four

Olivia walked into their bedroom with a towel draped around her. Her hair was still wet from her shower and she took the towel from her body and rubbed her hair. It pleased her to walk naked in front of Lloyd these days.

'How was Brussels?' she asked.

'The usual,' Lloyd replied. 'Everything been all right here? You've been all right?'

'Of course.'

'What's that?' Lloyd had been sitting on the bed but he walked over to her. 'You're bruised.'

She tensed as he touched her back.

'Yes. When I was out shopping, I was jostled getting out of the lift. My back hit the rail.' She wriggled her spine. 'Actually, it's quite painful.'

'I'll massage it for you. Come here.'

She could see that her somewhat aloof attitude was worrying Lloyd, making him eager to please her. Good. Never again would he accuse her of 'suffocating' him.

In the past, when Lloyd had returned from a business trip, Olivia had raced into his arms to tell him how much she had missed him. She had pampered him and pandered to his every need. Not this time, though. She had heard him return and feigned concentration in her work. She had given him a vague greeting without leaving her computer. This was a new Olivia. If he wanted a marriage of convenience, then that's what he would have. Olivia no longer needed him. She wanted him, but she didn't need him. She would bide her time until he needed her. She was determined that day would come. Meanwhile, when she craved the things he was unwilling to give, all she had to do was take the Brighton train.

Lloyd kneeled on the bed beside her. Like Steve, he had very large hands. They felt huge as he massaged her back with infinite care. He had a firm, confident touch that she loved. She forced herself to lie completely still and not give him the satisfaction of knowing how his touch excited her.

'You've been working too hard,' he murmured. 'Your neck and shoulder muscles are knotted with tension.'

They were. Olivia felt them begin to relax as he massaged them.

'You should get that chap in,' Lloyd went on, 'the one Audrey Symington uses. I can't remember where he is but I'm sure she'd give you his phone number.'

'I might do that.'

Audrey Symington wasn't Olivia's favourite person. At thirty-six, Audrey was twenty-six years younger than her rich and influential husband. She was also an incorrigible flirt. Twice, Olivia had caught Audrey putting her hand on Lloyd's knee. Audrey was also a bore when it came to health and fitness. Mind you, she positively glowed with good health and energy, and this was mainly attributed to the regular massages she received from Henri. She employed his services twice a week, unless she had a migraine or some other complaint when he had to make an emergency visit to her home.

'Mmm. That feels good.' It felt very good. Olivia had to resist the strong urge to respond to Lloyd's touch. After a few more minutes, she could stand it no longer. 'Thanks.' She rolled away from him. 'I'm wonderfully relaxed now and so tired. I think I'll have an early night.'

'Well – of course, if that's what you want.'

'It is.' She slid beneath the covers. 'Goodnight, Lloyd.'

With a barely audible sigh, Lloyd left the bedroom.

When he returned, a couple of hours later, Olivia could smell whisky on his breath. She pretended to be asleep, but she knew he didn't sleep. She could feel his tension as he lay beside her. Every now and again he sighed into the darkness.

Two days later, Olivia phoned Audrey Symington.

'Livvy! Wonderful to hear from you. How are you?'

Audrey was the only person Olivia knew who called her 'Livvy' – thank God!

'Fine, thanks,' Olivia replied.

'And that gorgeous husband of yours?'

'Yes. Lloyd's fine, thanks. He's in the north-east for the next few days.'

'He mentioned it,' Audrey said. 'We must get together, Livvy. I'm busy planning Tony's birthday party. I'm thinking of making it fancy dress. Tony will hate it, of course, but I think it might be fun. What do you think?'

'I think it's a lovely idea,' Olivia lied.

'So do I! There's something wicked about fancy dress, don't you think?'

'Well, I don't really know.' Olivia didn't have a clue what she meant. 'I haven't been to a fancy dress party since my mother forced me to dress as Little Bo Peep. Anyway, Audrey, I was really ringing for a favour.'

'Ask away! Name it and it shall be yours.'

Olivia rolled her eyes to the heavens.

'I wondered if you'd let me have the phone number of your masseur. It's silly, really, but I've bruised my back and a massage seems to help.'

'Henri? You want Henri?' Audrey laughed in a secretive way. 'He's too busy to take on new clients –'

'Oh, in that case –'

'I'll have a word with him, Livvy. I'm sure he'll make an exception for you.'

'No, really –'

'It's no trouble. I'll ask him to call you . . .'

When Olivia eventually managed to end the call, she swore loudly. She wished she hadn't bothered. The last thing she wanted was to be indebted to Audrey, and she certainly didn't want Audrey using her influence to make the poor Henri take on work he didn't have time for.

Late that afternoon, however, Olivia answered the phone to the man himself.

'Mrs Symington gave me your telephone number,' he explained in a charming and very sexy French accent. 'You are wanting a massage – yes?'

Knowing he must think her a nuisance, Olivia explained about her bruised back.

'But I know you're busy,' she ended briskly, 'so perhaps you could recommend someone else?'

'I am never too busy for a friend of Mrs Symington's, madam,' he assured her.

Audrey must give him very large tips.

'That's very kind, but –'

'No butting. I will visit you tomorrow – yes?'

'If you're sure.'

'Eleven o'clock?' he asked.

'Thank you.'

'You are wanting –' he hesitated briefly, as if choosing his words with care '– the same treatment as Mrs Symington?'

'I don't know. I don't know what treatment Audrey – Mrs Symington – has. I only know that a massage relieves the pain in my back.'

'Ah! Then we shall – how you say? – play it by the ear, yes?'

'Yes,' Olivia agreed, smiling to herself.

'I see you tomorrow, Mrs Standish. At eleven o'clock. Until then, *au revoir*.'

Olivia was extremely curious about Henri now. He was certainly keen to please Audrey. Was that simply because Audrey paid over the odds, or was there another reason? Audrey couldn't be having an affair with him, could she? Surely not! On the other hand, it had to be said that for someone bursting with such health and vitality, she did suffer from migraines with an alarming frequency. Her husband was in his early sixties, he was away from home a lot, and Olivia had never believed that Audrey had married for love.

Henri arrived a few minutes before eleven the following day and, as soon as she saw him, Olivia felt sure her suspicions were correct. She could imagine Audrey having an affair with this gorgeous creature all too easily.

Normally, Olivia wasn't turned on by muscular men, but she made an exception in Henri's case. He was wearing tight black jeans that hugged his thighs and buttocks like a second skin. A white, short-sleeved T-shirt showed off a solid chest and incredibly well-muscled arms. His shoulders and neck were a little on the large side perhaps, and he wasn't particularly tall, but all in all he had a magnificent body. No wonder Audrey suffered from migraines!

It was difficult to guess his age. Olivia would have put him around the thirty mark but, looking more closely at the lines on his face, she decided he was closer to forty. His nose was crooked, looking as if it had been broken at some time. Thick, vibrant dark hair seemed to offer an invitation to restless fingers. His eyes were his best feature, though. They were a brilliant, penetrating shade of blue. Olivia wondered briefly if he wore tinted contact lenses.

'Mrs Standish! It is a great pleasure to meet you.' He lifted her hand and dropped a brief kiss on her knuckles. He had full, sensual lips and Olivia's skin tingled at the unexpected touch.

'Thank you for coming.' Her cheeks grew warm beneath what she could see was an appreciative gaze. 'Where – I mean –'

'What is your bed like?' he asked. 'So long as it is firm, that will be fine. If not –' he shrugged '– we think again. Mrs Symington prefers the floor. She has a rug, you see.'

Olivia stifled a laugh at the thought of Audrey's rug.

'There's a firm bed in one of the guest rooms,' she said. 'Please, follow me.'

He picked up his briefcase – heaven alone knew what was in that – and followed her up the stairs.

Olivia wondered if he was watching her as she walked. She wasn't wearing stockings and her skirt was short, giving him a good view of her slim legs if he wanted one. At the top of the stairs she turned right, trailing her hand along the gallery rail until she reached the small guest room.

'My mother-in-law has this room when she visits,' she explained, pushing open the door.

He followed her inside, shutting the door behind them.

'Let me see.' Henri sat on the bed, bounced a couple of times, and declared it suitable. 'Your mother-in-law is a wise woman. Only on a firm bed does the spine get the rest it deserves. To sag – it is not good. The bed sags, the spine sags.'

He got off the bed and took three small bottles from his briefcase.

'You undress now – yes?'

'Undress? What, all of me?'

'Of course.' He chuckled. 'The oil is for your muscles, not your clothes.' He looked at her and must have sensed her embarrassment. 'A towel – if you wish.'

Cursing her own stupidity, Olivia went to the adjoining bathroom and undressed. In her naiveté, she had expected to remove her blouse and bra, but nothing else. She was more than willing to lie on the bed naked for this man. However, she now felt obliged to return to the bedroom with a towel draped around her.

'Lie face down, madam,' Henri instructed.

She did as he told her, making sure that she wasn't lying on the towel. He would need to massage her lower back and he would have to move her towel for that.

'You must say if my hands are too cold,' he murmured. 'I have the cold hands and – what is it? – yes, the hot heart.'

'I see,' Olivia replied, smiling to herself.

She felt the bottom of the bed sag beneath his weight. Then, to her great amazement, he began rubbing oil into her feet.

'Relax,' he said, his voice hypnotic.

It was impossible not to. Olivia had never much cared for having her feet touched but this was heaven. He caressed her heels, stroked her insteps, and gently massaged each toe in turn. It really was heaven.

'That's better,' he said, 'but you are still tense. It is not good for the body. You must abandon this tension, madam. It is very important.'

Henri covered his hands with oil and began massaging her calf muscles. Olivia closed her eyes. His hands were strong and he wasn't afraid to apply pressure to her muscles. Then he stroked her skin with infinite gentleness, from her ankles to the backs of her knees.

'Your legs are perfect, madam,' he told her.

'Thank you, Henri.'

'There is no need for thanks. I speak only the truth. And now, I believe I shall need to remove the towel for a while, if I may.'

'Of course.'

Olivia reached behind her for the towel and tossed it to the floor.

There was no movement for a while and she thought he must be assessing her body. The thought both excited and embarrassed her. She soon realised he was putting oil on his hands, though. The perfume was heavy. He began to massage her thighs, working up a little way from her knees. Olivia's heart began to beat more quickly. His hands moved in a circular motion, each arc going a little higher than the last. His thumbs made deep, probing circles on her inner thighs and Olivia instinctively parted her legs a little. Higher and higher his hands went. Faster and faster Olivia's heartbeat raced. His hands caressed the tops of her thighs and her bottom. His thumbs still concentrated on the inside of her thighs. Her hips, her waist, the long length of her spine . . . his touch did the most amazing things to her senses. Her hands, wrists, forearms, elbows, shoulders, neck . . . he was relentless.

'If I could ask madam to turn over,' he said, his voice sounding as if it was coming from a long way off.

Olivia rolled over, flinging her arms above her head. Already her breasts were tingling in anticipation of his caress. Her nipples stood out hard and pointed.

He started on her feet, as before, then rubbed the heavily perfumed oil into her shins, knees and thighs. Desire burned within Olivia. It was as much as she could do not to thrust her body towards him. She could feel a trickle of perspiration running down the valley between her breasts. She was damp between her thighs.

His hands were working their magic on her waist now. They moved up her ribcage until the weight of her breasts was on the backs of his hands. Her breathing was rapid and shallow. A sigh of gratitude escaped her when he began rubbing oil into her breasts and she gasped aloud as he lightly touched her aching nipples. Her shameless body arched towards him slightly. She was powerless to stop it. With one hand, he stroked her breasts in sweeping, circular movements, occasionally flicking his thumb over her nipples. With his other hand, he massaged her lower abdomen. His fingers ran through her bush, and her hips lifted off the bed to obtain more pressure. As if sensing her need, the flat of his hand increased the pressure while his thumb went between her thighs. Olivia's orgasm came from nowhere to explode within her. Somehow, she managed to stop herself crying out. In fact, the only tell-tale sign that she had experienced such pleasure was in the way her heels drummed the bed for a few seconds.

Her eyes flew open, but Henri wasn't looking at her face. He was rubbing oil into her knees. Surely he knew! If he did, he gave no indication.

'I think that is all I can do today,' he said briskly. 'That should give your back the relief it needs.'

'I – yes. Thank you, Henri.'

'The pleasure was mine, madam.'

Not entirely, Olivia thought, the colour still burning in her face.

'If I may make the suggestion, madam – perhaps you will need another massage in two or three days' time.'

'I'm sure I shall. May I play safe and make an appointment now?'

Henri checked his diary and wrote her in for Friday morning.

'I will see myself out, Mrs Standish,' he said, giving her a small bow. 'You should relax – yes?'

'I will, Henri. Thank you.'

She closed her eyes and drifted into a deep sleep.

That evening Olivia felt restless. Lonely, too. She wished Lloyd wasn't in Brussels.

It was an ideal opportunity to settle down to some uninterrupted writing, but she couldn't concentrate on the world of politics. Her head was reeling with far more interesting thoughts: Steve; Henri; the pleasure her body had experienced and the way it ached for so much more; the way it ached for Lloyd.

One day he would want her. One day he would damn well beg her. But not this evening, alas.

She wandered into her study, switched on her computer, and checked her e-mail. There was a message from Steve.

Hi, Jane.

How are things? I'm up to my neck in galleys at the moment. Donna and the boys are staying with her parents for five days so at least I can get on with work.

I'm really writing to let you know of a website I came across today. It's very interesting, with lots of good links.

Best, Steve.

The message disappointed her. What the hell did she care about websites?

However, she spent half an hour online, checking out the site. He was right; it was impressive. She marked it for a future visit, but she couldn't concentrate on it now.

If Steve was alone, which he was, she could phone him. It would be good to hear his voice. It would be good to know if he wanted to see her again, too. Perhaps he would talk about that dreamlike train journey. It would be fun to talk about it, to tell him how it had felt to have his fingers working such magic on her needy body, and to tell him how it had excited her when the stranger had walked past them.

That was the problem, of course. Olivia couldn't talk about such things. Jane might be able to, at a push, but Olivia couldn't.

Still, it would be good to hear his voice again.

She was still deciding whether to call him or not when her phone rang.

'Livvy? It's Audrey. Can you meet me for lunch tomorrow?'

Normally, Olivia would have claimed pressure of work, but it would be amusing to bring up Henri's name and watch Audrey's reaction.

'Yes, I'd like that.'

'Great! Twelve-thirty OK?'

'Fine.'

Olivia wore her favourite dress. It was short, understated and black except for a tiny silver butterfly motif across the bodice. The matching jacket had an even smaller silver butterfly woven into the lapel. She knew it suited her and that fact alone gave her confidence. Whenever she wore it, heads turned.

Today, however, all the turned heads were looking in Audrey's direction. Audrey was noted for her bold use of colour and today was no exception. Her dress – even shorter than Olivia's – had a scarlet skirt and orange bodice. The bolero jacket was scarlet edged with orange. With her auburn hair, Audrey should have looked frightful. She didn't, though. As always, she looked far younger than she actually was, and very, very sexy. Olivia envied her.

'I love your outfit,' she said truthfully.

'But you wouldn't wear it yourself,' Audrey replied with a knowing laugh.

It was true.

'Black suits you.' Audrey lowered her voice. 'It gives

you an air of mystery. Whereas I –' she laughed, a deep, husky sound '– dress to shock. And to draw attention to my figure. I work hard to keep in shape so I make sure people appreciate my efforts.'

Several male diners were appreciating her efforts as she spoke.

'You mean you exercise?' Olivia asked. Somehow, she couldn't imagine Audrey sweating it out on a treadmill.

'In a manner of speaking.'

The waiter came to their table.

'Hang it, we'll have champagne, shall we?'

Before Olivia could decline, or even reply, the champagne was ordered. Their food, too, was ordered with little input from Olivia. She felt like a child out for a Sunday treat with a maiden aunt. Not that there was anything maiden-auntish in the way Audrey flirted with the waiter.

As soon as they were alone again, they chatted about mutual acquaintances. They were half-way through the consommé when Audrey returned to the subject of her fitness regime.

'I never liked games at school,' she confided to Olivia. 'I was more interested in the boys.'

'We didn't see any boys,' Olivia said.

'God, poor you. The boys' school was attached to ours. We weren't supposed to mix, of course, other than at a couple of special functions in the year, but that simply added spice to our meetings. As I've grown older –' she shrugged '– my tastes haven't changed. I still prefer boys – men, now – to sport.'

'So how do you keep so fit?' Olivia asked curiously.

'By taking my exercise in the way I like best,' Audrey replied softly.

'What – you mean –'

'Indeed. Tony isn't as young as he used to be and to be honest, he's never been very adventurous in bed.'

That shrug again. 'I have to look elsewhere for my exercise. Tell me,' she said suddenly, 'how did you enjoy Henri?'

'Henri?' Olivia's cheeks burned with colour at the memory of Henri using his skilful hands to give her an unexpected orgasm.

'He didn't leave you unsatisfied, I trust?' Audrey said, frowning.

'No – not – but I only wanted a massage.'

Audrey's burst of laughter had several men looking wistfully in her direction.

'So did I, until I saw him. He is gorgeous – yes?' she asked in a wonderful imitation of Henri's accent.

Now it was Olivia's turn to laugh.

'Is that accent for real?'

'God knows, but it works wonders,' Audrey responded with a laugh.

'He's good-looking too,' Olivia pointed out.

'He is. He's also very willing. With Henri, you only have to ask. The soul of discretion too, of course.'

'Ask?' Olivia murmured blankly.

'Ask!' Audrey repeated firmly. 'God, Livvy, you don't get anywhere in life if you don't ask. Of course,' she went on, 'we have to be discreet, which is why I have my regulars.'

Just in time, Olivia stopped herself repeating the word 'regulars' in shocked amazement. She was beginning to sound like a parrot. She took a sip of champagne to moisten her mouth.

'I see Henri twice a week, and sometimes more,' Audrey explained. 'I have chess lessons once a fortnight. My gynaecologist gives me a thorough examination once a month –'

She broke off as the waiter attended to them, but Olivia suspected there were more.

'Discretion is everything,' Audrey said when they were alone again. She looked at Olivia's complexion which was changing from crimson to deathly white. 'You're shocked?'

'Not at all. Well, a little surprised,' Olivia admitted.

'And you? Are you satisfied with Lloyd? Like Tony, he's away from home a lot. Don't you get lonely?'

'A little,' Olivia answered slowly, 'but I wouldn't – I mean, I haven't –'

But she would like to. She would like to so much.

Before she knew she was doing it, she was telling Audrey about Steve. Surprisingly, Audrey was disapproving.

'You need to be so careful, Livvy. Is he discreet? You don't know, do you? The tabloids would have a field day with his story. You need men who have to be discreet, either for the sake of their marriages or their professions, and preferably the latter. Most men are far more careful with their careers than with their wives. When you find someone like that then, and only then, you make it plain what you want.'

'I find it difficult to talk about such things,' Olivia confessed.

'Really? God, and I always had you labelled as the spoiled little rich kid who always took what she wanted.'

'I suppose I am a bit like that, but not when it comes to – sex. I just can't talk about it, somehow.'

'I was like that, once. Like you, I'm an only child of strict, elderly parents. It's a pain. I had the most sheltered, boring upbringing you can imagine. But there's no need for these childish inhibitions.'

Audrey laughed softly.

'I'll have to introduce you to Clive, my chauffeur. He's a magnificent lover who I always say should be available on prescription. He'll soon get rid of your inhibitions. Yes, together, Clive and I will show you a new world of pleasure.'

Olivia protested for almost an hour. She neither

wanted nor needed to meet Audrey's chauffeur. Nor did she need any instruction in what was such a basic act!

'Soon, you'll know exactly how to get what you most desire,' Audrey promised. 'And I hope,' she added in a whisper, 'that one day you'll desire me.'

Olivia's head flew up.

'Has a woman ever made love to you, Livvy?'

Audrey's voice was lowered, but Olivia still checked to make sure other diners weren't listening. Confident they weren't, she gave a slow shake of her head.

'Do you think you'd enjoy that?' Audrey persisted.

'I don't know,' Olivia replied, but the thought excited her. It wasn't the first time she had thought about it, either.

'I think you would,' Audrey murmured. 'I know I'd enjoy making love to you . . .'

That startling statement remained with Olivia on the short journey home.

When she let herself in, Dorothy was crossing the hall, dragging the vacuum cleaner behind her.

'That came – hand delivered,' Dorothy greeted her in the usual curt manner, pointing at a large manila envelope on the hall table.

'Thank you, Dorothy.'

Olivia had been about to make herself a coffee but she couldn't bear the thought of Dorothy watching her every move. Instead, she strode into the hallowed ground of the kitchen, grabbed a bottle of wine from the rack, and picked up a glass. She would drink her wine and think about Audrey's shocking proposition in privacy.

She picked up the envelope on the way to her study.

As she walked, she frowned at it. Only her name was printed on the envelope. There was no address, no nothing, only a PHOTOGRAPHS – DO NOT BEND sticker.

When she reached her desk, she picked up her letter opener, sliced through the flap and took out the single monochrome photograph.

The envelope fell to the floor as she stared at the contorted black and white figures.

Chapter Five

*A*udrey pushed the door shut with her bottom and kicked off her shoes. It had started to rain and she shook a few droplets of water from her hair, glad to be home.

She loved their home. When she had first moved in with Tony, the house had struck her as dark and oppressive, but she had soon changed all that. These days, his stuffy ancestors frowned down disapprovingly at her from light beechwood frames that broke up the large expanses of white walls. The stern faces had been in evidence all over the house but Audrey was slowly moving them to out-of-the-way corners. She had even managed to sneak a couple off to the attic.

Luckily, Tony adored her, and had given her free rein when it came to decorating. Everywhere was white. It was an excellent backdrop for the splashes of bright colours she liked to create. Oriental rugs were shown off against thick white carpets. She loathed gardening, but had a passion for flowers. She loved the red, orange and pink blooms that drew the eye straight to them and demanded attention.

Wearing black jeans and a tight scarlet shirt, Audrey

felt like an exotic bird against the soothing white. Not that the white felt particularly soothing today; she was bored.

The answer machine's zero was blinking at her to show there were no messages. She had hoped Olivia would phone her, had been hoping that for days, but she wasn't really surprised that she hadn't. Disappointed, but not surprised. Not too disappointed, though. Audrey had always enjoyed a challenge, and if Olivia wanted to play hard to get, so be it. One day, she would be hers. Just as Lloyd had once been hers. Yes, it would be very satisfying. If she couldn't have Lloyd, then she would have his wife.

She and Lloyd had been lovers for eight years and Audrey missed him still. What hurt, what still hurt, was the way Lloyd had ended it so abruptly. One minute they were enjoying each other's bodies on a regular basis, the next it was over and Lloyd was announcing his plans to marry Olivia.

Audrey was no fool. She knew Lloyd too well to believe he had become squeamish about cheating on his wife. He had cheated on his first wife for years without a qualm. Nor could she believe that their lovemaking had grown boring for him. No, something had frightened Lloyd into his squeaky clean lifestyle, and she would love to know what that something was. Or perhaps he wasn't so squeaky clean. Audrey couldn't imagine that the repressed Olivia was satisfying his whims.

She picked up the receiver and tapped out Olivia's number. She knew it by heart.

It was answered on the fourth ring.

'Livvy? It's Audrey. How're things?'

'Oh – hi, Audrey. Fine, thanks. How are you?'

'Bored,' Audrey replied. She hadn't missed the wary edge to Olivia's voice. 'I wondered if you felt like coming over for dinner this evening. Lloyd's away, isn't he?'

'He is.' There was a slight pause. 'I'm sorry, but I have plans for this evening.'

Audrey waited but there was no elaboration.

'How about tomorrow?' she persisted, struggling to keep the impatience from her voice.

'Tomorrow? I'm not sure. Can I get back to you?'

'Of course.' Audrey decided to try another approach. 'Or how about Friday evening? Tony's in Paris, but he'll be back on Friday and I'm sure he'd love to bore us both to tears with his enthusiasm for the city.'

'Yes, OK. Thanks, Audrey. I'll look forward to it.'

Audrey heard the relief in Olivia's voice.

'Me too,' she said lightly. 'Seven-thirty suit you?'

'Lovely. Thanks again.'

Audrey replaced the receiver with a satisfied click. She couldn't wait to see Olivia's expression when she discovered that Tony was still in Paris . . .

There had been no special deliveries for Olivia today. She had no idea who was sending the photographs to her, or who was delivering them. She knew only that they made her feel sick. The people featured were the same – a woman with dark hair, a man with fair hair, and Lloyd. They were indulging in some sort of sexual orgy, and at times it was difficult to see where one naked body ended and another began. Despite spending hours on watch at the window, only once had she seen a figure push one of the familiar manila envelopes through the letterbox. She had thought the figure was male but it was difficult to tell. Male or female, they had walked smartly from the corner of the road, wearing full motorcycle leathers and a black crash helmet, ran up the steps, pushed the envelope through the door and then hurried on to be lost in the crowd. The envelopes – there had been six to date – had arrived at different times of the day. Last night's, or this morning's, had landed on the carpet at a few minutes after midnight.

She assumed that someone intended to blackmail her, or blackmail Lloyd. She couldn't understand why the photographs were addressed to her. Such incriminating material could end Lloyd's career, so surely it would have made sense to send them to him?

Every time she opened an envelope, she expected to find instructions on where to leave a holdall full of used, non-consecutive notes, and every time the telephone rang, she expected to hear a threatening, muffled voice. Nothing happened, though. Perhaps she had been watching too much television lately.

Something had to happen though, she knew that. What she didn't know was how she would react. It would depend on what demands were made, she supposed, but if they thought she was going to bankrupt herself to protect Lloyd, they were very much mistaken.

Whoever was behind this was playing right into her hands. She still had the video, and now she had the photographs. It hadn't crossed her mind until the photographs started to arrive, but the video gave her power over Lloyd. The photographs merely added to that power. She could wreck Lloyd's life – his whole reason for being – so very easily.

A satisfied smile crossed her face. Lloyd would soon discover that his marriage wasn't quite as convenient as he had thought.

She glanced at her watch. Her taxi wasn't due for another ten minutes – more than enough time for another glass of wine. It was Dutch courage. She wasn't looking forward to dinner with Audrey and Tony. Tony was boring, and Olivia knew all too well what Audrey would be thinking about. She could bear that, though. What she couldn't bear was the humiliation of Audrey introducing her to Clive, the chauffeur-cum-stud.

She wished she was taking her own car – it would be easier to escape – but she'd had too many glasses of wine so that was out of the question now. It didn't matter, though. She would chat to Tony about Paris and leave as early as was polite.

'Your taxi's here, Mrs Standish,' Dorothy shouted up the stairs.

'Thank you, Dorothy.'

Olivia emptied her glass in one swallow, put on her jacket and picked up her bag. It was absurd but she couldn't help thinking of lambs and slaughter.

The taxi was warm and comfortable, and she sank back against the upholstery. Her shoes were new. She'd worn them in the house but now they were pinching her toes, so she eased them off her feet and wriggled her toes.

'Bloody 'ell!'

The driver's heartfelt exclamation made her forget her feet.

'Look at that daft prat!'

'Yes.' As Olivia didn't know which daft prat he was referring to, it seemed easier to be on his side.

'A bomb scare earlier,' he said, turning his head to speak to her. 'It was all sorted hours ago but the roads are still clogged. It's not surprising with daft bloody prats like that on the road.'

'Ah.'

He was about Olivia's age, she supposed. He had long fair hair tied back in a ponytail and was wearing a denim shirt. He looked clean, as if he had recently stepped out of a shower. There was no resemblance whatsoever but he made her think of Steve.

'Sorry about this, love. Don't worry though, we'll be moving in a tick.'

'I'm in no hurry,' Olivia told him, turning her head to look out of the window.

Her mind wasn't on the damp streets outside, it was

73

on Steve. She owed him an e-mail. He had written to tell her about a small studio flat he had bought in Brighton – 'easier to work away from wife, kids and all things domestic' – and said he hoped she would visit soon.

She would. She wanted to see him again. Audrey didn't approve, she knew that, but so what? Olivia was more than capable of running her own life.

'At bloody last!'

The taxi jerked forward, did a sharp right turn and gathered speed.

Fifteen minutes later, Olivia was stepping inside Tony and Audrey's home. The white came as a shock; it always did. To Olivia, it was a mixture of futuristic and sterility, spaceships and hospitals. Hospitals mostly, she decided. The huge displays of red roses in the hall were like splashes of blood.

'Livvy! Wonderful to see you!' Audrey kissed her cheek. 'I thought I'd be eating alone. Tony's stuck in Paris.'

'Oh!' Damn and blast!

'I thought you were going to desert me, too,' Audrey scolded lightly.

'Sorry. The traffic was bad. The taxi driver said something about a bomb scare.

'Another? Here, let me take your jacket.'

Silently cursing Tony's absence, or Audrey's deviousness, Olivia shrugged out of her jacket and handed it over. Her blue dress was short, showing off her long legs. She wished now that she had worn something more concealing. Audrey was wearing scarlet – another splash of blood.

'Come into the dining room. Are you ready to eat?'

'Yes, of course.' Olivia wasn't convinced she would be able to swallow a morsel.

The dining room was white, of course, but Audrey

flicked a switch and the room was immediately bathed in a warm, pink light.

'Audrey – that's lovely!'

'Isn't it? I called in a lighting designer – marvellous woman. I can change the colour to suit my mood. Look!'

The room changed from warm pink to cool, ice blue, to dangerous red, to reverent purple, to safe green. Olivia was very impressed. It amazed her that the colours could change the room, and the mood, so dramatically.

'Tonight I'm in the pink!' Audrey laughed as she flicked the switch again, bathing everything in that warm pink.

Olivia hardly touched her food. She was too nervous, and too busy knocking back wine. It seemed, though, that the more she drank, the more sober she felt. *Pull yourself together*, she told herself firmly. She had visited Audrey alone dozens of times and Audrey had never leaped on her yet. The idea made her smile to herself. That wasn't Audrey's style.

'Let's have coffee in the sitting room,' Audrey suggested, 'and I can show you the lighting in there.'

Olivia followed her along the hall to the sitting room.

'This is Clive, my chauffeur.' Audrey introduced the stranger who was sitting in an armchair looking completely at home. 'He'll drive you home. It's the devil's own job getting a taxi on a Friday night. Now – look at the lights in here.'

Clive? Clive! Olivia's heart hammered out the name as Audrey played with the lighting controls. Whether bathed in pink, red, white, blue, green or Audrey's final choice of purple, Clive looked very masculine, and very threatening.

'You should think about the lighting in your study, Livvy. According to my designer, you need blues for creativity.'

Olivia forced her mind back to the subject of lighting.

'My work's not particularly creative,' she replied. 'It's more a case of digging up the facts and putting them in some kind of order. It's more methodical than creative.'

'Perhaps green, then,' Audrey mused.

Olivia sat down. She had to. Her legs felt as if they belonged to someone else. Her heart was still hammering, but Audrey poured coffee as if it were the most natural thing in the world for the three of them to be tinted a holy shade of purple. She looked at Clive. He hadn't said a word, but Olivia could feel him watching her, assessing her. He was different to how she had imagined him. He was probably around forty, but it was difficult to tell. He was wearing black jeans and a blue shirt. Even sitting, he seemed tall. Dark hair grew back from his face. There was nothing special about him, nothing that would have made him stand out in a crowd.

Audrey handed her a cup of coffee and Olivia tried to relax her hands so that it didn't rattle in the saucer. No way would she let Audrey know how nervous she was.

'Coffee, Clive?' Audrey asked.

'Sure. Why not?'

It was the first time Olivia had heard his voice. The lazy, almost insolent drawl was quite attractive.

Audrey poured him coffee and handed him a cup. She poured herself a cup and stretched out on the sofa. Olivia, trying to give the impression that she was relaxed, slipped off her shoes and flexed her toes on the now purple-tinted oriental rug.

They all took their coffee black, she noticed.

A phone rang – but not in the sitting room.

'The machine can get it,' Audrey murmured, taking a sip of her coffee. 'Is it too warm in here?'

'I'm fine,' Olivia replied. In truth, she was very warm

but she wasn't convinced the heating system was to blame. 'Do you need a chauffeur, Audrey?' she asked, changing the subject. 'Don't you enjoy driving?'

'Enjoy it? Not particularly. Do you?'

'I love it. I hate being driven.'

'Really?' The idea seem foreign to Audrey. 'It is hot in here, you know.'

Olivia watched spellbound as Audrey unfastened the buttons on her dress, from neck to waist. Beneath the dress was a scarlet, lacy bra. At least, Olivia thought it was scarlet. It was difficult to say; everything looked purple.

As if this happened everywhere she had coffee, Olivia sipped her drink and forced herself not to be shocked.

She finished her coffee and returned the cup and saucer to the tray.

'More coffee?' Audrey asked.

'No, thanks.'

They were playing games, Olivia realised. Audrey was trying to shock her, and Olivia was refusing to be shocked. Audrey poured herself another coffee. She didn't ask Clive if he wanted one. He clearly did, though. He stood up – he was even taller than Olivia had thought – and took a couple of lazy strides to the tray. Instead of pouring himself some coffee, he held out his cup and waited for Audrey to do it for him. As she did so, his eyes never left her.

Olivia was intrigued by their relationship. Clive acted as if he were the master of the house.

They spoke of Olivia's writing, Audrey's latest shopping binge, Tony's health, Audrey's garden – still Clive didn't speak.

It struck Olivia with some surprise that, although she could ask to be taken home or call a taxi, she no longer wanted to leave. She had to know what was going to happen next. Apart from the strange lighting, and a sense of anticipation hanging in the air, the atmosphere was quite normal. And yet she knew that something would happen.

Clive finished his coffee and put the cup and saucer on a nearby table. Audrey finished hers and returned her cup and saucer to the tray.

'Phew – it is hot.'

Audrey stood up and took off her dress. No one spoke. Olivia was too busy marvelling at Audrey's firm body. It looked as if it should have belonged to an athletic eighteen-year-old. Olivia simply couldn't take her eyes off Audrey. She was wearing a scarlet bra and skimpy scarlet briefs. A lacy scarlet suspender belt held dark stockings in place.

'I'll get you a lighting brochure,' she said, skipping out of the room.

When she came back, she put the brochure by Olivia's handbag and returned to stretch out on the sofa.

'Thanks,' Olivia murmured.

Still Clive said nothing. He too was watching Audrey. Her skin was tinted purple. They were all tinted purple. It was bizarre.

While this thought was going through Olivia's mind, Audrey unfastened the clasp at the front of her bra. Her breasts, round and very firm, sprang free, and Audrey absently ran her fingers over her nipples. Olivia felt a sharp tingle in her own breasts. She glanced at Clive. He was watching Audrey with a look of something approaching lack of interest on his face, but as he shifted position and stretched his long legs out in front of him, she could see from the bulge in his jeans that he was far from uninterested. Olivia couldn't seem to get her breathing in order. Either she held her breath for long seconds, or she was taking in huge lungfuls of air and almost choking. Only Audrey looked totally relaxed. She suddenly looked straight at Olivia and continued to tease her nipples. The rosy peaks jutted out hard and pointed. Olivia licked her lips and swallowed with difficulty. Audrey lifted her hips off the sofa and pulled her panties down her long, slender legs before kicking them to the floor. The crinkly hair of her mound was the same colour as that on her head. It was a shame it had purple tinges to it.

'Don't look so alarmed, Livvy. I'm not going to seduce you . . .'

'I'm not alarmed.'

'. . . yet.'

Olivia wasn't alarmed exactly. Embarrassed, yes. Fascinated, certainly. Shocked, definitely. The wine she'd had earlier was helping at last, though.

She sucked in her breath. Audrey's fingers had slid down her body and were running through her crinkly pubic hair. Audrey threw back her head and slipped a finger inside her sex. Olivia knew an almost overwhelming desire to touch her own body.

'Clive, lie on the floor,' Audrey said without looking at him.

Without saying a word, Clive lay on the rug, his hands linked nonchalantly beneath his head. The hard length of him was evident in his jeans. Olivia's heart was racing.

Audrey continued to pleasure herself. She was taking no notice of them, but suddenly she looked straight at Olivia.

'Isn't he delicious? And so willing.'

She half-rolled off the sofa and kneeled beside Clive. She had an amazing body.

Slowly, very slowly, Audrey unfastened the buckle of Clive's belt. She unthreaded it and pulled it free. Laughing, she gave him a couple of flicks across his bulge before throwing the belt aside.

Olivia ached to see him naked but Audrey was determined to take her time. Olivia felt detached. It was like watching the video of Lloyd. She was nothing more than a spectator. She was safe.

The zip on Clive's jeans was finally lowered and he obligingly lifted his hips so that Audrey could slide his jeans and underpants down his legs. His penis – freed at last – stood upright, thrilling Olivia.

'Mmm. What do you think, Livvy?'

'Very impressive,' Olivia murmured, embarrassed, and Audrey laughed.

'I agree. It's knowing what to do with it that counts, though. And Clive knows what to do with it – don't you, my love?'

'Yes, I know.'

'He tastes good too, Livvy.' As if to demonstrate, Audrey bent her head and sucked hard on the tip of his cock. 'I can never resist him,' she murmured, letting her fingers slide along his length. 'Not,' she added with a wicked laugh, 'that I've ever tried.'

Olivia couldn't sit still; she was highly aroused. How she envied Audrey's total lack of inhibition.

She watched spellbound and torn apart with jealousy as Audrey straddled Clive and sank down on his cock. Sadly, or so it seemed to Olivia, her back was to Olivia, so she couldn't see the expression on Audrey's face. She swayed backwards and forwards, lifted herself almost completely off him and then sank down on to him again. She lifted herself off him again, giving Olivia a full view of his long, hard penis before sinking down again.

'It will be your turn to enjoy him next, Livvy,' Audrey said, slightly breathless as she began to bounce up and down on him.

The sharp protest died on Olivia's lips. What was the point? She *did* want to enjoy him. She would love to feel him inside her as Audrey could. Any woman would.

It was obvious that Audrey was enjoying him. Her

movements grew so frenzied that Olivia wondered how he could lie there so impassively. Amazingly, his hands were still linked behind his head.

After a series of short, sharp cries, Audrey collapsed on top of him with a satisfied gasp.

When, a minute or so later, she climbed off him – reluctantly, it seemed to Olivia – Olivia was amazed to see that his penis was longer and harder than ever.

'Livvy's turn,' Audrey told him, giving him an affectionate slap on the thigh. 'Be the perfect gentleman, Clive.'

He laughed. 'I'm always the perfect gentleman.' He looked at Olivia, and she was grateful that the purple lighting hid her blushes. 'The pleasure will be mine.'

He sprang up and moved to kneel in front of Olivia's chair. Very gently, he lifted a hand and lightly stroked her face.

'Allow me.' He pulled her forwards slightly and lowered the zip at the back of her dress. His voice dropped to a whisper. 'Relax. Don't worry about anything – forget Audrey. Let me make love to you.' His words were gentle and hypnotic in her ear. 'Come and lie beside me.'

She stood up, as if in a trance, and her legs felt unsteady. Perhaps the wine was responsible.

He pulled her dress down so that it fell to the floor, then took her hand so that she could step free of it. She stood like an obedient child as he deftly took off her bra and pulled her panties down, leaving her wearing just her suspender belt and stockings.

'Come here,' he whispered again. 'Come and lie with me.'

She lay on the rug and he lay on top of her, taking his weight on his elbows.

'Let me make love to you,' he murmured, covering her face with kisses.

She could feel his long, burning rod against her belly,

81

and he pressed it hard against her. Shielding her from Audrey's view, he lifted himself off her slightly and touched her eager sex. He slid a large finger inside her, and the effect was so electric that she had to bite her lower lip to stop herself crying out. She wanted him and she wanted him now. With her eyes tightly closed, and her hands gripping his shoulders, she was aware of every breath he took. His finger found her aching bud and tugged on it, making her gasp. Still his cock was hard and hot against her hip. She felt it jerk as he lowered his head to suck on her eager nipple. Her fingernails dug into his shoulders, hurting him probably, but she couldn't release her grip. He didn't appear to be in pain though, because he lifted his head and, when she opened her eyes, he smiled a secret smile.

'Do you want to feel me inside you?' he asked in a low voice.

She nodded, her eyes pleading with him. She was desperate for him.

He moved over her, took his cock in his hand, and guided it to her wanton sex. The hot, moist tip nudged against her before he pushed a short way inside her. He was so huge that it was a little painful, but it was a pain she welcomed. Her hands instinctively went to his buttocks as if to prevent him withdrawing.

'I won't leave you unsatisfied,' he promised softly.

'Good.' She had intended her reply to sound sassy, but it hadn't. She had almost thanked him.

As he pushed deep inside her, Olivia could feel every bump and every vein of his hot cock. Her muscles contracted sharply making him twitch inside her. He thrust slowly – gently. It was a joy to feel each movement. It was almost as erotic to feel his buttocks clenching beneath her hands.

'You have a marvellous body.' He spoke as if in wonder. 'It's so responsive – so tight around me. It tries to suck me deeper and deeper inside you.'

She could feel her body responding to his words. The walls of her vagina clenched around his shaft, and she shuddered as again she felt him jerk inside her. He withdrew, almost to the tip, then pushed deep inside her.

'It's so exciting to sink into you. Feel me –' he withdrew again, then plunged inside her '– can you feel me?'

'Oh – yes.' She had never been so aroused in her life.

As his movements gathered momentum, she saw that sweat was forming on his brow. His face showed his excitement. The fact that it was her body causing his arousal excited her still further if that were possible. He had a hand planted either side of her and he arched his back, keeping his arms at full stretch.

'Look,' he said, and she followed his gaze to where his huge cock was sliding in and out of her wet sex. 'That is so erotic. Watch – and feel.'

Olivia watched and she felt. His movements became fast and urgent, and she gazed at his long prick sliding into her. Tiny shockwaves went through her body, each more powerful than the last. She wanted to urge him to go faster, but she didn't need to. It was as if he could read her body's needs. She lifted her hips slightly and thrust up at him, wanting every part of him filling her.

'God, you're good,' he said with a groan.

She increased her thrusting. Their hips banged together.

'Oh!' She couldn't bear it. She was so close – so very close. 'Oh – yes!'

Her orgasm exploded suddenly, catching her unawares and making her cry out loudly. She fell back, breathing hard, while the aftershocks rippled through her body.

When she was completely still, Clive withdrew. His cock was still huge and it pointed at the ceiling.

Without taking his eyes off Olivia, he began manipulating it roughly with his hand.

'I want to come all over you.' His breath came in short, ragged gasps.

Olivia watched his skilful hand moving rapidly along the length of his shaft. The sight excited her. She longed to put her hands on him, and her fingers twitched longingly. As if he really could read her mind, he used his free hand to reach for hers. He clamped it around his busy hand so that her hand was between both of his, moving with his. Three hands moved in rapid unison on his rod. How could he bear it? Olivia's neck was aching with the effort of keeping her head raised so she didn't miss anything.

She felt the power of his climax, delighted in the long, deep groan of pleasure and relief that accompanied it, and rejoiced at the spurt of hot come that splashed on to her belly and into the valley between her breasts.

'I suppose you've both forgotten I'm here.'

The sound of Audrey's voice, sharp with jealousy, made Olivia jump. She *had* forgotten Audrey. She peered around Clive's body and saw that Audrey was using her fingers to pleasure herself.

'Lick my pussy,' she ordered Clive, adding sarcastically, 'if you've got the energy.'

Despite the sharp prod he received from Audrey's high-heel clad foot, Clive laughed.

'I've always got the energy for you, my love.'

Olivia watched him caress Audrey's thighs before spreading them wide. His dark head lowered to obey Audrey's command.

Olivia's sex throbbed at the memory of his body, and at the thought of the pleasure he was now giving Audrey. Olivia wanted him again. Never had she experienced such intense pleasure.

'That's enough.' Audrey pushed him away and got

to her feet. She crossed the room to a set of drawers, pulled open the bottom one and delved inside. 'As you're not much use to anyone at the moment . . .'

The sentence trailed away as she held up a huge vibrator. It was probably black, Olivia decided, despite the fact that, like everything else, it looked purple.

Audrey moved to stand in front of the kneeling Clive with her legs wide apart. She handed him the vibrator. Olivia was still marvelling at the size of the thing when she realised that there was no need for it; Clive's penis was stiff again.

Audrey and Clive had obviously played this game before, Olivia decided. Clive ran the vibrator up Audrey's thighs, then held it against her sex.

'Put it inside me,' Audrey ordered him.

He did. He used it expertly and all the while his cock grew more hard. Olivia wished – God, she wished for anything anyone would give her.

Audrey climaxed quickly and loudly.

'Don't stop!' she gasped and, within minutes, she climaxed again.

Olivia was torn apart with jealousy, but no one was taking any notice of her. She thought longingly of Lloyd, and she thought of Steve with equal longing. She wished either or both of them were here.

'Use it on Livvy,' Audrey told Clive.

Olivia hated being discussed as if she were a piece of the furniture. She couldn't object though; every nerve in her body was screaming out its need. Apart from propping her head on her hand, she hadn't moved. She was still lying on the floor where Clive had left her.

He came to her now and kneeled by her side, the vibrator in his hand. When he finally pushed it inside her, she could have wept with gratitude. It filled her completely, stretching her. Despite being so highly aroused, she couldn't find the satisfaction she craved. It jerked and pulsed inside her, but it wasn't what she wanted.

'I often think my toys give you too much pleasure, Clive,' Audrey said, sounding petulant again.

As if to prove her point, she lifted her foot across Olivia's body and pressed her shoe against his hard cock. His short groan thrilled Olivia. The fact that Audrey could inflict a lot of pain with the long, thin heel of her shoe didn't seem to bother him at all.

'If you're good to us,' Audrey said, pressing harder and making him gasp, 'I might give you my shoes.'

He looked at her questioningly.

'Livvy first,' she told him, 'but don't wear yourself out.'

He handed the vibrator to Audrey, and grasped his penis in his hand as he straddled Olivia.

'You want me?' he asked her.

'Yes.' God, did she want him!

He pushed his way gently inside her and she had to cling to his shoulders with the sheer joy of it. Why did it never feel this good to have Lloyd inside her?

Clive was teasing her. He withdrew completely, leaving her aching, then plunged inside her again. Olivia couldn't stand it. She grasped his buttocks and pulled him close. She lifted her hips to meet and embrace each thrust. Her heart was racing. The blood was pounding in her ears.

She wished it was Lloyd giving her such nerve-jangling pleasure. No, she wished it was Steve.

Once again, the strength and suddenness of her orgasm took her by surprise and she screamed out loud.

She slumped back on the rug, exhausted, but it was good to feel him inside her still.

'My turn,' Audrey said sharply, and he withdrew.

With a lazy laugh, he stood up and lifted Audrey off the floor, impaling her on his hard rod. Audrey's arms circled his neck as tightly as her legs wrapped themselves around his waist.

Again, that jealousy surged through Olivia. Clive was holding Audrey tight as he pounded into her, and it seemed so unfair. Audrey's head was thrown back in wanton abandonment. Clive's thrusting pushed them forward until Audrey's back was pressed against the door. Clive pounded into her, hard and fast, and Olivia felt sure Audrey must be in pain. She didn't look – or sound – as if she was, though. The sounds she made were those prompted only by intense pleasure. She climaxed loudly, making Olivia shiver with jealousy.

'Your shoes,' Clive reminded her.

He lowered her to her feet, but Audrey hadn't finished with him yet. She looked exhausted but she returned to the drawer where she kept her vibrator and took out a short riding crop.

'Where are your manners? People who ask don't get,' she said sharply, flexing the crop in her hands. She kicked off her shoes, picked them up, and held them in her left hand. 'What do you plan to do with them?'

'I'll take good care of them.' His voice was pleading with her.

Barefoot, Audrey walked around him in everdecreasing circles, then she lifted the riding crop and brought it down with a stinging crack on his buttocks, making Olivia jump.

Clive moaned as if with great pleasure. His cock was hard, and ramrod straight.

'Dogs play with shoes,' she told him, lashing out again with the riding crop. 'Perhaps I should get a collar and lead and take you for walkies.'

'Oh – yes.' Clive seemed delighted at the suggestion.

Olivia was surprised by the disappointment she experienced as Audrey tossed the riding crop aside. After her initial shock, it had excited her to see Audrey whipping him.

Audrey was soon waving something else in front of him, though. Something that looked like a collar and lead.

She kneeled in front of him and, to Olivia's fascination and pleasure, fastened the leather harness around his penis. It looked painfully tight. She then hooked a long chain to it and, laughing, began to lead him around the room. Clive's chest was rising and falling with excitement. His cock kept twitching in its confinement.

'So what do dogs do with shoes?' Audrey snapped at him. 'They chew them. Are you going to chew mine?'

'Oh, no.'

'No. I know exactly what you want to do with mine.'

He shuddered with pleasure.

'Don't I, Clive?' Audrey gave a sharp tug on the lead.

'Yes!'

'Here –' She handed him a shoe. He caressed it longingly, lovingly – he put it to his nose, sighing happily as he inhaled her scent. 'Walkies are over,' she told him, unfastening the leather contraption.

Olivia could hardly breathe for excitement. She watched in fascination as he ran the shoe over his cock. Amazed, she watched him try to slide his hard pleasure-giver into the shoe. It was an open, strappy sandal, but it would never fit. Surely he was far too large.

Clive soon proved her wrong. He pulled the straps over his cock, one by one, until the shoe was clamped on. Then, with his hands on his hips, he walked around the room with the shoe on his prick. It should have looked absurd but Olivia found the sight extremely exciting.

She was still lying on the floor, and Audrey joined her. Neither of them could take their eyes off him.

As if he'd resisted long enough, he towered over them, and held the shoe in both hands. He began to thrust. His whole body shuddered with pleasure and small moans escaped him.

Olivia suddenly noticed that Audrey was pleasuring herself as she watched Clive. Olivia could feel her own sex throbbing its need. She held off for as long as she could, but the sight of Audrey's fingers working rapidly, coupled with the sight of Clive gaining such pleasure from Audrey's shoe, soon became too much for her. She, too, used her fingers to bring herself to orgasm as Clive finally despoiled Audrey's shoe.

Chapter Six

Steve was composing an e-mail to Olivia when his phone rang. He reached for it.

'Hello?'

'Steve? It's Jane.'

He swung his legs off the desk. Well, well, well!

'Hi, Jane. What a coincidence. I was just writing to you. How are you? I haven't heard from you for ages.'

'I'm fine, thanks – although very busy.'

'I should be busy too,' he murmured, 'but I've been struggling to forget our train ride.'

There was a pause. Was she shy? Or was she simply frigid? Steve couldn't make up his mind what the hell she was, but she certainly wasn't the Olivia that Carmen remembered.

'I'm coming to Brighton tomorrow,' she said, surprising him. 'I wondered if I could look round this new studio I've heard so much about.'

He was even more surprised at the unexpected request.

'You certainly can. I'll even cook you lunch. Now there's an offer you can't refuse.'

'Thanks.' She laughed. 'I think.'

'Yes, well. Don't expect too much,' he warned her. 'Of the studio, or lunch. I'm a struggling writer – remember? – which means a studio is just another word for a hovel. It gives me peace and quiet, though. Oh, and I'm a lousy cook.'

Another long pause.

'What time's your train?' he asked. 'I'll meet you at the station.'

'No need. I'm driving. I've got your address so I'm sure I'll find you.'

'I don't have your address,' he pointed out – lying.

'No.'

'It doesn't matter, though.' The last thing he wanted was to scare her away. 'I'll look forward to seeing you tomorrow. What time?'

'About twelve?'

'Great.'

When he replaced the receiver, he looked around his new office. It was the usual tip. He had always been able to work surrounded by clutter, ever since he wrote his first novel at the age of sixteen while sitting at his mother's kitchen table. That fact was unlikely to impress Olivia, though.

He picked up the receiver again and tapped out a number. It rang and rang before Carmen finally answered it.

'You sound half asleep,' he greeted her.

'I was fully asleep until you woke me,' she complained.

'At this time of day?' Carmen often took naps during the day, though. 'Listen, I won't be home tonight. Olivia's phoned. She's paying me a visit tomorrow.'

'Is she?' Carmen was fully awake now. 'I wonder why.'

'It must be my body she's after,' he said with a wry laugh. 'Anyway, I'll need to tidy up here.'

'You will. And for God's sake, see if you can dig up

91

more dirt on Lloyd Standish, MP. Talk money, too. She must be loaded.'

'I'll do my best,' he promised. 'Anyway I'll need to stay the night here. I've got loads of work to do and the place looks as if a bomb's hit it.'

When the call was over, Steve began tidying his studio. It was small, thank God, just two rooms and a bathroom.

He used the large room as a study, with one desk set aside for writing. He had always preferred to write first drafts on paper before transferring them to his computer, which sat on the other desk. The walls were lined with books – or should have been. Currently, and usually, books were scattered in piles around his desks.

The smaller room housed a single bed, complete with tatty bed-linen, cooker, fridge and sofa. He rarely used the bed or the cooker, only when he worked late and was too tired, or too lazy, to go home.

He pulled on his jacket and made a mental note of items he needed from the shops: bed linen, food, wine . . .

'Rumour has it,' Jack confided in a low voice, 'that Michael's voting against it.'

'Why shouldn't he?' Mark said, lighting another cigar. 'Unlike the rest of us, he's got nothing to lose.'

'He's always been a subversive,' Jeremy put in. 'Every party needs one and Michael is ours. It gives us a more human face. Joe Public feels a lot happier if someone is thought to be bucking the system.'

'What do you think, Lloyd?' Jack asked.

Lloyd reach for his glass of Highland Park. He had been more than happy to keep out of the conversation.

'I think Michael's right,' he replied slowly. 'Subversive or not, we'd all be voting against it if we had a grain of sense. It's bloody ludicrous!'

'It's the silly season,' Jack said in a matter-of-fact

way. 'The election looms and we start panic voting. If the country wants free beer and skittles, that's what we'll give it.'

'I'm sure the country would love free beer and skittles,' Lloyd remarked with a wry smile.

'I've got this blasted television grilling in the morning,' Jeremy said. 'Perhaps I'll drop a few hints. A vote for us means free beer and skittles.'

'Another drink?' Mark suggested.

'Why not?' Jack replied heartily.

Why not indeed? Lloyd thought. They would sit in their cosy club, drink their drinks, make meaningless noises about the way they *should* vote, go home to their cosy wives, then leave for the House to vote as the obedient 'yes men' they were. Having voted for free beer and skittles – or a better, if totally unaffordable and impractical, deal for the health service, in this case – they would have another few drinks and make meaningless noises about how they would like to put the country right if only they had some say in the matter.

Another glass of Highland Park appeared in front of Lloyd and he picked it up and stared at the smooth amber liquid. Try as he might, he couldn't shake off his feelings of gloom. There were times, and today was one of those times, when his life seemed pointless. He spent half his waking hours waiting for all hell to break loose – he was no further forwards in discovering who was blackmailing him over that stupid blasted video – and he spent the other half of his day toeing the party line, doing what he was told to do and saying what he was told to say.

'I daren't get involved in that one.' Jeremy's voice filtered through his thoughts. 'I've got far too many shares in that particular company . . .'

Was this it? Lloyd wondered. Were they destined to spend the rest of their lives protecting their backs?

He took a swallow of his whisky, enjoying its

smoothness as it slid down his throat. No more alcohol, he reminded himself. It was only a short drive home, and the roads would be relatively clear, but he didn't need some smart-arse constable breathalysing him. In the last six months he'd been stopped twice and, although he'd been fortunate in being able to pay them off, he knew his luck had to run out soon.

He knew why he felt so restless. It was the shock of reading that Erica was dead.

She had died four months ago, but he had only read about it that morning. If she hadn't left a surprisingly large sum of money to a local rescue kennels, her death wouldn't even have warranted that small paragraph.

According to the newspaper, Erica had been fifty-six. He had never known her age, never even thought about it until now.

He could remember the first time he saw her as clearly as if it had happened yesterday. It hadn't, of course. It had happened thirty-four years ago, when he was just ten years old.

He had been walking along the road with his mother, only a few hundred yards from their house, when he saw her. She had been wearing a short, black leather skirt, white knee-length boots, a tight, red frilly blouse and a tiny white jacket. Her long hair had been blonde with dark streaks at the crown. Her lips had been painted scarlet and her eyes, huge and blue, had been edged with thick black liner. She had held a cigarette in her hand and had shivered violently as she inhaled. Lloyd had been fascinated. He had never seen anyone like her.

When they drew level with her, she had smiled at Lloyd. It had been a warm, friendly smile that had sparkled in her eyes. Lloyd, remembering the manners that had been drummed into him since birth, had smiled back and said: 'Good morning.'

The sting in his mother's hand as it connected with his ear had shocked him.

'We don't talk to people like that,' she had hissed furiously, dragging him along the road.

'Like what?' Lloyd had asked, confused.

'Like that! Now – not another word, young man.'

Over the years, Lloyd saw her many times, always standing on the same corner, always shivering in her skimpy clothes and always with a cigarette in her hand. And always with that ready smile that warmed his heart. Months would pass and he wouldn't see her. Either Lloyd was away at school or she simply wasn't there. Then she would be back in her usual spot. Her absences hadn't worried him too much. He had liked to believe she was holidaying in the Mediterranean or the Caribbean – anywhere that was warm.

He was fifteen years old when he stole an old coat that belonged to his mother. It was woollen – long and blue – and he couldn't recall seeing his mother wear it. When he knew his friend would be there, he crept out of the house with it.

'Hello there,' she greeted him with that lovely smile.

'I've brought you this,' he said, suddenly shy now that he was actually talking to her.

'That's for me? Why?'

'I – er – thought it would keep you warm,' Lloyd stammered.

'Warm?' Her sudden burst of laughter was not unkind. 'Well – bless you. Did you steal it?'

Lloyd thought for a moment before answering.

'I suppose so,' he admitted, 'but it's a very old coat. My mother never wears it. She has lots of coats anyway.'

'Then she's very lucky. Lovely coats and a wonderful son.' She ran painted fingernails over the coat. 'I'd never live long enough to afford a coat like this.'

'Don't you have much money?' Lloyd asked, curious.

She smiled at him.

'I've got enough to live on. That's all that matters.'

She lit a cigarette, shivering as she did so.

'Here.' He stood behind her so that she could slip her arms into the sleeves. 'Put it on and see if it fits. You'll feel a lot warmer.'

She had pulled it tight around her and huddled into its luxurious warmth. Then, to Lloyd's horror, she had started to cry. She had sank down so that she was sitting on the pavement, and covered her face with her hands. Lloyd, not sure what else to do, had sat beside her and put what he hoped was a comforting arm round her shoulders.

It had been the start of an unusual, but very special, friendship. Lloyd visited her home on several occasions. He could still remember the complicated network of buses she caught to get from the crumbling building where she had two rooms to the area where she 'worked'.

Strangely, at that time, Lloyd hadn't known she was a prostitute. All he knew was that he found more warmth in her smile, and more happiness talking to her in those dingy rooms, than he had ever found in his own home.

He often took her presents or gave her money, but on his seventeenth birthday, Erica gave him a present. Erica, dear street-wise Erica didn't think it 'proper' to take his virginity so, instead, she had arranged it with a friend of hers, a young red-haired girl called Naomi.

Lloyd had had sex with prostitutes and he'd had sex with what his mother called 'nice young girls'. He had always preferred the uninhibited, uncomplicated times he spent with prostitutes. He still did.

And now Erica was dead.

It was inevitable that they would lose touch over the years but the news of her death still saddened him.

He would have liked to attend her funeral but, even

had he known of her death, it would have been out of the question. He couldn't be seen at the funeral of a common prostitute. And that knowledge saddened him more than her death.

It was for Erica, and the thousands like her who struggled from day to day to find a week's rent, that he had entered politics in the first place. And now look at him – a performing bloody monkey!

'You OK, Lloyd?' Jeremy asked.

'Fine, thanks.' Lloyd tried to shake off his irritation. 'It's time I was heading home, though. And about next week – I might just join Michael and vote against this bloody débâcle.'

Three pairs of shocked eyes turned on him. How they hated anything to threaten the safety of their cosy little world. The room at large was checked to see if anyone had overheard his shocking statement.

'Are you mad?' Mark demanded in a low voice.

'Mad? I'm bloody furious!' Attempting a smile at the tired old joke, Lloyd got to his feet. 'I'll be seeing you.'

He felt their eyes on him as he left the room and heard their shocked whisperings.

Lloyd didn't drive straight home. He drove round the City, not caring that he had more than the permitted level of alcohol in his blood, and admired the familiar landmarks. The City always pleased his senses at night.

After driving for about half an hour, he reached a busier, if seedier, part of the City. Prostitutes strolled along the pavements, their hungry eyes assessing passing cars. He had intended to go home but there was no hurry. No doubt Olivia would be fast asleep by now. The thought struck him again that she was changing. She was becoming aloof, uninterested in him. The really strange part was that for the first time he was beginning to fancy her like mad. He had always been impressed by her beauty, but he had struggled to think of her in a sexual way. These days, he was struggling to think of her in anything *but* a sexual way.

A prostitute caught his attention. Dressed in a short, tight, red leather skirt, red leather jacket and red knee-length boots, she couldn't fail to. Why not? Lloyd slowed the car and opened the passenger door for her.

'Get in.'

She did so without hesitation and stretched out against the leather upholstery.

'Nice car.'

'I'm delighted you approve,' he replied with amusement.

It *was* a nice car though. As part of the 'be-seen-to-be-driving-British' campaign, he had exchanged his Mercedes for the Aston Martin.

'Is that a CD player?'

She was the wrong side of thirty, although still attractive, and she made her living on the streets. Somehow, that made her childish delight even more appealing.

'Yes.' He showed her his selection of CDs. 'Help yourself.'

She chose Dire Straits.

Lloyd drove to a secluded street, stopped the car and switched off the engine.

'I don't have much time,' he told her.

She looked disappointed.

'But I pay well,' he added with amusement.

He adjusted his seat to the recline position, unzipped his trousers and took out his penis. Putting his other hand at the back of her head, he gently pulled her face into his lap.

She was an expert, but Lloyd had expected nothing less. Her mouth was like a tight velvet glove around his cock. He held her head, running his hands through her bleached hair as her red-painted lips worked their magic. Her teeth teased him as her tongue flicked over his glans with lightening speed. She cupped his balls through his trousers as his cock hardened and throbbed beneath her skilful ministrations. He thrust deeply into her throat and she willingly took all of him. With a few powerful thrusts, he came inside her mouth.

'You really are good,' he murmured appreciatively. 'I'll have to make sure I have more time in future.'

'I'd like that.'

'A nice hotel room, perhaps.'

Lloyd adjusted his clothing and his seat, then reached for his wallet. He took out a wad of notes and gave her two hundred pounds.

'As I said, I pay well.' It was worth it just to see the delighted surprise on her face. 'Buy yourself a new lipstick.'

And thank one of your colleagues, he added silently, remembering his old friend Erica.

Olivia's heart was racing with a mixture of anticipation and nerves as she stopped her car outside Steve's studio. Her nervousness annoyed her. She had no need of him now; it wouldn't matter a toss if she never saw him again so there was no excuse for nerves. She was already pretending she was Jane, so she could just as easily pretend she was Audrey. She would treat him with the same disdain with which Audrey treated Clive. On that train journey he had led the way, but not this time. This time it would be her turn to call the shots.

She climbed out of her car, hit the remote to lock it, got half-way up the steps to an imposing blue front door, then had to go back for her handbag.

Feeling a complete fool, and praying he wasn't watching her, she took a few deep breaths and, this time, got to the front door and rang the bell beside Steve's name.

She heard him bounding down the stairs and was reminded of the way he had of moving.

'Jane! Welcome to my humble hovel. You found it OK?'

'Easily, thanks. Your directions were spot on.'

He was wearing jeans this time. They looked new, as if the dye hadn't had time to fade. They were tight too; Olivia could see every muscle in his thighs. He was wearing a black T-shirt which also hugged his body.

He took her into his study and Olivia was impressed. It was neat and tidy, and plenty of daylight streamed in through two windows. An inexpensive but attractive pine desk was clear except for a shorthand notepad, a glass paperweight and a framed photograph.

'Your wife?' she asked.

'What?' He frowned at the photograph and looked surprised to see it there. 'Oh, yes. Yes, that's Donna. Here – let's have your coat.'

He helped her out of her coat and hung it on a hook on the study door.

'She's younger and prettier than I imagined.' It was a head, shoulders and enviable cleavage pose. She had full, pouting lips and an inviting smile. She reminded Olivia of someone but for the life of her she couldn't think who that someone was.

She tried to take an interest in the rest of the room but it was difficult.

'Come through here,' Steve suggested.

Olivia followed him into another room, smaller than his study. This room was far more intimate. The light wasn't as good, creating shadows everywhere. A small bed with crisp, new-looking dark blue sheets, a sofa complete with brightly coloured throwback, a fridge, a cooker, two small cupboards – and that was it.

'Red or white wine?' he asked. 'Or would you prefer coffee?'

She shook her head. She needed something a lot

stronger than coffee. 'White wine would be nice. Thanks.'

Disdain, she reminded herself, but it wasn't easy.

She watched him take the chilled wine from the fridge and pour some into two glasses. He really did have the most beautiful hands. She remembered the feel of them on her skin and she shivered.

'Cold?' he asked.

'Not in the least.'

She was warm. Her body felt as if it was on fire. But she was shaking with nerves.

'Is steak and salad OK for lunch?'

'Perfect,' she replied.

'How do you like your steak?' he asked.

'Medium rare.'

'Right.' He grinned at her. 'One lump of charcoal coming up . . .'

Olivia did nothing but watch him. He prepared the salad and cooked the steaks as if he were used to looking after himself. The steaks were perfect, and the salad crisp and fresh. As there was no table, they sat side by side on the sofa with the plates on their laps.

'Do you realise,' Steve mused, 'that I know absolutely nothing about you? I know your name, I know you're married and I know you live in a flat in London. That's it. You're a complete mystery to me, Jane.'

'What else is there to know?' she replied with a shrug.

'I don't know.' He thought for a moment. 'Tell me about your husband. What's his name? What does he do? Do you love him? Does he love you?'

'His name is Neil and he's a lawyer.' The trouble with lies, Olivia thought, was that it was so difficult to remember what you had said. 'He loves me, of course, and I love him. That's why we married. Satisfied?'

'It looks like I'll have to be,' he replied with a wry

smile. 'I can't picture him, though. I can't even imagine you being married.'

Olivia thrust her left hand under his nose.

'One wedding ring.'

She glanced at his left hand. It was bare.

'You don't wear a ring,' she noticed.

'No. When Donna and I got married, we could only afford one ring.' He laughed. 'Things aren't much better now. My publisher keeps describing me as a best-selling novelist, but unfortunately my royalty statements don't back up that claim.' He glanced at her. 'I don't suppose you have financial worries. Lawyers make plenty, don't they?'

'Enough,' she answered. 'You're a good cook,' she added in an attempt to change the subject.

'I have to be. Donna's hopeless. She struggles to boil an egg. What about you? Do you cook? Or is Neil the cook?'

'We manage between us.'

'What sort of car does he drive?'

'What?' His questions were making her uneasy, but she was forced to laugh at the absurdity of that one.

'OK. Let me guess. Porsche? BMW?'

'A BMW,' she lied. 'A blue one with four wheels, four doors . . .'

'OK. I know when I'm being told to mind my own business,' he said with a laugh.

As soon as they had eaten, Steve refilled their glasses. The atmosphere was suddenly tense.

'May I use your bathroom?' Olivia asked.

'Of course.'

The room was small but clean. She soon discovered that the door didn't even close, let alone lock, and she had to sit on the loo with her foot outstretched to keep the door pushed against the jamb. The sound of her pee hitting the bowl was deafening. She took her time washing her hands, splashed cold water on her face, then held her wrists under the cold tap for a full minute to try and cool herself down.

When she emerged from the bathroom, she was too embarrassed to look at Steve so she wandered over to the window and gazed out. The buildings opposite were the same as this one; tall and imposing. Most had been converted to flats, she guessed. She pressed against the glass and her breasts tingled at the pressure.

She could sense Steve watching her. This time, she would make the first move. What had Audrey done? Simply taken off her blouse. That didn't sound too difficult.

Still with her back to Steve, and with her body pressed against the window, she carefully unfastened the buttons on her blouse. Very slowly, she turned around.

'It's hot in here.'

Steve nodded his agreement, his gaze on the swell of her breasts nestling in the lacy white bra.

'You're incredibly beautiful, Jane. You really are.'

Beautiful, but not sexy. She could see something in his eyes though, something that emboldened her sufficiently to push her blouse aside and run a finger across the white lace.

'Not as beautiful as the whores you write about though,' she replied lightly.

'You could act the whore if you wanted to.' He shrugged. 'Any woman can.'

Not this woman, she thought. Not convincingly at any rate. And certainly not with an audience.

'You're doing it now,' he went on. 'You're showing me your body, trying to arouse me.'

She didn't like that 'trying'.

'On the contrary,' she replied airily. 'I'm just hot.'

He gave an unconvinced murmur in response.

'Why?' she asked. 'Are you aroused?'

'Of course.'

Encouraged by this, she slipped off her blouse and threw it on the sofa. She couldn't look at him; instead she reached behind her, unfastened her bra, shrugged out of it, tossed it aside and walked back to the window. Again, she pressed against the glass. Her nipples tingled and hardened at the feel of the cool glass against them. The sensation was delicious, making her move her breasts across the glass in search of more pleasure. She doubted if anyone could see her; people walking along the street would have to crane their necks too far, and the road was wide so that the buildings opposite were too far away. Not that it mattered if people *could* see her. In fact, the thought excited her. Perhaps someone in the building opposite had a pair of binoculars or a telescope trained on her. The notion made her smile. Or a camera. She thought of the photographs of Lloyd that kept dropping through her letterbox. That thought wasn't so amusing.

A movement was reflected in the glass. Steve was moving towards her. Her muscles tensed. He stood quite still behind her for a few moments before running his hand across her right shoulder.

'Did I say you could touch me?' she demanded.

'No. Sorry.' There was a tightness in his usually lazy drawl that she had never heard before.

'Then don't!'

A shiver ran down to her navel as she sensed him stepping back from her. She was in control. She was actually in control!

When she turned round, she didn't quite know how she expected him to look – bored perhaps, or annoyed, amused even. There was no sign of any of these, though. Instead, she could see a hunger burning in his eyes. She knew he wanted her. Don't they say that you always want what you can't have?

'You invited me to lunch,' she reminded him. 'You didn't say you expected more.'

'I wasn't – I'm not expecting more,' he replied.

'Good.'

Olivia lifted both hands and toyed with her hard nipples. It felt so good. She often touched herself when she was in the privacy of her home but it was far more exciting to do it in front of Steve, especially when she heard his breath catch in his throat.

'Another glass of wine?' he asked.

'No, thanks.'

While he poured himself a glass, Olivia unzipped her skirt and let it fall to the floor. She stepped aside and slipped off her white panties.

Steve said nothing, but he took a large gulp of wine and Olivia suspected he was struggling to swallow.

'I suppose,' she said, 'that you think you did something very clever on our train journey? You didn't.' She covered her bush with her hand and slipped a finger between her thighs. 'I do what you did all the time. I didn't need you.'

He inclined his head slightly before murmuring, 'But wouldn't you prefer to feel something larger than your finger inside you?'

At that moment, strangely, she wanted nothing more than her own touch. Steve wanted her, she knew it, and the knowledge thrilled her. She was no longer a piece of jewellery that men liked to show off; she was desirable. She was sexy.

'Sometimes,' she replied, 'but I can always improvise.'

Full of a daring she didn't know she possessed, she walked over to the cupboard and chose the largest banana from the fruit bowl.

'This is quite acceptable,' she told him as she slowly started to peel it.

'But soft,' he pointed out. One hand cradled his wine glass and he put the other hand in the pocket of his jeans. 'Which I'm not,' he added.

She shrugged, not knowing how to respond to that. She'd had great plans for her banana but, for a moment, she was tempted to eat the damn thing. She couldn't do that, though. She would lose control. Averting her gaze from his, she ran the cool, flesh-like banana across the top of her thigh and then rubbed it against her sex. Already the banana was warm from her skin. It was also very soft, and if she wasn't careful it would break. She slowly – and very carefully – pushed the tip inside and heard Steve's sharp intake of breath as she did so. Again, that previously unknown feeling of being in control thrilled her and she looked up at him, pushing the banana further inside herself as she did so. The banana itself did nothing for her – it was too thin and too soft – but the desire burning in Steve's eyes was highly arousing.

She was surprised and disappointed when the banana turned to mush so soon.

'Why don't you eat it?' she suggested. 'It seems a shame to waste it.'

'Sure.' He didn't move.

'You'll have to come and get it.'

He crossed the room in an instant and immediately dropped to his knees in front of her. With those large hands on her thighs, he began to eat the mushy remains of the banana. When the banana had gone, he moved back a couple of paces, although he still remained on his knees. He was aroused; Olivia could see the evidence pulling his jeans tight. It was tempting to ask – no, *order* – him to undress. She longed to see him naked, longed to feel him hard inside her. She wouldn't, though. Not yet.

'You may touch my breasts if you wish,' she said.

He stood, like an eager-to-please puppy, and was about to take her nipple into his mouth.

'Touch with your hands only,' she said sharply.

A soft sigh escaped him and Olivia suspected he was

enjoying her show of dominance as much as she was. His hands caressed her breasts, long fingers stroking and tugging lightly on the hard, pointed peaks. When he swayed slightly, she felt the hard length of his cock press against her belly. His jeans felt rough on her skin, but she enjoyed the sensation. Then she wondered if he had brushed against her on purpose.

'Hands only,' she reminded him.

Her skin was warm, but his hands were very hot. They were slightly moist too, and glided over her heavy breasts.

'You may touch the rest of my body,' she said in an authoritative tone.

His hands slid down her ribcage and around her hips as he obeyed her. *As he obeyed her.* Olivia loved this. Never had she known such power. It was so easy, too.

Moisture was oozing between her legs and she pressed her thighs together. She didn't want Steve to know how aroused she was.

'That's enough,' she told him, and she rejoiced in the way his hands immediately dropped to his sides.

She reached for his belt, unfastened the buckle and pulled it through the loops. She licked her lips as she tossed it aside. Then she lowered the zip and tugged his jeans over the hard bulge that so excited her. His fully erect phallus sprang free. Olivia could do nothing but admire it for a few moments. It wasn't particularly thick – not that she had much knowledge of such matters – but it was very, very long.

'You want me?' he asked, almost pleading now.

For answer, she made him kneel on the floor, so that his face was level with her sex, grabbed his hand and pushed his middle finger inside her. His expert movements immediately transported her back to their train journey and she climaxed almost immediately.

The pleasure of her orgasm was short-lived though.

She wanted more, much more than his finger inside her.

'Stand up,' she commanded.

He did so.

'Suck my nipples.'

His hands went to her hips, hesitantly, as if he expected her to remonstrate, and then his mouth fastened itself around her nipple He sucked noisily, greedily, letting his tongue flick over the peak. All the while Olivia could feel his shaft hard against her belly. It jerked against her. They were both breathing hard.

On an impulse, Olivia grabbed Steve's hand and dragged him to his study. She pulled his chair from under his desk and made him sit so that his long, beautiful cock pointed at the ceiling.

He was waiting for her to impale herself on his pleasure-giver, she guessed, and, although the idea was very appealing, she resisted. Instead, she perched herself on the edge of his desk with her legs spread wide apart. She wanted to feel his tongue inside her but the words refused to come. Steve reached for her and she held up a threatening hand.

'You may touch me with your tongue only.'

He lunged for her hungry sex with an eagerness that thrilled her. She *could* make demands.

She moaned softly as his tongue probed inside her. The fire within her burned fiercely and she knew she had to feel him inside her to get the satisfaction her body craved.

'Enough!' The tone of her voice surprised her. It brooked no denial.

She moved away from the desk, straddled him, and slowly impaled herself on his deliciously long prick. It was thicker than she'd thought. It filled her, spreading her.

'Preferable to your banana?' he asked with a knowing laugh.

'I've seen better,' she retorted, refusing to lose control.

With her feet planted firmly either side of his chair, she began moving up and down on him. She neither knew nor cared if he was finding the experience pleasurable. The only thing that concerned her was satisfying her own cravings. She rode him faster, her hands on his shoulders, fingernails digging into his flesh.

Steve threw back his head and moaned. As she bounced up and down on him, she felt his cock jerk inside her. Feeling desperate to come herself, she released one hand from his shoulders and rubbed frantically between her legs. When her orgasm finally came, crashing over her in wave after wave, she screamed out with pleasure – and triumph – before flopping exhausted against him.

With a couple of thrusts and a long, deep shuddering groan, Steve climaxed too.

Their breathing slowed to a more normal pace. Beads of sweat were clinging to his face, she noticed.

'You're right,' he said, 'it is too warm in here. Would you like a glass of wine?'

And that was it, Olivia thought. She had made her demands, claimed what she desired, was feeling fulfilled and content – and now they were discussing wine, as if nothing had happened.

'I'd like a mineral water, if you have one.'

'I think so.'

He gently lifted her off him and went through to the other room.

Olivia leaned back in his chair. As far as he was concerned, she supposed nothing *had* happened. Or nothing out of the ordinary. He would have no idea that this was the first time Olivia had felt in control. Nor would he know just how much that feeling of power had thrilled her. OK, so it hadn't been terribly imaginative, but it hadn't been so bad for her first attempt. Practice makes perfect, she reminded herself, and she intended to get lots of practice.

She glanced across Steve's desk to the photograph of his wife. Perhaps she should have felt guilty, or perhaps Steve should feel guilty. Who the devil did the woman remind her of? It didn't matter – Olivia didn't care that she'd just had sex with the woman's husband – but the question niggled and she knew it would continue to niggle until she came up with an answer.

Chapter Seven

When Olivia arrived home, she went straight to the sitting room, kicked off her shoes and threw herself down on the sofa.

Every now and then, shivers ran down her spine as she remembered special moments, but she wanted to relive every astonishing second of the day. *Suck my nipples.* Had she really said that? Yes, she had, and her breasts still tingled at the memory.

Smiling to herself, she stretched out and hit the remote to switch on the television.

Her smile vanished immediately and she sat upright, frowning as she tried to catch what was being said. She had recognised Lloyd immediately, despite the flock of reporters crowding round him with their cameras held high, but she couldn't tell where he was. He was wearing a stiff smile for the benefit of the flashing cameras, and she heard him say 'No comment' several times before he pushed his way past the reporters and climbed into a waiting black car. The news reporter then introduced the weatherman.

Olivia scanned the teletext pages but there was no mention of Lloyd in the news. What had he done and why were reporters hassling him? Could it have anything to do with the photographs that kept arriving? Perhaps whoever was responsible for sending those had blackmailed Lloyd. If he hadn't paid up, and God knows he had a stubborn streak, perhaps they had decided to expose him.

She fiercely hoped it wasn't that. It wasn't the thought of the government facing another sleaze scandal, or even the thought of Lloyd having to resign that troubled her. What really worried her was the thought of losing the hold she had over him. Those photographs signified power and she didn't intend to lose it without a fight.

Her mind racing, she phoned Audrey to see if she had heard anything. The gossip that Audrey missed wasn't worth hearing.

'I did hear something,' Audrey told her, 'but it was very vague.' Audrey, too, sounded very vague, as if her mind was on more important matters. 'Something to do with a vote. I think Lloyd was threatening to vote against the government.'

'Is that all?'

'As far as I know. Why?' Audrey asked curiously. 'What's he been up to?'

'Nothing, as far as I know.' Olivia wondered if it had been a mistake to call Audrey.

'I'll let you know if I hear anything else, Livvy.'

Olivia decided her luck was in, because Audrey sounded keen to get back to whatever her call had interrupted . . .

The phone rang as soon as Olivia replaced the receiver.

'Is he there?'

The sound of her father's angry voice infuriated her. She had hoped it was Lloyd calling her.

'Lovely to hear from you, too, Father,' she replied,

her voice heavy with sarcasm. 'And if you're referring to your son-in-law, then no, he isn't here.'

'What in hell's name is he playing at?' he demanded. 'His mobile's been switched off, all day.' Before she had a chance to reply, he barked out, 'Tell him to call me!'

The connection was cut.

'Bastard!' Olivia muttered, banging down the receiver.

All pleasure in the day was slipping away from her. She had felt so powerful; For the first time in her life, she had felt powerful; she had known she could use her femininity for her own satisfaction. She had felt desirable. Not only beautiful, but desirable. Now, she simply felt worried.

What the devil *was* Lloyd playing at? If, as Audrey had suggested, it was a big fuss about a vote, she supposed that wasn't too bad. If, on the other hand, it was tied up with those photographs, it was a different matter entirely. In her mind, she could see her own face on television, her arm linked through Lloyd's as she made the obligatory sickly-sweet comments about standing by her man. Steve would be sure to see her and he would know that he had been screwing Lloyd Standish's wife. For how much would that little gem sell?

'Oh, shit!'

Audrey's words came back to haunt her. *'You need to be so careful, Livvy. Is he discreet? You don't know, do you? The tabloids would have a field day with his story . . .'*

Of course she didn't know. She could guess, though. Steve had made dozens of references to the money he made – or didn't make – from his novels. Only today, he had asked about Lloyd's income. Somehow, she couldn't see him having scruples. Why should he? All she had done was use him so, if he had a grain of sense, he would use her to line his own pockets.

She spent the rest of the evening in front of the

television with a bottle of wine for company, but there was no further mention of Lloyd, and she was about to go to bed when she heard the front door open and then slam shut. She went to the hall to see if Dorothy had come back for something. It wasn't Dorothy, though, it was Lloyd.

'I wasn't expecting you tonight.'

'A change of plan,' he muttered. 'God, what a bloody day!'

He strode into the sitting room, shrugged out of his jacket, pulled off his tie and poured himself a large Scotch.

'I've spent half the bloody night trying to give reporters the slip. I expect they'll be camped out on the sodding doorstep by morning.'

He took a swig of whisky and undid the top two buttons on his shirt.

'What's happened?' Olivia asked. 'I saw you on TV this evening and –'

The telephone rang before she could finish the sentence.

'I'm not here,' Lloyd warned as she went to answer it.

For the second time that evening, Olivia heard her father's angry voice.

'Is he there yet?'

'I've no idea where he is, Father.'

Lloyd's eyebrows beetled into a frown when he realised who was calling.

'Is there a message for him?' Olivia asked.

'Tell him to get in touch – stupid bloody fool.'

Again, the connection was cut.

'What was the message?' Lloyd asked.

'He said, "Tell him to get in touch – stupid bloody fool." I'm not sure if the stupid bloody fool referred to me or you.'

Lloyd smiled at that, and Olivia felt a familiar pang

of longing for him. He had a very sensual smile that never failed to touch her.

'I suspect it was me,' he murmured, 'although it might have been you, for marrying me.' He got to his feet and refilled his glass. 'God, you can't even take a piss without the whole bloody world wanting to know what colour it is. I was overheard saying I might vote against the government next week,' he answered her earlier question. 'Someone got in touch with the press and – bingo. I have an appointment at Number Ten on Friday to have my knuckles rapped.'

The telephone rang again.

'Ignore the damn thing,' Lloyd said irritably as Olivia once more rose to answer it, 'or let the machine get it. Where the hell's Dorothy, anyway?'

'It's her night off.'

Olivia unplugged the telephone. They could hear the one in the hall ringing out, and those upstairs, but the sound was bearable. She would unplug those later.

'I thought you'd been caught committing some terrible crime,' Olivia remarked.

'Like what?'

'I've no idea. How would I know what you do?'

His gaze rested on her face for a few moments.

'Well, I haven't done anything wrong,' he said at last. 'I merely said I might vote for good sense, for a change.'

Before their marriage, Olivia had admired what she thought were his principles. She had admired his stubbornness, too. Since then though, she had learned that he had only married her to help his career, and she had watched him suck up to her father and to Monty at every opportunity. His sudden change of attitude surprised her. Perhaps he had scruples, after all.

'I hope you do,' she said. 'I'd hate to think I had married a younger version of my father. God knows, he would do anything for a pat on the back from the PM.'

Lloyd nodded, but Olivia could see that his thoughts were miles away so she left him with his drink and went to run a bath.

Lying back in the scented, foaming water, she tried to recapture every moment she had spent with Steve. Her only regret was that it couldn't be allowed to happen again. Audrey had been right; Olivia needed to be discreet. Today's little scare had taught her that much. For all that, it was good to remember those magical moments. At first, she had thought he wasn't particularly interested in her, but the more she had toyed with him, the more he had wanted her –

Olivia sat up so suddenly that water sloshed over the side of the bath.

Carmen Blake!

The woman in the photograph on Steve's desk was Carmen Blake.

Olivia's mind raced with a dozen questions, none of them pleasant. Unless Carmen had changed her name to Donna, which seemed highly unlikely, then Steve had lied to her. Her breathing slowed to a more normal pace. Why on earth would he do that? He didn't – couldn't – know that Olivia had known Carmen or Donna or whatever she chose to call herself these days. Nor could he know that Jane was in fact Olivia Standish.

Carmen Blake! Olivia couldn't believe it.

It had been twelve years since the two girls had seen each other. Carmen had left school at sixteen, on her sixteenth birthday in fact if Olivia's memory served her right.

'I'll get you back, you bitch!'

With a shudder, Olivia recalled the last words Carmen had thrown at her. But they had been prompted by teenage bravado. Carmen would have forgotten all about her by now. Or would she? In the same position, would Olivia had forgotten her? Probably not.

Olivia lay back in the water again and recalled those schooldays with little pride. Carmen had arrived midterm, she remembered, when the rest of them had already found their way around and made friends. Any newcomer would have struggled to fit in but Carmen, arriving in a uniform that was obviously second-hand, and speaking in an accent that was pure East End, had come to them gift-wrapped. Full of their own superiority, they had picked on her relentlessly. They had teased her because she never had any money, because no relatives ever visited her, because she had no friends, because she spoke so badly, because she often had to spend the holidays at the school. Olivia had often felt small twinges of guilt at their treatment of her but, having spent so much of her life without friends herself, she hadn't wanted to lose those she had found at the Queen Alexandria.

Olivia hadn't thought of those days for years but she could remember one particular day as clearly as if it had been yesterday.

'I think I've lost forty pounds!' In complete astonishment, Olivia had uttered those words to Victoria, her best friend.

'Carmen!' Victoria said immediately. 'Didn't I say we'd have to keep an eye on things before Sticky Fingers got her hands on them?'

'Vicky! I'm not even sure I've lost it, let alone had it stolen.' Olivia sat on her bed in the small dormitory and tried to think how much money her parents had given her and how much she had spent. 'I could have left it in my pocket. Let me check.'

After a thorough search, though, she knew the money was lost.

'You need to report this to Miss Rigley,' Vicky declared. 'I bet that little madam's had it.'

Olivia protested but she had finally been persuaded

to visit Miss Rigley's study. She didn't mention their suspicions, only said that the money had been lost.

'If anyone hands it in, I'll let you know,' had been Miss Rigley's response, 'but in future, Olivia, I suggest you take better care of your money. It all comes far too easily for you girls. In my day . . .'

The lecture had gone on and on.

The money wasn't found and the girls chose to blame Carmen. Their taunting was cruel, no matter how many times Olivia reminded them that they had no proof that the money had been stolen in the first place.

Carmen, not surprisingly she supposed, had assumed that Olivia was behind the accusations and, one day, when they had been alone in the library, she stopped in front of Olivia.

'Don't you *ever* call me a thief again, you stuck-up, prissy-nosed bitch!'

The words had sounded menacing and Olivia had known real fear.

A couple of months later, Olivia's watch vanished. It was a slim, gold wristwatch, a Christmas present from her parents, and although it held no sentimental value, it was an attractive piece of jewellery. She had taken it off when she went to bed and put it in her bedside cupboard, as she did every night. The following morning, however, it had vanished. Olivia searched through her cupboard, behind the cupboard, under her bed, everywhere.

'You know where it is,' Victoria had scoffed as Olivia continued to search.

'Carmen wouldn't take it,' Olivia had retorted. 'How could she wear it here? She's not stupid. Everyone would know whose it was.'

'She could sell it.'

'She wouldn't!' But it was a possibility and Olivia knew it.

Miss Rigley was at the end of the corridor and

Victoria, in her own inimitable way, acted Best Pupil of the Year and asked their headmistress if she could spare a moment of her valuable time.

'Olivia's watch has been stolen, Miss Rigley.'

'Stolen?' Poor Miss Rigley had struggled to grasp this notion. Theft at the Queen Alexandria was unheard of. 'Are you sure? That's a very serious allegation, Victoria. Very serious indeed.'

'I know, but we're quite sure,' Victoria said before Olivia could answer. 'Several things have gone missing,' she went on. 'We haven't liked to say anything, Miss Rigley, but if you could search Carmen Blake's property –'

'Vicky!'

'– before she realises Olivia has noticed the watch is missing,' Victoria went on, ignoring Olivia's interruption, 'I'm sure you'll find the culprit and be able to deal with this – er – problem before it gets out of hand.'

'Carmen Blake?' Miss Rigley's face had turned white.

'Yes, miss.' Victoria had nodded.

Later, when Carmen's belongings were searched, it had been difficult to say who had been the most shocked, Miss Rigley, Olivia, or Carmen herself. The only person who made no show of surprise was Victoria. Carmen had insisted the watch had been planted there and Olivia had never been entirely convinced that she wasn't speaking the truth.

And now, all these years later, their paths had unknowingly crossed again. Carmen would be furious if she knew that her husband had spent part of his afternoon on his knees eating the remains of a banana from Olivia's secret place . . .

The press had been hovering around Lloyd all day like vultures. He had finally lost them – for the moment – but he could feel the tension in every muscle in his body. His head ached, his neck and shoulders ached, even his teeth ached. Perhaps he needed a massage. The wonderful Henri, whose amazing talents he had first heard about from Audrey and now heard about from Olivia, could get rid of tension within seconds, apparently. Lloyd, however, preferred to find his relaxation elsewhere.

'This will be fine, thanks.' He tapped on the glass to tell the driver to stop. 'Anywhere here.'

To avoid the press and their army of cameras, he'd had to don jeans and an old jacket and dive into three different taxis.

He took a note from his wallet and handed it to the driver. 'Keep the change.'

'Thank you, sir.' The chap would have touched his forelock if he'd had one.

Lloyd had no real idea where he was. At night, one area of London looked very much like any other. It was the abundance of pubs that had attracted him to the street.

A car drove up and parked in the spot the taxi had pulled away from but Lloyd paid it no attention. Only as he walked along the damp pavement did he hear a woman's heels tapping on the ground behind him. He hesitated outside a pub and stood for a moment until she walked past him. Her heels were high and her legs long. So long as she wasn't a journalist wielding a camera, though, Lloyd couldn't care less how long her legs were.

The windows of the pub let a small amount of light spill on to the pavement but it was impossible to see inside. Oh, well – he pushed open the door to The Fountain and stepped inside.

It was one of those pubs that normally he wouldn't be found dead in. What it lacked in style and comfort, it made up for in noise. From a jukebox in the corner, Stevie Wonder was telling everyone that he'd just called to say he loved them. Two girls in their twenties were dancing drunkenly to the music and, while Lloyd was having a pint of beer poured for him, they pulled an elderly lady to her feet. Dressed all in green, with a green beret perched on top of her grey hair, there was something of the leprechaun about her.

He paid for his pint and took it to a table in the corner. From there, he watched the other drinkers enjoying themselves. A brief fight broke out between a black guy and a white guy but within minutes the two antagonists had their arms draped around each other and were practically crying into each other's beer. No one took any notice. Lloyd could only assume it was fairly normal behaviour for this place.

It was far removed from the offices of Number Ten where he had spent an uncomfortable hour, that morning. He had known the outcome of course; either he toed the party line, and more importantly was seen to be doing so, or he found himself promoted to some foreign backwater.

Trying to ignore the thought of the germs clinging to his smeared glass, he took a large swig of beer.

Blackmail, that's all it was. In some ways, it was easier to sympathise with the scum blackmailing him over that damn video.

He was making little progress in that direction. Peter, Linda's brother, was working hard but, as yet, they had no idea who had made the video, or where it had been made. The letters demanding money had been printed on a laser printer, one of the many thousands of laser printers in the country, so no clues were on offer there. The demands had been relatively small, but the blackmailers were getting greedier. The last letter, demanding a payment of five thousand pounds in cash, had told Lloyd to take a taxi to Paddington Station where he would be given instructions as to where he was to drop the money. This time, Peter planned to be right behind Lloyd to see who picked it up. Not that the 'who' mattered; Lloyd could hardly have them marched off to the nearest police station. No, the important thing was to destroy all copies of that damn video.

He finished his pint and went to the bar to order another. For now, he wanted to forget his problems.

He was returning to his table in the corner when a young woman walked into the pub. Lloyd tried to place her; he felt sure he'd seen her somewhere before. She ordered a white wine, paid for it, then looked around for a vacant table. Not seeing one, her eyes rested on Lloyd for a moment before she walked over to him.

'Do you mind if I share your table?' Her accent held traces of the East End.

'Please – be my guest.'

He realised then where he had seen her before. She was the woman who had parked in the taxi's spot, the one he had watched walk past him on those incredibly high heels.

'You look out of place in here,' she remarked after a while.

Lloyd looked around him. 'Everyone looks out of place in here,' he replied with a wry smile.

'It's a dump, isn't it?' Laughing, she added, 'Do you come here often?'

'I've never been here in my life,' he told her truthfully. 'A drink's a drink when you're thirsty, though.'

'True.'

She didn't look particularly out of place. Her hair was dark and well-cut, framing a face that boasted incredible cheekbones and very little make-up. Her skirt was short, showing off those long, slim legs. She wore a skimpy, low-necked top that revealed a delicious amount of very tempting cleavage. Lloyd felt the first stirrings of desire.

'I've been in here half a dozen times,' she said. 'I

have business nearby and this is as good a place as any to unwind.'

He nodded, his gaze still on her full, milky white cleavage until she crossed her legs and he caught a brief glimpse of smooth, white flesh at the top of her stocking.

'It's always noisy,' she added, 'but I quite like that. If you have to drink alone, it's nice to have a bit of life around you.'

'Do you often drink alone?' he asked.

'It depends.'

It was too noisy for any real conversation and Lloyd was more than happy to watch her drinking her wine. She oozed sex appeal and he suspected she knew it.

'Would you like another?' he asked when her glass was empty.

She glanced quickly at her watch before nodding and smiling. 'Thanks.'

He wondered if she noticed the bulge in his jeans as he stood up and went to the bar. There was nothing he could do about it. He wanted her. He wanted to feel his cock sliding along the valley between those beautiful breasts.

He carried her wine back to the table and sat opposite her. She glanced at her watch again.

'Are you meeting someone?' he asked. He hoped not.

'No. No, it's not that. I've booked myself into a nearby hotel and I don't want to be too late getting there. The streets around here are a bit creepy at night.'

'I'll walk back with you, if you like,' he offered.

'Would you mind?'

'Of course not.'

'Thanks.' She laughed softly, her eyes sparkling as they met his. 'Rape is supposed to be every woman's secret fantasy and yet half of us are too scared to walk the streets late at night.'

'Is it your secret fantasy?'

'I think it's every woman's fantasy.'

Lloyd wasn't so sure about it being every woman's fantasy, but he was more than prepared to go along with it. Normally, Lloyd preferred the women in his life to take a very active role, but nothing would give him greater pleasure tonight than to have her body at his disposal to do with as he pleased.

'I don't know your name,' he said.

'Jill.' She answered quickly, too quickly. 'What's yours?'

'Jack.'

She laughed. They were both lying, and they both knew it. Lloyd couldn't care less what her name was, though. He had his reasons for lying, and she was equally entitled to her own.

He saw the mark left by her lipstick on the glass and thought how good it would be if she left a similar mark on his cock. God, he was hard. He noticed that her nipples were showing hard and pointed through her top. For a moment, he wondered if rape was Olivia's secret fantasy. Lately, he didn't know what to make of her. She was changing. She seemed to get some thrill out of walking naked round their bedroom. She also seemed to get a thrill from telling him she was too tired when he made any advance towards her. And, despite claiming she was tired, she spent a torturous amount of time tossing and turning before sleep finally claimed her. Her thigh would brush against his, or her breast would touch his arm. It was driving him to distraction. The less interest she showed in him, the more he wanted her. Last night, he had felt a strong urge to spank her until her skin was red and take her by force . . .

'Are you ready?' his companion asked.

'Of course.'

'Don't feel you have to walk me back to the hotel,'

she said quickly, 'if you'd rather stay here and have another drink.'

'I'd rather walk with you.' He was so aroused he would have trouble walking at all.

'Thank you.'

Her car wasn't where she had left it, but Lloyd assumed she had parked it at the hotel. The building was a couple of hundred yards away.

'Here you are, safe and sound,' Lloyd remarked when they reached the door.

He held his breath and waited.

'Would you like to come inside for a drink?' she asked, as he had guessed, and hoped, she would.

'I'd like that. Thank you.'

She collected her key from reception and took a quick look at the hotel's bar.

'It's very crowded. Shall we have a drink in my room?'

The bar was almost empty.

'That would be good.'

They took the lift to her room on the second floor. It was a large room with a double bed and a single. The TV had been left on, although the sound was muted, and apart from this a single lamp offered the only light. An overnight case was open on the dresser. Several stockings dangled over the back of a chair.

Not bothering to offer him a drink, she walked to the window and stood peering out into the darkness, her back to him.

Lloyd didn't intend to play games. He wanted her and he wanted her now. He strode across the room, grabbed her hips and pulled her roughly back against him so that she would feel his arousal. She gasped, but made no attempt to move. With one arm round her waist, holding her captive, he yanked down her briefs.

'Oh, no – please.'

The half-hearted protest was part of the game she

wanted to play. She could have escaped his hold easily enough had she wanted to.

'You're asking for trouble, lady,' Lloyd said heavily. 'If you invite men to your room, they won't assume they're there for cocoa.'

'But I only thought –' She gasped again as he pulled her tight against his erection.

'You'll get what you want,' Lloyd promised.

'Please, no. I beg you.'

Lloyd unfastened the button on his jeans, undid the zip and pushed his jeans down around his knees. He took his stiff penis in his hand and jabbed it against her milky-white thigh.

'No, please –'

Strangely, he found her false protests arousing.

'Oh, yes,' he retorted. 'You've been teasing me all night – showing me your cleavage and making sure I caught a glimpse of your stocking tops.'

'I haven't!'

'Turn around.'

'Oh, no – please.'

'Turn around.' He yanked her round so that she was facing him. Her cheeks were flushed pink, her nipples standing out hard and erect against her flimsy top. 'Do as I say or I'll have to get really rough with you.'

A soft sigh escaped her.

'What are you going to make me do?' she asked.

'I'm going to give you what you deserve. I'm going to give you what you've been asking for all night.' She went to protest, but Lloyd put a hand over her mouth. 'Feel that?' He jabbed his cock between her thighs. 'That's what your teasing has done to me. Feel it. Hold it in your hands.'

'No – I couldn't.'

Lloyd slapped her lightly across the face. He wondered for a moment if he'd gone too far but she threw back her head with a soft moan before groping for his cock. Her hands were light and motionless around it.

'Hold it properly,' he snapped out.

Her grip increased slightly.

'Tighter,' he said, trying to make his voice sound menacing. 'Stroke it – before I get really rough with you.'

She followed his instructions.

'Faster!' Lloyd ordered.

'I will, but please don't hit me again.'

Lloyd almost laughed out loud. He didn't, though; he was too aroused to spoil her little game. He slapped her across the face again, just hard enough to leave a pink tinge to her cheek but not hard enough to hurt. He felt her hands tremble as they moved rapidly along the length of his cock.

He pulled her away from the window, clamped a hand across her mouth and slapped her on the bottom. Her gasp of pleasure was hot against his hand. He slapped her again, enjoying the way she showed her pleasure by working her magic on his cock. Occasionally her long fingernails would lightly scratch the underside, making him groan with pleasure. Moisture was oozing from the tip and she rubbed it against the softness of her belly.

He remembered the red imprint of her lips on the wine glass and knew he had to feel those lips around his cock. Reaching behind him, he tugged one of her stockings from the chair, then turned her around and tied her wrists together. Grabbing her roughly by the arm, he spun her round and threw her on the bed. She lay back, hands tied behind her back, eyes wide, and her skirt around her waist so that Lloyd could see the triangle of hair covering her secret place. Lloyd took off his clothes, watching her all the while, but she made no attempt to move. Her gaze was fixed on his erection. He climbed on to the bed and straddled her chest, making it impossible for her to move even if she had wanted to. Thrusting himself at her face, he took her hair in his hand.

'Take it in your mouth. All of it. Every inch.'

She made little whimpers of protest until Lloyd slapped her thigh. He slapped her again and again, and each time she writhed beneath him.

'Take me in your mouth,' he ordered harshly.

Her lips formed a scarlet 'O' and she raised her head slightly as she sucked his cock into her mouth – deeper and deeper. She sucked hard on him, and ran her tongue over the bumps and veins. Lloyd's heart was pounding as her mouth slid up and down his hot, aching penis. His knees were trembling and he put one hand on the wall behind her head to support himself. He reached back and slapped her thigh with his other hand. The effect was electric; she writhed and sucked vigorously, making him groan with pleasure.

He wanted the pleasure to last much longer, though, and had to pull out of her mouth before he lost control. Still straddling her, he pushed her flimsy top over her breasts. Her bra fastened at the front and with a quick movement, he undid the clasp and pushed the lace cups aside. Taking her breasts in his hands, he pushed them together to form a perfect cushion and then watched his cock slide up and down the soft valley of milky cleavage. Her tongue flicked out whenever he neared her mouth and she continued to squirm beneath him. Her breasts were gorgeous – swollen, heavy but oh, so soft. He flicked her nipples with his fingers. Her breathing was fast and irregular.

Her knees were raised and he pushed them flat. He moved back, raised her skirt so that it was around her waist and admired her triangle of dark hair. He slipped a finger into her sex. She was very wet. All thought of protest had gone now. He knew she was close to orgasm and he slipped another finger inside her eager sex and used his thumb to stroke her clitoris while his fingers plunged deep inside her. Her orgasm was quick and powerful, her hips rising off the bed to push hard against his hand. She closed her eyes and let out a long, grateful sigh of pleasure. Lloyd watched her for a moment, but he was too aroused to let her lie still. Her silly protests had excited him and he wanted to hear them again. He moved to her side.

'Roll over.'

He pushed her over, so she was lying on her front. Her skirt had fallen down and he pushed it up around her waist again so that her bottom was clearly visible. The sight of her hands, still tightly bound, thrilled him.

'Open your legs.'

'Oh, no – no more, please.' But she spread her legs wide. 'Please, don't hit me.'

Smiling to himself, Lloyd spanked her bottom. A red mark appeared where his hand had touched her. It excited him and he spanked her again, harder this time. Each time he spanked her, she moaned softly and lifted her bottom off the bed slightly.

His cock was aching, begging for the relief it craved, and he stroked it while he continued to spank her. Her bottom was covered in red marks. He ran his cock along the valley between her buttocks; it jerked as he slapped her and felt her response.

'Stop – I beg you!' She was breathing hard and she lifted herself off the bed to press against his cock. 'Please take pity on me!'

'Shut up!' He slapped her hard and felt a shudder of pleasure in his navel at her groan.

He slipped a hand beneath her to raise her hips off the bed. Only too eager to please, she was on her knees, thrusting her bottom high. Lloyd wanted the game to last for hours yet but he was dangerously close. He nudged her anus with his finger, then pushed it a little way inside.

'Oh, no – not that!' she cried.

'Whatever I want,' he retorted, the idea exciting him.

'You're too big. You'll hurt me . . .'

'Yes, I'll hurt you.'

She moaned softly.

With his free hand, he lightly spanked her. Her anal muscles clenched around his finger and he pushed in still further. His cock was straining for her and he pushed the moist tip against her forbidden place. He pushed it a little way inside, opening her. She was so tight that the breath caught in his throat. Grabbing her hips with his hands, he pushed in deeper. He pushed deep inside her and withdrew almost to the tip before forcing his way deep inside her again and again.

Tired of games, and desperate now for relief, he withdrew and climbed off her. He lifted her off the bed, untied her hands, dragged her to her feet and pushed her up against the wall.

'What – what are you going to do to me?' she demanded, still breathing hard.

'I'm going to fuck you senseless,' he told her, his own breath coming in short, ragged gasps. He slammed his hand against her mouth. 'I'm going to shove my cock in your cunt and fuck the living daylights out of you!'

Her body was trembling against his as he used a hand to spread her and then pushed his penis deep inside the warm, welcoming wetness of her sex. Her tunnel walls were a perfect silk sheath for him. Her protests were over and he moved his hand from her mouth and put both hands on her buttocks, his fingers digging deep into her flesh. Her feet were off the ground, and her arms snaked around his neck as he took her weight and rammed into her. There was no way he could have held back, even had he wanted to. He had passed the point of no return long ago. He bit her neck and she pulled his hair and bit his ear. He lifted her higher off the ground and she locked her legs around his waist, letting the wall behind her take her weight. Sweat formed on Lloyd's forehead and chest as he continued to thrust. He felt his orgasm building up, felt he would explode, and involuntary grunts escaped him at each thrust. The noises he made were drowned out by the sound of her cries. She screamed loudly as she climaxed again, her vaginal muscles shuddering around his cock until, with a loud, deep groan, he came inside her.

His legs trembled with relief and when their breathing slowed slightly, he carried her to the double bed and dropped her on to it.

'Boy, did I need that,' she said, exhaling on a long, contented sigh.

'So did I.' He sat on the edge of the bed, exhausted but wonderfully relaxed. All his earlier tension had melted away.

'You make a terrific rapist,' she murmured.

She was smiling as she spoke but her eyes were closed and, within minutes, Lloyd knew she was sleeping. He watched her for a while, then slowly, with a pang of regret, he dressed. The regret was because he would like to experience the delights of her body again and knew he never could.

He flicked on the main light, blinking as his eyes adjusted to its harshness, to check the room in case he had forgotten something. Satisfied, he let his gaze linger on her sleeping form for a few final moments. It was then that he noticed the small butterfly tattoo on her neck. He hadn't noticed it while they were in the pub, but he supposed he hadn't paid much attention to anything above cleavage level. Tattoos on either sex had never appealed to him before but he found this one quite attractive.

Chapter Eight

*O*livia didn't pay too much attention to the photograph that came in the familiar manila envelope. She was far more interested in the letter that accompanied it: *There is no need to remind you of the damage that could be done to your husband's career should certain negatives fall into the wrong hands. Unfortunately, negatives have their price. Arrange to collect ten thousand pounds in cash from your bank. You will be given further instructions in 14 days.*

It was early, just after seven o'clock, and she wasn't even dressed. Clad in her dressing gown, she had been on her way to get her first coffee of the day when the envelope had dropped through the letterbox.

She sat in the hall to read the letter again. She had been waiting for something along similar lines, but the letter's tone infuriated her. Who the hell did they think they were? To make her wait a whole fortnight for further instructions was sheer malice. They were toying with her just as a cat toys with a mouse before going for the kill. If they thought they would get the better of her and blackmail her for the rest of her days, they were very much mistaken. She *might* pay for the negatives, but only when she was certain she had every single one in her possession. Then again, she might call their bluff and save her money. She already had the video and photographs; the negatives were no big deal.

She examined the photograph more closely. Monochrome, about eight inches by ten, the quality was excellent. It was her guess that the pictures had been taken by a professional photographer, someone with an artist's eye for light and form who took pride in their work rather than a snoop who used his camera as a means to an end. This particular photograph showed a threesome; Lloyd and the other man were screwing the dark-haired woman.

'Did you want something, Dorothy?' she snapped, aware of Dorothy's presence behind her.

'I wondered if it would be convenient for me to clean your study, Mrs Standish?'

Did you hell, Olivia thought irritably. You're curious about the contents of these manila envelopes more like.

'Yes. Thank you.' Olivia shoved the photograph and the letter back in the envelope.

While Dorothy flicked a duster round her study, Olivia went to the kitchen for coffee and croissants. Every now and again, she took the photograph out of the envelope and studied it. Each time she looked, she saw another detail. It didn't look as if the threesome were in a normal room; the cramped space was more indicative of a caravan, or a boat perhaps.

It was the expression on Lloyd's face that fascinated her the most, though. His companions' faces weren't so clear. The woman was sitting on the other man's penis. Her head was down and his face was turned away from the camera. Only Lloyd, gripping the woman's hips and with his penis inside her, was facing the camera. Never had Olivia seen an expression of such intense pleasure on his face . . .

Later, when Olivia was in her study, trying and

failing to concentrate on her work, Dorothy buzzed through to tell her she had a phone call from Clive, Audrey's chauffeur. Olivia welcomed the distraction. She was curious too as to why he was calling her.

'Mrs Symington's away for three days,' he explained, 'and she asked me to offer my services in her absence.'

Olivia didn't know quite what to make of that. Exactly what services was Clive offering?

'Well – thank you,' she replied slowly, 'that's very kind, but as Audrey knows, I drive myself. In any case, there's nowhere I need to go at the moment.'

'Fine. If you change your mind, though, there's a car and driver at your disposal, Mrs Standish.'

The way he called her Mrs Standish and referred to Audrey as Mrs Symington amused her. Considering he'd fucked them both, and had been fucking Audrey on a regular basis for years, the show of respect was incongruous.

'I'll remember, Clive. Thank you.'

When she replaced the receiver, she had even more problems concentrating on her work. Her mind insisted on flitting back to the evening she had spent with Audrey and Clive. Whenever she recalled that evening, it had a dreamlike quality to it. A dreamlike quality with a purple haze.

She began to wish she had taken Clive up on his offer. A car and driver were no use to her, but she didn't think for a moment that his offer had been restricted to that. If she closed her eyes, she could hear his voice: 'You have a marvellous body. It tries to suck me deeper and deeper inside you . . .'

After an hour of torturing herself with similar memories, she gave up all thoughts of work. Her body craved things that a completed manuscript couldn't offer. Clive could, though.

She tapped out Audrey's telephone number and

Clive answered almost immediately, as if he had been awaiting her call. Perhaps he had.

'Clive, I've changed my mind,' she told him. 'I would love to go for a drive. I don't really care where, although somewhere in the country would be nice.'

'I know the very place, Mrs Standish. What time would you like to leave?'

'Give me an hour.'

An hour later, Olivia had showered and changed, and Clive was waiting outside for her.

He opened the door for her and Olivia slid into the back of Audrey's Rolls Royce. Once inside, she slipped off her long coat and put it on the seat beside her. She wasn't wearing panties; the leather was cold on her bottom and it sent a delicious shiver through her.

As Clive drove, Olivia sat back and tried to relax. It was difficult, though. She had spent the last hour thinking about what she wanted to do with Clive, and what she wanted him to do to her. Already her heart was racing with anticipation.

Olivia had no idea where they were going and she cared even less, but the buildings of London were soon exchanged for green fields. She soon lost track of time and had no idea how long it was before Clive swung the car off the main road and on to a tree-lined driveway.

They were in a park, she realised. There was a formal area ahead of them with ornamental fountains dotted among landscaped gardens.

Clive stopped the car, got out and walked round to open her door for her.

'Would you like to walk, Mrs Standish? It's a lovely spot. There are usually deer to be seen among the trees.' He pointed to the large wood.

Olivia got out of the car, reached back for her coat and slipped it on.

'Would you stop calling me Mrs Standish?' she said irritably. 'Given past experiences, it sounds ridiculous.'

'You'd prefer Livvy?'

'No!' She smiled, and felt her spirits lift. 'I'd prefer Olivia.'

'Right.' He smiled that lazy smile of his in return. 'Are you going to walk? Would you like me to walk with you – Olivia?'

'Yes and yes.' They fell into step. 'I'm surprised Audrey doesn't make you wear a uniform,' she remarked after a moment.

The last time she had seen Clive, he had been dressed casually, but today he was wearing a dark suit with a grey shirt and blue tie. He looked smart, but Olivia could easily picture him in a uniform complete with chauffeur's cap and jackboots.

'You'd like me to wear a uniform?'

She thought for a moment.

'Yes,' she said at last. 'It's nothing to do with me but, if you were my chauffeur, I think I would probably insist on it.'

He smiled, but said nothing.

They walked deeper into the wood where narrow paths wound their way round old trees. Apart from the sound of birds, all was silent.

'Look.' Clive nudged her arm and pointed.

Olivia looked. She didn't know what she expected to see but it certainly wasn't a deer. She had assumed he'd been joking. Several deer darted across the path in front of them as they walked deeper into the wood.

'I'm not really interested in deer,' Olivia told him.

Realising he wasn't going to take the initiative, and surprised to find that she didn't want him to, she stepped off the path and stood, leaning back against a tree. Clive looked at her briefly, but he didn't need to be told what she wanted. He moved to stand close in front of her. She unfastened her coat, grabbed his hand

and pulled it beneath her full skirt. His hands were cold against her thighs. She saw that lazy smile of his as he moved his hand upwards to discover that she was wearing nothing under her skirt. Olivia lifted her hands to his shoulders, and let her head fall back gently against the tree. When he pressed his hand hard against her vulva, she let out a sigh of pleasure. He was so close that his masculine scent filled her nostrils. It was intoxicating. Her breathing increased its pace as he slipped a cold finger inside her. His touch was light but intense and she felt her flesh clench. The pleasure she desperately craved was so close, and she parted her legs to encourage him. He touched her aching bud, pressing on it with his index finger. A moan rose in her throat, and she cried out with joy as she climaxed. Clive stopped moving his hand for a while, and when he resumed, Olivia climaxed again, almost immediately.

'Stop,' she said, her voice shaking.

He removed his hand and put his fingers to his lips. She watched in fascination as he slid his fingers into his mouth and licked them.

'You taste so good,' he murmured lazily.

Olivia was still reeling from the pleasure he had given her. Her heart was still pounding. She wanted to walk but couldn't – not yet. Her legs were weak and she felt sure that if she took her hands from his shoulders, she would collapse.

She had to walk, though. She had to be in control, of Clive as well as herself. With shaky steps she began walking along the path, even deeper into the wood. Clive followed, his hands in the pockets of his trousers. As they walked, she wondered about him. He walked by her side as if he didn't have a care in the world. Back there, he had given her the pleasure she needed, then stopped when she asked him to. If he found her desirable, wouldn't he have been more pushy? Perhaps he didn't desire her.

137

A young couple walked towards them, taking Olivia completely by surprise. She hadn't expected to see other people, had forgotten they were in a public park. Her heart quickened as she was reminded of that magical train journey with Steve. She had been wearing her long coat then, too. She remembered the man carrying the coffee. Had he guessed what Steve was doing to her when he walked past?

'Don't worry,' Clive broke into her thoughts. 'Not many people come here. And if they do, they're not here to see the deer.'

'I wasn't worrying,' she replied. 'Far from it.'

'You like your pleasure in public?' he asked, sounding surprised.

'Sometimes.' She nodded, a touch of pink in her cheeks.

'Come with me.'

He took her arm and began leading her back the way they had come. After a while he took a path to the left that led to another road. They soon emerged from the wood and were by the side of a busy main road.

Olivia saw a long, low building set back from the road with several cars parked outside.

'A drink?' Clive asked. 'Something to eat?'

'A drink would be good.'

Olivia needed a drink. She needed Clive's touch more, though. Her heart was pounding as he led the way into the crowded bar of The Traveller's Rest. It was a typical country pub, with seats and stools covered with dark red velvet, and walls dotted with horse brasses and prints of hunting scenes. A real log fire crackled at the far end of the room.

'Sit down.' Clive nodded at a velvet-covered bar stool. 'What would you like to drink?'

'Southern Comfort, please.'

Her coat almost touched the floor behind her and she arranged her skirt so that her bare skin touched the velvet stool. She had one foot on the floor, and the other resting on the brass rail that ran round the bar. Someone jogged her elbow as they stood to order a drink. She looked around her. There were about thirty people in the bar, she calculated. A few were enjoying bar snacks, but most were drinking and talking. She took a gulp of her drink as soon as it was placed in front of her.

Clive, with a glass of mineral water in his hand, moved closer to her and pulled her open coat aside slightly.

'Your nipples are stiff,' he murmured. 'Anyone looking at you could see what you want.'

Olivia didn't know how to respond. She stared at her drink, feeling her cheeks burn. When she risked a look round, she saw that no one was taking any notice of them. The barman was deep in conversation with a couple of men at the other end of the bar. A sudden burst of laughter from a group sitting around the fire startled her, but they were laughing at their own joke.

'Is your clitoris stiff, too?' he asked provocatively.

He slipped his hand under her skirt. His fingers burned against her skin. This was madness. It was also incredibly exciting. No one could see anything; the overhanging bar hid her lap from view and Clive was too close for anyone behind them to see anything. It didn't matter though; her need overcame all common sense. She parted her legs instinctively and gasped as he touched her. She felt his fingertips on her wet flesh; felt them hot and stiff as they dug into her folds and parted them. She was breathing too quickly but she could do nothing about it.

Clive lifted his glass and took a look round the room but his fingers continued to pleasure her. Olivia wondered again how he could recognise her needs so easily. He seemed to know exactly when to increase the pressure.

She became aware of a man standing at the bar on her left, waiting to order a drink. She wondered if he could smell the scent of her sex. She put a hand in the pocket of her coat and pulled it across to shield herself. The barman came across to serve the man and, while he took the order, he looked straight at Olivia. What did he see? A flush in her cheeks? Could he guess why her breathing was so fast?

Clive increased the pressure on her clitoris as if guessing at her heightened excitement. She was so close. And still the barman was looking straight at her. Her orgasm came fiercely and she had to cling tightly to her breath to stop herself crying out. Only the quick throbbing of her thighs gave any hint of the pleasure that thudded through her body, but the barman wouldn't see that.

He gave her a quick smile and turned away to pour the customer's drink.

Clive removed his hand and Olivia reached for her drink. She drank it in one swallow, welcoming the warmth of the amber liquid as it slid down her throat. Her body was still trembling violently.

'Another drink?' Clive asked.

She needed to escape, to feel the cool, calming air on her face. She also wanted another drink, and as she didn't feel capable of walking out of the bar, she nodded.

When the barman came over to serve them, he looked straight at Olivia again. He had a knowing smile on his face as if he knew exactly what Clive had been doing to her. That was absurd, though. He couldn't possibly know. And yet when Clive handed him a note to pay for the drinks, he waved it aside.

'It's on the house.' With a final, almost wistful smile at Olivia, he went to serve another customer.

'He's definitely got the hots for you,' Clive murmured, sounding amused. 'I'm not surprised, either. You look very, very sexy.'

Olivia looked at him, searching and finding the truth of that in his eyes. She wanted him, wanted any man. She drank her Southern Comfort quickly.

'Let's go,' she suggested.

The chilly, fresh air cooled her face when they stepped outside, although the rest of her body still felt as if it was on fire.

'I'm sure that barman saw something,' she said.

'No, he just fancied you like mad. You looked as if you were hungry for sex.' He glanced at her as they walked. 'You still do.'

'I am,' she confessed, her voice shaky. 'Is it so very obvious?'

'Yes. It's also very exciting,' he answered at length.

They walked quickly, winding their way through dozens of tall chestnut trees. When they reached a thick clump of bushes, Clive grabbed her hand and pulled her off the path and into the bushes. Grateful for his understanding, Olivia took off her coat and threw it to the ground. She was still struggling with her blouse as Clive roughly kissed her. She wanted him fiercely, and knew he wanted her just as much. He pushed her down. The ground was soggy from overnight rain and she could feel damp leaves sticking to her back. She didn't care. She gripped his upper arms, creasing his jacket in her hands as he groped for his zip and slid it down. He entered her with no warning, but she was more than ready for him. His trousers were half-way down his thighs; they were rough against Olivia's flesh as he pounded into her. He made short grunting sounds with each thrust, deep thrusts that pushed her along the damp ground.

Unseen, but clearly heard, a couple walked along the path, laughing together, and Clive sat up quickly.

Olivia felt bereft. She felt the cold air invade her hot sex and she pulled him back to enter her again.

He rolled her over, nuzzled the leaves from her back with his face, and put his arm under her belly to raise her bottom so that he could enter her from behind. Hard and hot, he plunged into her. There was no gentleness in his movements; only a sense of urgency that Olivia welcomed. She was so wet that his thrusting made slurping noises. She could sense the tension in his body, could tell from the frantic way he pounded into her that he was about to come. He was wild for her, completely out of control. They came together, in one shouting, shuddering mass . . .

Several male heads turned as Audrey strode out of the airport terminal with a small suitcase in her hand. She was frowning, but it did little to mar her appeal.

She stepped outside the building and stood for a moment, still frowning, and now tapping a high-heeled foot impatiently. She was reaching into her handbag for her mobile phone when she saw the Rolls Royce being driven into the car park. Instead of walking the twenty yards to it, she waited for Clive to come and meet her.

'You're late,' she said, her displeasure evident.

'Sorry. The traffic was murder.'

'Then you should have left earlier,' she snapped.

'You're right,' he agreed, lifting her suitcase as if it weighed no more than cotton wool. 'I'll remember for next time.'

It was impossible to be angry with him for long. With his couldn't-care-less attitude, he could usually make her smile. And he really couldn't care less. Oh, he enjoyed screwing her but she knew that if she as much as threatened to fire him, he would leave without so much as a backwards glance. She was lucky to have him. He was a good driver and an excellent lover. There was no point quibbling about his time-keeping.

He opened the front passenger door for her, and waited until she had her seat belt fastened before closing it. When he'd put her suitcase in the boot, he slid behind the wheel and fired the engine.

He was whistling softly as he pulled out of the car park.

'You sound happy with life,' she remarked dryly.

'I am. The sun's shining and all I have to do is drive a gorgeous woman home in a gorgeous car.'

'Flatterer!'

'It is a gorgeous car,' he retorted, deliberately misunderstanding her. 'For a short time, as a child, I was friendly with a boy who had very wealthy parents. One day, the boy asked me if I'd like to go with them to collect the Rolls.' He laughed at the memory. 'I was so excited at the thought of my first ride in a Rolls Royce that I could hardly contain myself. So off we went – to the local bakery. They were collecting bread rolls for a party they were throwing.'

Audrey laughed. She enjoyed Clive's easy sense of humour, and found it impossible to be cross with him. His time-keeping was hopeless, but she was so glad she had him.

'Did you call Olivia?' she asked.

'I did.'

'And?'

He checked the mirror and pulled out to overtake a slower-moving vehicle before answering.

'I took her to the park, and to The Traveller's Rest.'

Audrey waited but nothing more was forthcoming.

'And?' she prompted again with increasing impatience.

'She had an enjoyable time.' He smiled suddenly. 'So did I. You were right; she shows great promise. She's insatiable.'

'Insatiable?' Audrey experienced something that was suspiciously like jealousy. 'You didn't leave her unsatisfied, I hope?'

'No,' he answered slowly, 'but the more she has, the more she seems to want. She's a very sexy lady. I thought the barman in The Traveller's Rest was going to leap over the bar and take her by force. Oh – and she enjoys sex in public places.'

'She does?' Audrey was amazed. 'Are you sure?'

'I'm sure. I gave her an orgasm right in front of the barman. She loved it.' He took his eyes from the road briefly and grinned at her. 'I reckon he did, too.'

Audrey knew real jealousy now. She was jealous of Olivia for having Clive – despite the fact that she, Audrey, had told him to approach her – and jealous of Clive, too. People thought Olivia was cold and unapproachable but Audrey had longed to make love to her almost from the first time they had met.

'I wonder if Lloyd knows that,' she remarked curiously.

'Who knows?' Clive shrugged. 'Although it's my bet that she's not getting what she wants from him.'

'Oh, no. That's ridiculous. God, Lloyd is an amazing lover. Believe me, I know. I speak from personal experience.'

The more she thought about it though, the more sense it made. The only reason Audrey had introduced Olivia to Clive was to try and rid the girl of her inhibitions. Not that those inhibitions had been in evidence at The Traveller's Rest by all accounts, she thought grimly.

'I shall have to do some fishing.' She leaned back in her seat with a smile on her face. 'I think I shall enjoy that. It's been a long time since I spent any time with Lloyd.'

'You're incorrigible.' Clive grinned.

'I know.'

* * *

144

It was three days before Audrey managed to reach Lloyd. Olivia, she knew, was attending a friend's book launch on Wednesday and would be away for the night.

'Lloyd,' she greeted him when their little woman eventually found him and brought him to the phone. 'It's Audrey. How are you?'

'I'm fine, thanks. You? And Tony?'

'Yes, we're well.' She hesitated a moment. 'I was really calling to invite you to dinner on Wednesday night. We haven't seen you for ages, Lloyd, and I know Olivia's away that night. I thought it would stop you dining alone.'

'Thanks. Yes, I'd like that, Audrey. You're right. It has been ages.'

It had!

'I know how busy you are these days,' she said smoothly. 'I've seen quite a bit of Olivia, though.'

'Yes, I know. She's pretty busy at the moment too. She's got a couple of TV interviews coming up. You heard that Tony Clements had died?'

'Yes. Oh – of course. She wrote a biography on him, didn't she?'

'That's right. The publishers are hyping it like mad at the moment so she's got TV and radio interviews and a couple of signing sessions lined up.'

'How exciting.' Audrey wasn't in the least interested. 'You must tell us all about it on Wednesday. Seven for seven-thirty suit you?'

'I'll look forward to it, Audrey.'

But not as much as I will, Audrey thought with a satisfied smile as she replaced the receiver.

She hadn't said in so many words that Tony would be dining with them so Lloyd couldn't blame her when he discovered she had something far more intimate in mind.

It had been six months since Lloyd had ended their

145

affair, and she missed him dreadfully. He had said he intended to be faithful to his new wife but, if Clive was right and there were problems in the marriage, perhaps he would have changed his mind. If not, Audrey felt sure she could change it for him. She knew him well, and she knew his body even better.

What would he say, she wondered, if he knew that his precious Olivia had been fucked by Clive? Audrey would dearly love to find out.

The smart new television studio had been alive with activity but now it was fairly quiet. Olivia had been abandoned with only a glass of white wine to calm her nerves.

Strangely, she wasn't nervous about the interview. She had never appeared on television before, but the producer had given her a rundown of the questions she was to be asked, and she had given him her replies. In any case, it was being recorded for transmission later so, if anyone got it wrong, they could record it again. No, it was Steve that worried her, and she wasn't sure why. It was highly unlikely that he would see the programme as it was only being broadcast in the north of England, so there was no need to worry on that score. Yet, still she worried. Even if he *did* see it, all he would see, along with all the other viewers in the north of England, was Jane Marshall promoting her biography of the late Tony Clements, MP.

It was the photograph of Carmen Blake on Steve's desk that had unnerved her. She could think of no reason whatsoever for Carmen to change her name to Donna, or for Steve to lie about his wife – unless, of course, he knew that Jane Marshall was in fact Olivia Standish, and that she and Carmen had once been sworn enemies. That idea seemed ludicrous. There had to be a perfectly innocent explanation but for the life of her she couldn't think of one.

'Jane Marshall?'

Startled, Olivia turned to look at the young girl who had stuck her head round the door.

'Yes?'

The girl bounced into the room and slammed a black box on the table in front of Olivia.

'Make-up,' she explained. 'I'm Sharon, by the way.'

Beneath the layers of heavy make-up she was wearing, she was probably no more than eighteen years old. She looked straight at Olivia, then walked around her, viewing her from all angles.

'I'll just take the shine off you,' she said at last.

'Thanks,' Olivia murmured.

'Nervous?' Sharon enquired cheerfully.

'Not really. Should I be?'

'I would be. I love working on this side of the camera, but I'd hate to be on the other. Some folk are physically sick beforehand.' She dabbed at Olivia's face with very orange-looking powder. 'There are folk who do it every day who are sick before they go on. Lift your chin – there. Perfect.'

'Thanks,' Olivia said again.

'My pleasure.' She snapped the black box shut and bounced over to the door. 'Gavin's on his way to see you.'

'Oh, right.'

'Talk of the devil,' Sharon added cheerfully.

Gavin Peterson, the show's presenter, glided into the room, ignoring Sharon.

As Olivia had never seen his show before, she had no idea how he looked on the small screen, but in real life he was a huge disappointment. He was late forties, she supposed, and wore a thick, dark toupee that looked at odds with his greying eyebrows. He had a gold tooth too and Olivia's gaze kept straying to it. Added to that, it seemed that Sharon had treated him to the orange-powder look. Earlier, he had been wearing jeans and an old T-shirt but he was now wearing a dark blue suit, pale blue shirt and brightly coloured, wide tie.

'Nervous?' he asked.

Olivia wondered if interviewees were ever asked a more original question.

'Not at all. I'm quite looking forward to it.'

'Good. That's the spirit. There's nothing to it. Just be yourself.'

'I always am.' Right down to the hair and teeth, she thought with a small smile.

'Good. That's the spirit.' He looked at the huge clock on the wall behind Olivia. 'We're on a five-minute countdown. We'll make our way to the studio, shall we?'

Olivia finished her wine in one swallow and got to her feet.

He led the way along a long corridor that was again buzzing with activity to the small studio. From then on, it was straightforward.

After lighting and sound checks Gavin, still looking to Olivia as if pieces might drop off him at any moment, asked his questions and she answered them. Fifteen minutes later it was all over.

'You're a natural,' John, the producer, told her as she left the studio. 'Let me know if you ever want a job in television.'

'I'd love one!' Olivia laughed at herself, but it was true. She had loved every second of it. There was something exciting about flirting with a camera and knowing you were flirting with thousands of people in their living-rooms. 'Let me know when you have a job for me.'

'Are you serious?' he asked.

'I think so.' She nodded. 'But it would have to be the right job. I couldn't read the news or the weather. I'd like to do something interesting, something in the political world, something that involved digging up the truth.'

Olivia gained the distinct impression that he lost interest at that point. She certainly hadn't, though. There were plenty more television companies in the country!

There was a knot of nervousness in Lloyd's stomach and it irritated him. Tomorrow, he was to deliver the cash to whoever it was who was blackmailing him and, hopefully, discover their identity. He would be greatly relieved when it was all over.

He wished Olivia was home, but she wasn't. She rarely was these days.

He poured himself another whisky, picked up the phone and tapped out Peter's home number. What was it that Linda had said about her younger brother? That he did a cracking Philip Marlowe impression, but was not what people would call successful? Her words certainly hadn't inspired confidence. Lloyd knew he could trust Peter, though, and that was worth a great deal. Peter, like Linda, had simple tastes. There was no hint of greed in either of them. And without greed, Lloyd thought, there was no deceit.

'All set for tomorrow?' Peter asked him now.

'I suppose so. That's why I was ringing, to see that you were.'

'Oh, I am. Don't worry about me.'

'Me too, I suppose.' Lloyd glanced across at the table. 'I've wrapped five thousand pounds in brown paper, as instructed, and put it in a Sainsbury's carrier bag. God, it's like something from a *Boys' Own* cops and robbers story.'

'Blackmailers usually like to have their fun.' Peter was sympathetic. 'You're OK with your microphone?'

'Fine.' It was bizarre. He was going to be 'wired', as

Peter put it, so that Peter would hear exactly what was happening at all times.

'I'll be right behind you,' Peter said, sounding a lot more confident than Lloyd felt. 'I'll be wearing a jogging suit, and I'll have personal stereo earphones on so that I don't miss anything.'

Lloyd took a large swallow of whisky.

'Are you going straight to Paddington?' he asked.

'Yes. I'll be by the flower stall. When they give you instructions, make sure you repeat everything.'

'I will.'

'And keep your eyes peeled,' Peter added. 'Nine times out of ten, blackmailers are people you know.'

The thought made Lloyd shudder.

'I will,' he promised.

'And don't be surprised if they have you chasing round London half the day,' Peter warned him. 'They'll probably want to play safe and try to shake off any company you may have.'

'Just make sure you don't get shaken off then.'

Peter laughed into the receiver.

'I won't. Don't worry, Lloyd. We'll get them, this time.'

'We'd damn well better!'

Lloyd felt no better when he replaced the receiver. Worrying wouldn't help matters though. All he could do was take a taxi to Paddington Station as instructed and wait for the phone call.

Lloyd hadn't slept well, but he hadn't expected to. He pulled back the curtains and sighed as he gazed out at the damp streets of the City. If it was going to rain all day, they hadn't better have him chasing around.

Dorothy served him breakfast but, for once, he was in no mood for flirting with her. He tried to read the newspaper instead, but he was in no mood for that, either. He simply wanted to get the day over and done with.

His taxi pulled up outside. Lloyd patted his microphone to make sure it was still in place and picked up the Sainsbury's carrier bag that contained five thousands pounds. Why they had chosen a Sainsbury's bag, God alone knew. Lloyd certainly didn't. He would have felt – and looked, he suspected – far less conspicuous with his briefcase.

'Paddington Station, please,' he instructed the driver.

The weather was foul. It didn't know whether to rain or not. The driver switched on the wipers several times, only to switch them off when they began to squeak on the near-dry windscreen.

At least the driver was the sullen, silent type. The last thing Lloyd wanted was to be forced into inane conversation.

The traffic was clogged in places so that Lloyd began to think they might not arrive in time. They did, though. It was exactly nine fifty-five when the driver stopped the taxi.

'Thanks very much. Keep the change.'

He jumped out and strode into the station. He had been told to go to the phone booth facing the flower stall. Terrific. There were four of the damn things facing the flower stall. Fortunately, none were in use.

Lloyd stood there, his carrier bag under his left arm, checking his watch every few seconds, and trying not to pace.

He looked around and spotted Peter. True to his word, he was wearing a sloppy, blue jogging suit and was tapping his foot as if to some music that might be playing in his earphones. He didn't look out of place. He checked the departures boards, looking like all the other folk milling around who were waiting for their trains.

Lloyd was watching everyone when he suddenly

spotted another phone booth – one that really did face the flower stall. He marched over to it. The phone was ringing.

Licking his dry lips, he lifted the receiver. His heart was hammering loudly.

'Hello?'

'Take a cab to Speaker's Corner and wait there.'

The connection was cut and Lloyd swore beneath his breath. Remembering Peter, he took a handkerchief from his pocket and pretended to blow his nose.

'I'm to take a taxi to Speaker's Corner and wait there,' he muttered.

As he left the building, Peter gave him a brief nod to confirm that he had heard.

Lloyd joined the queue for taxis, and fortunately didn't have long to wait. There was some confusion though, and at the exact moment that Lloyd got into the taxi, an elderly lady, clutching several large wicker shopping bags and a tiny dog, did likewise.

'Speaker's Corner, please.' They spoke in unison.

'Oh – er, sorry,' the old lady said. 'I was told this one was mine.' She was about to get out, but changed her mind. 'We may as well share. Shall we?'

'Why not?' Lloyd nodded, resigned.

He didn't care how many humans or animals were in the taxi so long as he got to Speaker's Corner and finally met someone. And they could hardly suspect the old lady of being his undercover police representative, he thought grimly.

The dog sat on her lap, shivering as small dogs always seem to, while she hunted through her bags.

'Would you like a mint, luvvie?' she asked Lloyd.

'No. No, thanks.'

'Oh, well. Suit yourself. My mouth gets dry – my hubby says it's because I talk too much –' she squawked with laughter '– so I like a mint.' She turned her attention to her dog. 'I expect you want one of your biscuits, don't you, Sally? Here – let Mummy find one for you.'

Lloyd stared out of the taxi window, refusing to offer her any encouragement. Instinct told him her husband was right. As she hunted through her bags for the dratted biscuit, she didn't stop talking. At times it was difficult to tell if she was speaking to the dog, Lloyd or the driver. It didn't really matter. None of them responded and she didn't seem to care.

The taxi came to a stop in the traffic.

'It's been like this all morning,' the driver complained.

'I think I'll get out and walk,' the old lady said. 'How much do I owe you?'

'It's OK. I'll take care of it,' Lloyd said immediately, relieved at the thought of having the taxi to himself.

'Well, thank you. You're a real gent. Not many of you left these days.' She opened the door and struggled out. 'Oh – look at me. I nearly walked off with your bag.'

'What!' Lloyd's heart was beating in his mouth. He'd forgotten all about the damn bag.

'Silly me.' She put his Sainsbury's bag on the seat beside him. 'As if we haven't got enough to carry, Sally. And you'll have to walk, my girl . . .'

The door slammed shut and she was gone. Thank God.

Lloyd wished he could walk too, as it would be quicker and a damn sight less frustrating, but he knew he had to carry out their instructions. If they said take a taxi, he had to take a taxi.

For the next ten minutes, the traffic moved a few yards a minute, but then they picked up some pace and finally reached their destination.

'Thanks.' Lloyd felt the familiar knot of tension in his stomach as he took a note from his wallet and handed it over.

He grabbed his bag and climbed out. The bag – it felt different. Still standing on the pavement, he looked inside.

'What the bloody – oh, shit!'

He lifted out the package. It was wrapped in brown paper, exactly as the cash had been, but the size, shape and weight were all wrong.

'Shit!'

That bloody woman – that old, rambling, doddering, stupid bloody woman had somehow managed to work a switch.

Lloyd tore off the brown paper, but he knew what it was long before he saw the words 'Master Copy' on the spine of the video case.

Chapter Nine

Dinner was superb. Audrey made a mental note to thank Mary and Julie for all their hard work. She had employed the two girls as she had wanted something special and Alice, her own cook, lacked imagination. Mary and Julie, however, were quickly gaining a well-deserved reputation for their catering skills. They were exceptionally pleasing on the eye, too. Audrey had noticed Lloyd's gaze wander longingly on more than one occasion. Both girls wore casual clothes to prepare and cook the food but the transformation when they served it was amazing. They looked delightful in their short black dresses, tiny white aprons and high heels. She would have to recommend the girls to Olivia. Their fees were a bit steep, and getting steeper by the week, but the end result was well worth it.

She suspected Lloyd had been a little annoyed to discover that he wasn't dining, as he had clearly expected to, with her *and* Tony but, of course, he was far too polite to say so. She also suspected that the sight of her pretty caterers had helped him to forget his annoyance.

'Let's have our coffee in the sitting room,' she suggested. 'It's cosier in there. Besides, you haven't seen my new lighting system.'

'No, but I heard all about it from Olivia.'

'Did you? And what else did she tell you?' Audrey asked.

'Stop fishing for compliments, Audrey,' Lloyd retorted with a smile. 'She was very impressed, as I'm sure she told you herself.'

Audrey laughed off his words, pleased but not in the least surprised that Olivia hadn't mentioned what had taken place beneath those lights.

Lloyd was, or pretended to be, impressed with her lighting, too. She bathed the room in a warm, pink glow.

Mary brought their coffee and, again, Audrey saw that Lloyd's gaze was irresistibly drawn to the girl's high hemline and long, slender legs.

'She's gorgeous, isn't she?' Audrey remarked when Mary had left them alone.

'Yes, she is. So are you, Audrey.' He made himself comfortable on the sofa while Audrey poured their coffee. 'Don't think I haven't noticed the way you've been flaunting yourself all evening.'

'Flaunting myself?' If that remark had come from anyone but Lloyd, she would have been highly offended – and furious. 'I have not!' She handed him his coffee. 'Although I have to confess,' she added quietly, 'that I do miss you, Lloyd.'

'I miss you, too,' he said, but Audrey guessed he was lying. 'I explained things to you –'

'You said you were going to be faithful to Livvy,' she scoffed. 'And if you think I believe that, Lloyd Standish, you're a fool. You couldn't be faithful if you tried.'

'Perhaps.' A coolness edged his voice. 'But I haven't – and won't – sleep with a friend of Olivia's.'

'Spoilsport!' She put a teasing note into her voice to

try and lighten the mood. 'Never mind, I'm happy to make do with Clive again for tonight.'

'Clive?'

'My chauffeur. Livvy hasn't mentioned him?'

'No.' He sipped his coffee. 'So how many men do you have running after you now, Audrey?'

'Enough,' she replied, 'but that doesn't stop me missing you.' She decided to change track. 'How are things between you and Olivia?'

'Fine.' The reply was abrupt.

'Good.' She could tell from his brusque response that things were far from fine but she wasn't going to push the issue. Yet. 'Doesn't this seem a waste, though? I know what you like, and you know what turns me on. Hey, you'd love my bedroom. I've had a little work done in there, including having a mirror put in. Well, it's a mirror from my bedroom. All I see is my own reflection. But it's a plain sheet of glass from my dressing room.'

Lloyd didn't speak, but he shifted position before drinking his coffee.

'I bet that appeals to you, Lloyd,' Audrey pressed on. 'I know how much you love to play the voyeur.'

He shrugged as if he could take it or leave it, but Audrey guessed she was on a winner.

'I bet you'd love to watch,' she murmured huskily. 'Clive's a marvellous lover – I'm only surprised Olivia didn't mention him. I bet you would love to watch him make love to me.'

He shrugged again, but was less convincing this time.

'Possibly,' he admitted at last.

'He has a beautiful cock,' Audrey confided. 'I think even you would be impressed, Lloyd. But even better, he knows exactly how to use it. I really love putting my lips round it and sucking on it.'

Lloyd's cup rattled on its saucer and he put it on the small table beside him.

'Are you thinking of my pleasure, Audrey?' he asked knowingly. 'Or does the thought of me watching excite you?'

'Of course it does.' She laughed. 'But I know you would enjoy it, too.'

'You're right. I would.' He sounded resigned.

'Come upstairs. Let me show you.'

She reached for his hand; it was hot and it trembled slightly. As they walked up the long, curving staircase, she could hear him breathing fast. Lloyd was a fit man, in the peak of condition, and she knew it had nothing to do with the slight exertion.

She pushed open the door to her bedroom and stood back to let him enter first.

Audrey couldn't guess his thoughts as he stood looking at the large, high bed with its blue silk sheets and pile of matching cushions. The curtains, in the same blue but dashed with yellow, reached from floor to ceiling. The mirror, which had now caught his attention, also reached from floor to ceiling. Lloyd gazed at her questioningly, and she unlocked the door to her dressing room. He walked inside, gazed at the huge pane of glass that gave a perfect view of Audrey's bedroom, then gave a deep laugh.

'My God! Isn't this so typically you, Audrey.'

'Do you like it?' she asked, knowing from his expression that she already had her answer.

'Yes.' He looked round the small room, touched the green leather couch, opened the door of the well-stocked drinks cabinet and laughed again. 'Yes. I love it!'

'Good. You make yourself comfortable and I'll go and find Clive.' She nodded at the drinks cabinet. 'You should find something there to your taste.'

She left him, locked him in the dressing room, and went downstairs and along the hall to the self-contained flat that was Clive's. He opened the door to her, his eyes widening in surprise.

'Has he left already?'

'No, he's in my dressing room.' She walked past him into the flat. 'Are you alone?'

'Of course.'

'Good – I suppose.' She went into his bedroom, ignored the untidy state of the room and opened the wardrobe. 'Give me thirty minutes, then come to my bedroom.' She took a dark suit that she had bought him out of the wardrobe and put it on the bed. 'And wear that.'

'Yes, ma'am.' He gave her a mock salute.

'Don't be cheeky.' But she was smiling. 'And I shall expect a good performance.'

'Have I ever let you down?'

'No. No, you haven't.' She reached up and dropped a kiss on his cheek. 'So make sure you don't tonight.'

She left him and returned to her bedroom. She kicked off her shoes and let her stockinged feet curl into the thick, white carpet.

Planning to give Lloyd an evening to remember, she stood in front of her mirror and brushed her hair. It was tremendously exciting to know he was watching her. She moved slowly, wanting to make him impatient, to tease him. She put down her hairbrush and reached behind her to slide down the zip of her dress. It fell from her body to the carpet. As she stepped out of it, she admired her well-toned body. Her underwear – bra, briefs and suspender belt – was a flimsy concoction of pale blue silk and lace. She made sure Lloyd got the best possible view as she bent to pick up her dress from the floor before hanging it in her wardrobe. When she was back in front of the mirror, only about twelve inches from it, she unhooked her bra and threw it over the back of the chair. She knew she had good breasts; large and full. For a few minutes, she caressed them in front of the mirror. Was Lloyd aroused? Was he touching himself? Her imagination excited her still further. She pulled on her stiff nipples and they hardened still more.

Still standing in front of the mirror, she pulled down her panties and threw them to join her bra. She stood, legs slightly apart, and continued to caress her breasts. Her sex was eager for her touch but she refused to rush things. She intended to make Lloyd as eager for her body as she was for his. In her mind, she could see him standing on the other side of her mirror, touching himself.

She suddenly thought of something and went over to the bed and picked up the phone. It rang for a full minute before Clive answered.

'Sorry, I was taking a shower.'

'There's half a bottle of wine in the kitchen.' She spoke in a low voice so that Lloyd wouldn't hear. 'Bring that and a couple of glasses in ten minutes.'

'OK.'

'Oh, and Clive – we'll warm the bottle. Right?'

'Right.' She heard him chuckle as he replaced the receiver.

Ten minutes . . .

Audrey stretched out on the bed, half-lying and half-sitting against the cushions, with her legs bent to give Lloyd a good view of her secret place. She caressed her breasts, teasing the hard, rosy peaks, then ran her hand along her stocking-clad thigh before slipping her hand between her legs. She threw her head back and parted her legs still further as she inserted a perfectly manicured finger. She kept the flat of her hand on her bushy mound and curled her index finger inside to give Lloyd the best view possible. It excited her immensely to know that he was locked in. She was so excited that she knew she was already close to orgasm. She wanted to hold back but it was too late. Her eager finger brought her to a quick orgasm. She wanted much more but she could wait for Clive.

For once, he was punctual. He knocked on the door and walked into her bedroom carrying half a bottle of wine and two crystal glasses.

'Couldn't you wait?' he asked, noting the flush in her cheeks.

'No.'

He poured her a glass of wine and sat on the bed with his back to the mirror.

'Take your clothes off,' she said, adding in a whisper, 'slowly.'

He nodded his understanding.

Audrey caressed her heavy breasts as she watched him remove his clothes, very slowly, in a way that was far sexier than any stripper. It was done so subtly that Lloyd wouldn't know it was for his benefit.

Clive stood beside the bed, completely naked. His body was wonderful; big and powerful without looking as if he spent hours a day on body-building exercises. His chest and shoulders were broad and strong, tapering to a narrow waist and hips. His thighs were firm and well muscled. His penis was wonderfully long, and it flopped against his thigh as he sat on the bed.

Audrey smirked with anticipation.

'Have a drink.'

She passed him the bottle but didn't offer him a glass. Normally, he would have kneeled between her legs but, ever mindful of Lloyd's watchful gaze, he kneeled by her side. Slowly, and very carefully, he nudged Audrey's sex with the neck of the bottle. The touch of the icy cold glass made her shiver.

'Don't spill any.' Her breath was ragged.

'I don't intend to.' He pushed the bottle a little way inside her.

'It's so cold!' she gasped.

'It will soon warm up.' Clive pushed it deeper inside

161

her, then removed it. He put the bottle to his lips and tilted it to drink the wine. 'You taste so damn good with a fine wine.'

When he had finished drinking, he licked the neck of the bottle and, again, slid it inside her, nudging and stretching the smooth walls of her tunnel.

Clive's penis stiffened as he played with the bottle. Audrey felt it jab her thigh.

She felt relaxed and mellow. At any moment she could take control but, for now, she was happy to let Clive take the initiative for a change. The cold wine trickled into her hot sex and drops spilled on the bed. She sighed with delight at the surprising hot-cold sensations.

Again, he removed the bottle and drank from it. Putting the bottle on the table, he bent his head and used his tongue to mop up the drops of wine on her thighs. She cried out when his tongue touched her sex. He licked her folds, parting them. His hot tongue moved rapidly over her flesh, the tip finding her bud. Audrey moaned loudly. It never ceased to amaze her how quickly he could bring her to a state of such high arousal. She moaned again as his tongue flicked relentlessly across her aching bud. Her orgasm was much stronger this time, and immensely satisfying. It left her feeling warm and lethargic.

'Was that good?' Clive murmured against her ear.

'Very.' She sighed happily.

'What would you like now?' he whispered.

Audrey thought for a moment.

'Lie on your back, sideways across the bed.'

He did as she asked, linking his hands behind his head so that his chest appeared bigger than ever. Audrey kneeled at his side, facing the mirror, then bent her head to take his ever-stiffening prick in her mouth. It twitched as her mouth circled it. She used her hand to stroke it, she sucked on it and felt it push into her mouth. She flicked her tongue over the glans and smiled with satisfaction at his soft moans of pleasure. She took more of him into her mouth. She outlined every bump and vein with her tongue, and his ever-responsive cock was soon at full stretch. She could feel his shudders of excitement but didn't want him too aroused – not yet. She climbed off the bed and reached for his hand.

'Dance with me,' she murmured.

He sat up and got to his feet. They embraced and began to move slowly, dizzily, around the room. Audrey was determined to take things slowly, to make Lloyd really ache with longing, but the feel of Clive's strong body beneath her hands was highly arousing. As they moved, he ran his hands down her spine and over her buttocks. His cock was tantalisingly hard against her belly. His mouth found hers and he kissed her hungrily, pushing his tongue between her teeth. He thrust with his tongue and she felt his cock jerk against her in response. His hands slid between them and he stroked her aching nipples.

Audrey's body was burning with longing. When he guided her to the wall, she welcomed its coolness on her back. He pressed tight against her, almost crushing the breath from her body, and her arms snaked around his neck, pulling him even closer.

'I want you,' she cried urgently.

He bent his knees a little and his beautiful, obedient cock needed no assistance. It found her wet opening and pushed its way inside her, making her cry out.

Clive took most of her weight, holding her thighs as he thrust into her. Each thrust forced her up the wall a little. She lifted her legs higher, affording deeper penetration, and crossed her legs behind his back. He made short, deep grunting noises with each thrust, the sounds running into each other as he increased his tempo. Audrey's fingernails dug into his shoulders and she screamed out as a fierce orgasm claimed her. Her heels drummed against his back until, finally, apart from the occasional tremor running through her body, she was still.

She had almost forgotten Lloyd. Almost.

'I feel sure he'd love to watch you come all over me,' she whispered against Clive's ear. 'Carry me to the bed.'

With his cock still inside her, Clive did as she asked. Only when he had to drop her on the bed did he – reluctantly, she knew – withdraw.

She lay on her back with her head towards the mirror and her feet at the head of the bed. Facing the mirror, and with a knee either side of her thighs, Clive straddled her and took his penis in his hand.

'You like to watch too, don't you?' he said gruffly, taking his cock in his hand and manipulating it with slow but firm strokes.

'Yes,' she confessed.

She loved to watch Clive masturbate; it always excited her. This evening was doubly exciting, though. She imagined, and hoped, that on the other side of the mirror, Lloyd was masturbating too. Fortunately, she knew only too well that his own hand wouldn't satisfy him; he would want her, need her.

Clive's hand was working rapidly on his cock. Audrey loved to watch, and she loved to hear the sounds he made. It was almost as if he were in great pain. His eyes rarely left her face, and when they did it was only to look at the hand that was giving him such pleasure. She could tell he was very close to orgasm.

'Does that feel as good as it looks?' she whispered.

Clive nodded, eyes closed and biting his bottom lip. With a long, deep cry of relief, he came, smearing Audrey from her breasts to her navel. He leaned back, his eyes still closed as his breathing slowly returned to normal.

Audrey patted his arm. 'You can go now, Clive.'

'Must I?'

'Yes!'

When he left her, Audrey went to her bedside table and picked up the keys to the dressing room. As she unlocked the door and pushed it open, she didn't know quite what to expect, but she was bitterly disappointed to find Lloyd looking quite undisturbed. He was fully clothed, not a hair out of place, and was pouring himself a drink.

'Well?' Audrey asked, somewhat deflated. 'What did you think of Clive?'

'An impressive performance.' He gave her a wry smile. 'But I expected nothing less from you, Audrey.'

'Did it excite you?'

'Of course. You knew it would.'

'Yes.' She felt relieved. 'Yes, I know what you like, Lloyd.' She reached out and touched him. Beneath the fabric of his trousers, she felt the power of his arousal.

She took the glass from his hand, set it down and slipped off his jacket. He made no protest. His tie was next. She threw it on the back of the chair.

'I need a shower,' she whispered. 'Will you soap my back for me?'

He was already unfastening his shirt.

'Yes.'

His trousers ended up on the floor with his shirt.

She gazed at his nakedness with a familiar ache of longing. He had a wonderful body. At one time, every inch of it had been hers on a regular basis, and the knowledge that this was no longer the case saddened her. Tonight, however, every inch of him would be hers again, albeit for a very brief time.

'Come on.' He grabbed her hand and led her to the shower room. It was familiar territory to him.

Audrey slid the glass doors closed behind them. There was plenty of room for two; she had made sure of that when she'd had it installed. She reached for the controls and switched it on, then adjusted the temperature slightly because she knew Lloyd liked his showers very hot. Two jets of water, one from either side of the large cubicle showered down on them. The hot spray made her skin tingle.

Lloyd grabbed the soap, worked up a lather and rubbed it into her shoulders. She loved his touch, and needed no proof of his arousal. She could see it for herself. He stood so that the main force of the jet hit his hard cock. God, she wanted him. How she envied Livvy . . .

'What would you say, Lloyd, if I told you that Clive had screwed your wife?'

His soapy hands stilled on her arm for a moment.

'I wouldn't believe you,' he replied evenly.

'That's what I thought.' She turned her back on him, standing close so that she could feel his penis on her body. 'Wash my back, Lloyd.'

'Olivia's not the type to –'

'So one would think,' Audrey cut him off smoothly. 'We never really know people though, do we? For instance, do you know she likes to have sex in public places?'

'Ha!'

'Indeed. Wash my thighs for me, Lloyd.'

He kneeled behind her and, although he soaped her legs with infinite care, Audrey could tell he was distracted.

'Now that Clive's screwed Livvy – not that you believe me, I know, but now that I've seen her with him, I want her for myself. I've always wanted to make love to her, from the first moment I laid eyes on her, but now that Clive's enjoyed her body, I'm more determined than ever to have her.'

Lloyd stopped soaping her thighs, stood up and turned her round to face him. He was frowning, Audrey saw, with a mixture of shock and disbelief.

166

'I hope you're not jealous of Clive,' she murmured. 'Mind you,' she added, teasing him, 'I would have thought you would have been more than enough to satisfy her, Lloyd.'

His eyes narrowed and a vein throbbed angrily in his neck.

'Is this true?' he demanded, and Audrey nodded.

'It is.' She linked her hands around his neck and pressed her body tight against his. 'When I make love to her – and believe me, Lloyd, I shall – would you like to watch?'

He didn't answer immediately.

Audrey was deliberately goading him. She only spoke the truth, but this was neither the time nor the place – except she wanted to goad him. She wanted to make him angry. Once before, years ago when he had been married to his first wife, she had made him angry. She couldn't remember how; she could only remember the forceful way in which he had made love to her. He had been rough with her and she had loved it. There was a touch of the mean, moody and magnificent about Lloyd at times.

'You won't get Olivia into bed,' Lloyd broke into her thoughts.

'Ah, but I will, Lloyd. Clive has – well, no, he didn't take her to bed. He took her on the carpet in my sitting room, and he took her in the bushes deep in the country.'

'Liar!'

'If you say so.' She shrugged. 'But if I do get her into bed, would you like to watch?'

'Of course!' He laughed, albeit a little shakily. 'But you won't.'

'We'll see.'

She put her hands between their bodies and grasped his cock. The hot water rained down on them.

'Let me wash you,' she murmured huskily.

She reached for the soap, coated her hands in lather, and slid them along the length of his cock. It was thicker and harder than ever. She dropped to her knees and took it in her mouth. Every inch, every bump was painfully familiar to her.

'I bet Livvy doesn't do this to you,' she said, sliding her tongue along his length. 'I'm sure she would love to, but she's too scared to take the initiative. She shows great promise, though.'

She took him in her mouth and sucked him vigorously, making him groan, and was surprised when he suddenly switched off the showers. When she looked up at him, he opened the cubicle and thrust a towel at her. Having dried himself briefly, and without giving Audrey time to dry herself properly, he pushed her in the direction of the bedroom and the bed.

'Is this a ploy to get me back into your bed on a regular basis?' he demanded.

'Is what a ploy?'

'All this talk about Olivia. I don't believe for a minute that she's had sex with your chauffeur. Good God, Audrey, I do know my own wife, you know.'

'Do you? I wonder.'

'Of course I damn well do!'

'If you insist.' Audrey lay back on her bed. 'And no, it's not a ploy. I'd love you in my bed on a regular basis, Lloyd, but there are plenty more men around who are eager to please.'

They were eager; they simply didn't please as Lloyd did.

'I'm sure there are.' She could tell he was angry – and confused. He pushed her legs roughly apart and kneeled between them. 'Everyone's a challenge to you, aren't they, Audrey? I'm a challenge; Olivia's a challenge.'

'A challenge is healthy for the mind,' she replied, her eyes taking in each glorious detail of him, from his broad, solid chest, to the way his hands were tensely placed on his thighs, and the way his eager penis jerked towards her. 'And the body,' she added softly.

'Did she?' he demanded.

'Yes.'

'And you watched?'

'Yes. She watched me with Clive, too.'

His soft groan turned to a gasp as she touched him; she knew he was incredibly aroused, and she knew that this was partly due to thoughts of his wife with another man. She grasped his beautiful cock with her hand, and felt a deep shudder run through his body at her touch. The knowledge that he would soon be inside her after so long was almost more than she could bear. Still gripping his shaft, she lifted her hips off the bed.

'Take me inside you,' he urged her.

Audrey sighed at the words she had longed to hear. She lifted herself on to his cock and rejoiced as he thrust into her.

'God, I'd almost forgotten how good you feel,' he said with a groan.

Audrey hadn't forgotten how good he felt. The hard length of him, the expressions that flitted across his handsome face, his movements, the sounds he made – she remembered it all.

'Hold me!' he pleaded.

Audrey held his cock tight as he rammed into her. Her hand banged against his balls, against her own sex – her orgasm came quickly, exploding through every nerve ending. With a deep shuddering groan, Lloyd came inside her.

That was the way it had always been with them. It was always fast and furious, and always over in a matter of minutes. And then – then they would make love very, very slowly . . .

Chapter Ten

Despite telling herself over and over again that she had no proof, Olivia knew, without any doubt whatsoever, that Carmen Blake, or Donna, or whatever she chose to call herself these days, was blackmailing her. She suspected that Steve was involved, too. It was an unpleasant thought, far better to think that they had met innocently enough over the Internet, but it was too much of a coincidence to ignore. How the devil could she prove it though?

Her favourite idea – her *only* idea, come to that – was to call Steve's home number when she knew he wasn't there, speak to Carmen and confront her with it.

She paced around her study, pondering this. No. It was no good simply confronting Carmen with it; that would get her nowhere. She needed something she could hold against Carmen. The only way to deal with a blackmailer was to blackmail them.

She swore softly to herself. There were grudges and grudges, but this grudge had been held for years. Olivia had forgotten all about Carmen and she found it hard to believe that Carmen still felt aggrieved by what happened when they were children. It was – well, it was downright childish. Profitable, though, an inner voice added. Carmen would assume, as most people would, that Olivia would pay well to protect her husband's name and career. She was doubtless thinking that she could make a fortune out of this. Well, she would have to think again. Olivia wasn't the soft touch that Carmen hoped she was.

All she needed was something she could hold against Carmen. There must be something. Everyone had skeletons in the cupboard; it was just a case of finding them.

An idea formed and she scribbled a few notes on a scrap of paper. It was ludicrous, but she had nothing to lose . . .

She sat at her desk and tapped out the number for Steve's office. He answered almost immediately. Olivia replaced the receiver without speaking. She had only wanted to check that he was there and not at home. With her heart hammering, she tapped out his home number but there was no reply. It was probably just as well. She needed more time to think about what she was going to say.

She tried the number at fifteen-minute intervals and it was finally answered.

'Oh, hello,' Olivia said in a bright and breezy, friendly tone. 'I don't know if you can help me. I've been trying to get in touch with a Carmen Blake and I've finally been given this number. Is she there by any chance?'

'Who wants to know?'

'Sorry – I'm Jenny Somerville – Jenny Smith as was. The name will mean nothing to her I'm afraid, but we were at school together. I know she won't remember me because I don't remember her. I have to confess that I've done my best to forget my schooldays – they weren't particularly pleasant. Anyway, the thing is, some of us are planning a school reunion – but you won't want to hear all this –'

'I might. I'm Carmen Blake.'

'Oh, really! That's wonderful. I've been chasing you all over the country.'

'I've moved home a lot.'

'So have I. God, that's a nightmare in itself. Most of the kids from school are easy to trace – well, let's face it, most of them could trace their ancestors back to Noah – but you were tricky. And the funny thing is, I don't remember you at all. Did you leave early?'

'When I was sixteen,' Carmen answered.

'Ah, that explains it, then. I would have started during the year you left, and then stayed for two years. I don't know about you, but I hated the place.'

'So did I.' There was a brief pause. 'If you hated the place so much, why are you having a reunion? It's the last place on earth I would want to see again!'

Olivia gave what she hoped was a chummy laugh.

'Me too, normally. A few of us are going to arrange a bit of a party for some of the others, though. They treated us like dirt when we were there, so we're planning to get our own back. Do you remember any of the girls? There was Victoria, for a start – God, she was a snooty piece. And she had a friend –'

'Olivia,' Carmen said softly.

'Yes! Yes, that's her. I couldn't stand either of them. Oh!' Olivia injected a note of apology into her voice. 'Me and my big mouth. You'll tell me now that they were your best friends.'

'Ha! I couldn't stand them either.'

'Phew!' Olivia laughed with relief. 'Thank goodness for that. That – what was her name? – Olivia? – is married to an MP now. Did you know?'

'Yes, I did. Lloyd Standish.'

'Probably. I know nothing about politics; it bores me to death. I can imagine her though, lording it over his constituents. She'd really look down on me now; all I've done is marry a builder and have three kids. What about you, Carmen? Have you taken the world by storm?'

'Not really. I've just opened my own shop – fashion. I design my own clothes.' Carmen was quite friendly now that they had a common bond. 'It's early days but business is good, so far.'

'How exciting! Is your shop in Brighton? My cousin often shops there and she's clothes mad. She's got pots of money, too.'

'Recommend me – please!' Carmen laughed. 'I need all the trade I can get.'

'I will,' Olivia promised. 'What's the shop called.'

'Carmen's Casuals. Very original, don't you think?' Another little laugh.

'It must be wonderful to have your name over the door though,' Olivia said. 'I'll tell Mags to call in and look round. Really, Carmen, she spends a fortune on clothes and hardly wears any of them.'

'Just the sort of customer I need. Financially, it's still a struggle, although – well, I've got something in the pipeline that should help considerably.'

They talked clothes for a while, far longer than Olivia wanted to.

'And have you married?' she asked.

'God, no!'

Olivia was thrown.

'No one serious in your life?'

'Not really. Well, there's one. He's far more serious than I am. He's the serious type, though. He's a writer and I think they're always a bit serious.'

'I don't know any.' So at least she was admitting to Steve, even if they weren't married. Olivia had noticed that he didn't wear a wedding ring, but a lot of men didn't. 'I'd better go, Carmen. It's been good to talk to you. I'll be in touch nearer the date and we'll see what we can arrange. Meanwhile, have a think about some means of getting back at snobby Victoria.'

'Oh, I will. Trust me. And that bitch Olivia. It was her I really hated. Actually, I've got a few ideas of my own but – well, that's personal . . .'

Olivia replaced the receiver and stared at it for a long time. It was an uncomfortable feeling to know that someone disliked you so intensely after so long. It was infuriating, too.

The following day, after a poor night's sleep, Olivia rang Carmen's number again. It didn't matter now if Steve was there or not. She didn't know if he was involved, and she didn't care. That wasn't strictly true; she hated to think of everything that had passed between them and know that it had been a lie. She guessed he was involved, though, which meant he had known all along who she was. But it didn't matter.

'Hello?'

'Carmen?' Olivia asked, her voice like ice. 'It's Olivia Standish.' Olivia could have predicted the stunned silence that met her announcement, but it still felt very good. Carmen Blake wouldn't get the better of her. 'It's been a long time, Carmen. Although perhaps not long enough.'

'Well, well.' Another long silence. 'How did you get my number?'

'Oh, I've had your number for a long time,' Olivia replied. She wanted to be suitably cool, distant and businesslike, but she could feel the anger inside making her heart pound. 'Your boyfriend – the one who's more serious about your relationship than you are – keeps a photograph of you on his desk. I happened to notice it when he was fucking the living daylights out of me.'

She was shocked to hear herself speaking the words, but Carmen merely laughed at her.

'I know he does,' she answered. 'He's devoted to me. Oh, well, at least we're square on that front. You've had Steve, and I've had your husband. Not that he knew it was me, of course. He's very, very good. You're lucky to have him, Olivia.'

Now it was Olivia's turn to be lost for words. Lloyd had slept with Carmen Blake? The thought repulsed her. She wished she could disbelieve Carmen, but she couldn't.

'So what can I do for you, Olivia?' Carmen asked.

'I think you know why I'm calling, Carmen. I'm not going to beat around the bush. I'll pay for those negatives, but only once, and don't kid yourself that I'm paying for them simply to save Lloyd's career. I have bigger and better ideas for Lloyd and the very last thing I care about is his career. But, as I said, I'm willing to pay for them. I want every negative, though, and because I wouldn't trust you as far as I could throw an elephant, I'll give you fair warning: if I'm ever contacted again, or if Lloyd is, you can forget Carmen's Casuals. You'll be finished, Carmen. I'll make sure of it. I have friends in high places and I have no scruples about using them. Is that understood?'

'Yes.' Carmen had lost a lot of her bravado now.

'Good. We'll meet at Steve's office so just make sure that he's there, too. I want to be certain that you both understand the consequences. Shall we say two o'clock on Monday afternoon?'

'If you like.'

'I like. And I dictate the terms now. For instance, you won't be getting a cash payment. Instead I'll write you a personal cheque, just in case we have any – problems in the future.'

'Er, right.'

'Fine. I'll see you at two o'clock on Monday. I'm sure you won't forget the negatives.'

Olivia cut the connection. She felt no real satisfaction from getting the upper hand over Carmen, or knowing that Steve would be present at their meeting. It would be strange and not particularly pleasant to meet at Steve's studio, but it was perhaps fitting.

The whole thing left Olivia with a bitter taste in her mouth. She could cope with that though, so long as she got those negatives. Once they were in her possession, she would use them to her advantage.

Lloyd had seen little of Olivia for days and it made a pleasant change to find that she was at home on Sunday evening. He had suggested going out for the evening, but she hadn't wanted to. She seemed distracted. Several times he'd had to repeat something he had said. He was equally distracted, though. Try as he might, he couldn't forget what Audrey had told him. Half of him was convinced Audrey had to be lying, and the other half knew for a fact that she wasn't. Olivia had changed dramatically since their marriage. In the early days, she had thrown herself on him at every opportunity, but these days she hardly seemed to notice whether he was there or not. The more he thought about it, the more convinced he became that she had a lover. Or several.

'I saw Audrey the other evening,' he remarked as he filled his glass with whisky. 'She'd heard you were away and invited me to dinner.'

'And no doubt she showed you her lighting system? What did you think of it? We were bathed in purple when I visited. It was strange, to say the least. I was half expecting her to start sacrificing virgins or something.'

'I know what you mean,' he answered with a wry smile. 'I had warm pink. It's completely over the top, of course, but that's Audrey. I suppose she gets bored and, God knows, it needs something to mask all that white. It's a strange house.'

'Yes.'

Lloyd watched her circling the rim of her wine glass with her finger. She definitely had things on her mind and he would dearly love to know what those things were. She was sitting on the sofa, her feet curled beneath her, and was doing little but stare into her glass and make conversation when she had to. Her skirt was long and full, and not one of his favourites, but she was wearing a white T-shirt that hugged her skin and emphasised the fullness of her breasts. In the early days of their marriage, when she had thrown herself on him at every opportunity, he hadn't found her particularly desirable. Attractive yes, but not desirable. Now that she had lost interest in him, he wanted her more than he had ever wanted any woman. Everything about her had changed, from the way she walked to the way she dressed, and it was driving him to distraction. The thought of Audrey's chauffeur getting his hands on her drove him to distraction.

'I met her chauffeur while I was there,' he remarked casually. 'Have you seen him?'

'Clive? Yes, I've seen him.'

'I can't think why she needs a chauffeur. She always used to manage to drive herself.'

'Who knows?' She shrugged. 'She told me she didn't like driving. She's always jetting off somewhere or other so perhaps it's easier to have someone on hand to take her to the airport and meet her again.'

'Perhaps,' he agreed. 'What did you think of him?'

'Who?' She frowned.

'Her chauffeur.'

'I didn't take much notice of him. Why?'

'Just wondered.' He didn't miss the tell-tale colour that invaded her cheeks. 'I think Audrey may be sleeping with him. Do you?'

'I've really no idea, Lloyd.' She finished her wine and got to her feet. 'I think I'll have an early night. I've got a lot to do tomorrow.'

'Fine.' Her confounded early nights were driving him insane, too. 'I've got lots of paperwork to sift through so I think I'd better retire to my study for an hour or so. Goodnight, darling.'

'Goodnight.'

Lloyd went to his study but he couldn't bring himself to look at any paperwork. He couldn't rid himself of the picture of Olivia with that bloody chauffeur. He knew, had known before he spotted her tell-tale blush that it was true, but he still found it impossible to believe. The truth was, he didn't want to believe it. What was Olivia like when she was with him? Did she beg him to take her? Did she straddle him? Did she suck on his cock as she had never sucked on her husband's? Did she play the submissive? Visions filled his mind, visions that tore him apart. Jealousy was an alien feeling for Lloyd and he didn't much care for it. And what about Audrey's ambitions to make love to Olivia? Surely Olivia would never go along with it. Lloyd knew only too well how persuasive Audrey could be but, even so –

Jealousy didn't figure too highly in his feelings when he thought of Audrey making love to Olivia. The idea excited him far too much. As Audrey had guessed, he would love to watch. More than that, he would love to join the two of them.

He sighed as he felt the familiar ache in his body. No one seemed to satisfy that ache, these days. He had no trouble finding attractive, willing women to fuck, but it was Olivia he wanted, Olivia he ached for. It was tempting to march into their bedroom and demand what was his. Damn it all, he was her husband; he had certain rights. That wasn't Lloyd's style, though. He preferred the women in his bed to be willing, to be as eager for him as he was for them.

One day, he promised himself. One day soon.

Olivia dressed with care for her meeting with Steve and Carmen. She wore a long, straight skirt in black-

and-white check that managed to look businesslike and, because of the slit at the back and side, showed off her legs at the same time. She chose a simple shirt and wore her most expensive jewellery with it. It was imperative to have the upper hand and expensive jewellery gave her added confidence. All the same, she was dreading the meeting. She wished now that she hadn't suggested meeting at Steve's studio. The place would be full of too many memories.

She took the train, then got a taxi from the station to Carmen's Casuals. The window display was impressive. Peering inside, Olivia saw that the shop was small, but there were three potential customers inside and the garments were displayed in an attractive way. The quality looked to be good, too.

With her curiosity satisfied, Olivia got back in her taxi and gave the driver the address of Steve's studio. Her nerves were jangling as she sat back and tried to relax. It was silly, really. They were the blackmailers; they were the ones who had been caught out and, hopefully, they were the ones who were going to look pretty silly by the end of the afternoon. On the other hand, Olivia was the one handing over the cheque, and she was the one whose husband featured in the photographs. It was a business transaction, she told herself. Nothing more and nothing less. In a short while, it would be over and she would never have to see either of them again.

The driver stopped outside the studio. Olivia took her time paying him, then climbed out. She felt even more nervous than she had on her previous visit.

She strode up the steps with her head held high, refusing to let any prying eyes see that she was nervous.

Seconds after she pushed the button beside Steve's name, she saw a dark figure approaching on the other side of the glass. It was Steve, and it was a painful reminder of her previous visit.

'Jane.' The door swung open and he gave her a broad smile. 'Or should I say Olivia?' he added softly.

She found his confidence surprising and very irritating. With the slightest inclination of her head in acknowledgement, she strode past him and up the stairs to his studio. Her heels clattered on the steps, keeping time with the pounding of her heartbeat. When she arrived at the door to his studio, she had to wait for him to let her in.

He pushed the door open and stood back to let her pass in front of him. She remembered every detail of the building, and walked straight into his office. Papers were strewn everywhere. Piles of books littered the desks. The wastepaper basket was overflowing with what looked to Olivia to be unopened mail. She took in all this during a split second.

Carmen was leaning back against the pine desk and Olivia looked straight at her. She, too, looked irritatingly unruffled. She looked irritatingly attractive, too. A figure-hugging, red T-shirt was tucked into the waistband of black, skin-tight denims.

'Carmen.' Olivia slipped her hands into the pockets of her skirt. 'It's been a long time. You have the negatives?'

'You haven't changed at all,' Carmen remarked, ignoring the question.

'You have.' Olivia felt slightly more calm as she thought back to their schooldays. Then, she'd had the upper hand over the scruffy East End child. She still had it today. 'When we were at school, I actually admired you.' She smiled as Carmen's eyebrows shot beneath her hair. 'Yes, I did. I had no friends before I went there and, because I was too frightened to lose the few I made, I went along with them. I was a coward in those days. You weren't, though. Despite everything, you maintained your dignity. I never believed you to be a thief, but perhaps I was wrong.'

Carmen clearly had no answer to that.

'The negatives?' Olivia prompted.

It was Steve who walked over to his desk, pulled open a drawer and extracted a large brown envelope. Without saying a word, he handed it to Olivia. She took out the sheet of negatives and held them up to the light of the window. The first few frames showed an old country church which looked innocent enough, and the last frames showed an elderly woman with a small dog. As satisfied as she could be that there were no more shots of Lloyd, Olivia returned the negatives to the envelope.

'And the prints?' she asked.

'You've had most of them.' Carmen handed her another envelope. 'You've certainly had the good ones.' She nodded at the envelope. 'He's very good in bed.'

'I know,' Olivia answered with all the coolness she could muster – which wasn't much. 'That's why I married him. So is this everything?'

'Yes.' Steve answered her question.

'Just the money,' Carmen reminded her.

'Ah, the money. Yes, against my better judgement, I'm going to pay you ten thousand pounds. As I said on the phone, this has nothing to do with saving my husband's career. I couldn't care less about that. I suppose I'm paying to clear my conscience. I've felt guilty about the way we treated you at school. But that's it, Carmen. After this, you won't get any more money out of me. If you try, or if I discover there are more negatives or prints lying around, I'll finish you. I mean it. I paid Carmen's Casuals a visit on my way here. You should be very proud of it. But if you try to double-cross me, there won't be any Carmen's Casuals. I have lots of friends that I'm not afraid to use when necessary. You'd be wise to remember that.'

Wishing she'd had the foresight to write out the cheque before she came, Olivia took her cheque book from her bag and looked around for a pen. In the end, Steve handed her a fountain pen. She took off the top and wrote out a cheque payable to Carmen Blake. After double-checking that she had remembered to sign it and had put the correct date and figures on it, she blew on it to dry the ink, then handed it to Carmen.

'I hope this is the last time we'll meet,' she said briskly as she returned her cheque book to her bag.

With the envelopes clutched beneath her arm, she turned and walked out of the room. Much to her annoyance, Steve followed her.

'I'll show you out,' he said.

'No need.'

'All the same . . .'

Her heels clattered deafeningly on the steps.

'I'm sorry it's come to this,' Steve said.

'Really? And why's that? You're ten grand better off; you should be pleased. I'm sure Carmen will be greedy, but you deserve your share for finding out about me, for bringing me here –' She was too angry to continue.

'Mmm,' was all he said.

Olivia yanked open the door and strode down the steps and into the street. When she was out of sight, she headed for the nearest bar. She needed a stiff drink.

Sitting with a glass of Southern Comfort in her hand, she slowly began to feel better. It was difficult not to remember her times with Steve, and it was difficult to swallow the bitter taste that the memories left, but she had to put it down to experience. It was time to move on, and she was ready.

In any case, her mind lately had been dwelling on Audrey. Audrey had made it plain enough that she wanted them to make love and, the more Olivia thought about it, the more the idea excited her. Ever since watching the video of Lloyd, she had tried to imagine how it would feel to caress another woman's soft skin, to have another woman caress her own . . .

Chapter Eleven

'*L*et's grab a coffee,' Audrey suggested.

'Good idea,' Olivia replied, sounding relieved. 'Shopping with you is exhausting, Audrey!'

They took the department store's lift to the top floor and were shown to a table by the window overlooking the City. Olivia was right, Audrey decided. Their shopping trips *were* exhausting. As yet, though, Audrey could think of no better way of getting close to Olivia. Only when shopping, and surrounded by other shoppers, did Olivia relax in her company. It was a safety in numbers thing, Audrey guessed. While out shopping, they had fun, but as soon as they were on a one-to-one basis, Olivia panicked.

Audrey was growing frustrated. She was convinced that Olivia wanted the two of them to make love almost as much as she did, but getting her to admit it was a different matter altogether.

'Let's just have a cake or something,' Audrey said when the waitress came to take their order. 'We can have a bite to eat when we get back to my place.'

'OK. I'm not really hungry at the moment, anyway.'

That was a step forwards and Audrey was mildly

encouraged. Olivia usually came out with a dozen excuses as to why she had to dash straight home. She did seem more relaxed today though. Perhaps today would be the day after all. Audrey's pulse quickened at the thought. She wanted to make love to Olivia, had wanted that for a very long time, but she also wanted to prove to Lloyd that she could do it.

Lloyd. If today was to be the day, Lloyd wouldn't be there to witness it. Audrey liked to believe that the first time would be the first of many, but she couldn't be sure. Olivia, she suspected, was keen to try new pleasures, but there was no guarantee that she would want to repeat the experience . . .

While they were drinking their coffee, Olivia inspected her purchases in what, to Audrey at least, seemed an exaggerated way. The dress she'd bought, a blood-red cocktail dress, was dismissed, as were the two pairs of shoes. It was the lingerie she seemed so pleased with. She held out a camisole in the palest of blue silks for Audrey's inspection.

'What do you think? Is it me?' she asked.

'It certainly is you,' Audrey replied with a smile. 'You like buying underwear, don't you?'

'It's not the buying of it,' Olivia replied with a thoughtful shrug, 'but I do like to have lots to choose from. My choice of underwear depends on my mood. I love to have silk next to my skin, though.'

'So do I,' Audrey said. 'And yes, that will look lovely on you. You can try it on when we get home.'

'Yes,' Olivia replied vaguely. She returned the camisole to its bag and took another from a different bag. This was altogether different; dark blue and more provocative. 'Which do you prefer, Audrey?'

'I love them both.' It was the truth. 'Try them on when we get home and make up your own mind.'

'Yes.' Again, that vague reply.

'Excuse me a minute, Livvy.' Audrey rose to her feet.

'I need to make a phone call and the battery in my mobile phone needs charging,' she lied.

She walked through the tables to the telephone booth near the door. As she tapped out the number, she smiled at Olivia.

'Lloyd? It's Audrey. I'm having coffee with Livvy and then we're heading back to my place.' She hesitated, very uncertain of herself for a change. 'I'm not sure what plans you have for the day, but I wondered if you'd like to make use of my two-way mirror again.'

There was a long, shocked silence. Audrey wasn't surprised. She was taking a huge gamble and only hoped that if he did take her up on it, he wouldn't be disappointed and she wouldn't be a laughing stock.

'You did say you wanted to watch,' she reminded him.

'Yes.' Another long pause. 'I just can't believe there will be anything to watch.'

'Oh, well. It doesn't matter. If you're not interested –'

Audrey was relieved. She had probably just imagined that Olivia seemed more relaxed and more eager for pleasure than usual.

'No. Yes. Yes, I'll be there, Audrey. What time will you be back?'

'About four, I suppose.' And now her nerves had her trembling. 'You know your way to my bedroom. The key to the dressing room is in the drawer by the side of my bed.'

'OK. I'll be there.'

'Lloyd – well, I can't guarantee –'

The sound of his laughter cut her off.

'Having doubts, Audrey? That's not like you!'

It wasn't, and she didn't like it.

'I just don't want you to be disappointed,' she said lamely.

'I won't be – either way.' Another long pause. 'I'll be there before four.'

The connection was cut and Audrey replaced the receiver and walked back to Olivia.

'Livvy, you can help me choose a new hat,' she said brightly. 'I hate buying the damn things, and they look ridiculous on me, but I need one to wear at Tony's nephew's wedding. Will you help me?'

'I'll do my best, of course. Our taste in clothes is very different, though, and I'm not keen on hats myself. I find they look lovely in the shop, but outrageous perched on your head.'

'Exactly!' Audrey laughed. 'Oh, well. It will be fun.'

It was, too.

Audrey knew she was right; there was definitely something relaxed and carefree about Olivia today. For once, her guard was down.

'You're looking at your watch again,' Olivia remarked with a frown. 'Are you in a rush to get home?'

'Not really.' It was after four o'clock, though, and Lloyd would be waiting. 'Well, I am a little tired. Shall I settle for this one?' She took a large, black hat that she'd tried on several times from its stand. 'It looks OK, doesn't it?'

'OK? Audrey, it looks stunning! You look stunning – very mysterious and very sexy.'

'That's good enough for me.' She laughed, feeling a little light-headed at the compliment. 'Let's go home, have a nice hot shower and relax with something to eat. Yes?'

'Sounds good to me.' Olivia reached inside her handbag and took out her mobile phone. 'I'll ask Clive to meet us outside. Your mobile needs its battery charging – remember?'

'Right.' Audrey nodded.

She hoped Olivia wasn't expecting Clive to play any part in their relaxation. It was too bad if she was; Audrey would give him the rest of the day off.

On the drive home though, Olivia paid Clive no attention whatsoever. She didn't so much as glance in his direction, Audrey noted. She was far too busy discussing their shopping expedition and laughing as if she didn't have a care in the world. Her attitude was exciting Audrey still more; she hoped she wasn't reading the situation wrongly.

'We can manage our own bags,' Audrey told Clive when he stopped the car outside the house. 'In fact, you may as well take the rest of the day off. Livvy has her car here, or if she doesn't feel like driving back we'll call a taxi, so we won't be needing you.'

'Fine,' Clive replied with a shrug.

Audrey let them into the house, and headed straight for the staircase.

'Let's take everything upstairs. You were going to try on that camisole, if I recall. Oh, and may I be very rude and have first use of the shower?'

It had been tempting to suggest they shower together, but Audrey wasn't going to push her luck. She was going to take things very, very slowly.

She threw her bags on the bed, then checked her bedside drawer. The key was missing. Lloyd was watching them. Her heart began to pound erratically at the thought.

Without a word, she took off her clothes, letting them fall in a pile at her feet, and headed for the shower room.

'I won't be long,' she called over her shoulder.

'Don't rush on my account,' Olivia replied.

The water was hot and refreshing. Audrey's body tingled all over with anticipation as she washed herself. If she had read the situation wrongly, and if nothing came of this, she felt sure that the disappointment would kill her . . .

When she walked back into the bedroom, it was to

see Olivia already undressed with a large, white towel wrapped tightly around herself.

'I helped myself to a towel. I hope you don't mind.'

'Of course not.' At times, there was something almost childlike about Olivia. It was the times when she was most unsure of herself. 'How many times have I told you to make yourself at home? Enjoy your shower.'

She lay back on the bed, aware that Lloyd would be watching her, and hoping that the small smile on her face looked more confident than she felt. In truth, she had never felt more nervous. She put her own bags on the floor, then emptied Olivia's. She laid out the two camisoles on the bed, together with the three bras and matching thongs that Olivia had bought. It was impossible to resist running her fingers over the silky material and wishing she was running them over Olivia's smooth skin.

When Olivia finally emerged from the shower room, the towel was still wrapped tightly around her. Her face was tinged pink, whether that was due to embarrassment or the heat of the shower, Audrey didn't know.

'Try them on,' Audrey said quietly, nodding at the garments on the bed. 'I'll go and get us a glass of wine.'

She thought, or hoped, that Olivia might relax a little if they had a glass of wine. Also, she suspected that Olivia would be more confident if she, Audrey, was out of the way while she tried on the first of her garments.

Whether her theory was correct or not, Audrey couldn't be sure, but when she returned to the bedroom with a bottle of wine and two glasses, Olivia was standing in front of the mirror wearing the pale blue camisole. She looked adorable. The garment showed off her lovely long legs but left so much of her body to the imagination. Audrey didn't need to imagine, of course; her memory was sharp. Lloyd, on the other side of that mirror, wouldn't need to imagine either. What would Olivia say, Audrey wondered, if she knew she was showing off her body to her own husband?

'That looks gorgeous,' Audrey said, sitting on the bed. '*You* look gorgeous. Try on the other one.'

Olivia did as Audrey suggested, but she kept her back to Audrey until she was wearing the camisole. In dark blue, this one was more provocative.

'You'll drive men wild in that,' Audrey told her truthfully. 'It is so sexy!'

Olivia looked pleased. She turned around in front of the mirror, viewing herself from all angles.

'How does it feel?' Audrey asked.

'Wonderful!'

'It looks it. Here – come and have a drink.'

Olivia, still wearing her camisole, kneeled on the bed, very much as a child would. There was nothing child-like about her body though. At that moment, Audrey thought it was the most beautiful body she had ever seen – male or female. Olivia didn't seem disturbed by Audrey's nakedness, but she avoided looking at it.

Audrey filled both glasses and handed one to Olivia.

'Are you going to try on your other purchases?' she asked. She very much hoped so.

'If you like.'

Olivia drank from her glass then put it on the table. She hopped off the bed and removed the camisole. Standing at the foot of the bed, completely naked, she looked straight at Audrey.

'Which first?'

'The red.'

Audrey's lips were dry and she took a sip of her wine to moisten them. She hadn't read the situation wrong; she couldn't have. Soon, their bodies would touch. Her breasts tingled with excitement at the thought. Olivia modelled each and every garment as if she were an expert on the catwalk. There was no sign

189

of nervousness, no hint that she would suddenly get dressed and run home. Wearing the last of the lacy bras and thongs, she sat on the bed once more and picked up her wine glass. Audrey wondered if she felt safer in the minuscule garments. Her body was exquisite and Audrey longed to reach out and hold her.

'Let me touch.' She reached out and touched the thin fabric of Olivia's bra. 'It feels fabulous. I bet it's great next to your skin.'

'It is.' Olivia nodded.

'You have lovely skin.' Audrey reached out and lightly, very lightly, stroked Olivia's thigh. To her relief, Olivia didn't flinch. 'So soft.'

'So have you.'

For one glorious moment, Audrey thought she was about to feel Olivia's hands on her skin, but Olivia merely reached behind her and unfastened her bra. She tossed it aside and then, much to Audrey's surprise and delight, pulled the thong down her legs and kicked that aside too. She sat on the bed, hugging her wine glass, with her knees raised to hide her breasts. Unless Audrey was mistaken, there was a hint of challenge, or perhaps it was merely acceptance, in her eyes. Audrey emptied her glass and set it aside. She had to make the first move; if they waited for Olivia, they would wait for ever. She would have been less worried about this if Lloyd hadn't been watching them. It would be too much if she frightened Olivia away. She didn't think that was likely, but it was a risk she wasn't prepared to take. Lloyd would never allow her to forget it.

'Let me touch your soft skin,' she whispered.

She put her hand on Olivia's thigh once more and ran her fingers down the silky smooth length of it. Olivia gazed at the hand, reminding Audrey of a fascinated child.

'Beautiful,' Audrey murmured.

Olivia emptied her glass and Audrey took it from her.

'Come and lie beside me,' she said softly.

Very hesitantly, Olivia turned round and lay back on the bed, her head on the pillows, and her arms crossed loosely on her stomach. Audrey stretched out beside her, lying on her side with her hand propping up her head to gaze at Olivia's loveliness. Audrey could feel her heart racing erratically with a mix of anticipation and nervousness, mostly the former. She ran her fingers across Olivia's arms, then very gently uncrossed them and moved them so that they lay by Olivia's sides.

'That's better,' Audrey murmured. 'I can see you now. You shouldn't hide such a lovely body.'

'Your body is far better than mine,' Olivia replied quietly. 'Your breasts are gorgeous – so full and heavy.'

'Touch them.' Audrey licked her dry lips. 'Touch my breasts, Livvy.'

Almost coyly, Olivia lifted her hand and traced a slow circle around Audrey's nipple. Her nipple hardened immediately at the gentle touch.

'Your skin's so soft.' Olivia spoke with a touch of wonder in her voice.

'It's exactly the same as yours,' Audrey replied, moving her own hand to caress Olivia's smaller but perfectly rounded breast. 'It feels good, doesn't it, Livvy? It's amazing to have your skin caressed by the same soft skin, don't you think?'

'It is. But, Audrey – I've never done this –'

'I know.' The words thrilled Audrey. It would be very, very special to be Olivia's first female lover.

'I'm not sure what I'm supposed to do,' Olivia admitted hesitantly.

'Just enjoy,' Audrey replied with amusement.

Before Olivia could voice any more doubts, Audrey lowered her head and took a rosy nipple in her mouth and sucked on it. Olivia's gasp of pleasure thrilled her, as did the way Olivia's hands went instinctively to Audrey's shoulders. Audrey moved closer so that their thighs touched. She wanted to take everything slowly, but already she was highly aroused. She sucked lightly on each nipple in turn and flicked her tongue across the rosy, hard peaks. It was obvious that Olivia was very aroused. Audrey began to stroke her thighs, her hand circling inwards, and then she ran her fingers through Olivia's mound. With a gasp of pleasure, Olivia lifted her head and sought Audrey's lips. It was so unexpected; intense joy flooded through Audrey as they kissed. Olivia's lips were soft and pliable against her own, her mouth eager for pleasure. They were both breathing hard. Audrey's finger slipped between Olivia's thighs and found her secret place. She inserted a finger, pressed lightly on Olivia's swollen bud, and was delighted when Olivia climaxed almost immediately.

'Oh, Audrey – I've wanted that for so long,' Olivia gasped. She flopped back against the pile of pillows. 'I'm sorry, but I've been aroused all day.'

'You have?' Audrey was intrigued.

'Yes. I knew this had to happen and I've been able to think of nothing else all day.'

'Good.' Audrey began to stroke Olivia's breasts again. 'Then we'll have to make sure you're not disappointed . . .'

Audrey was determined to make sure that Lloyd wasn't disappointed, either. She knew a great deal of satisfaction, making love to his wife while he watched helplessly. She could picture him; aroused but shocked, possibly angry and definitely jealous.

She forgot all about Lloyd though as Olivia lifted her head slightly and took Audrey's aching nipple into her mouth. She flicked the rosy tip with her tongue, then sucked gently. Her every touch had a gentleness to it that was highly arousing. She knew instinctively how to give pleasure, as every woman did.

They kissed again and Audrey moved closer, almost lying on top of Olivia. Her breathing was fast, she was very close to orgasm. Every caress from Olivia took her closer to the edge. Olivia's body arched towards hers; their breasts touched, sending delicious shivers down Audrey's spine. Olivia's hands were so soft on her bottom, so gentle on her waist, and so understanding as they sought Audrey's fully erect nipples. Her movements were fluid and slow, yet so exciting. Audrey had to fight the urge to caress herself; her aching clitoris demanded attention.

Olivia's lips took over from her hands, exciting Audrey still further. Her lips were cool in contrast to her hot hands. Audrey shivered as Olivia kissed her thighs and she parted her legs instinctively. Finally, just when Audrey thought she could stand it no longer, Olivia's lips brushed against the aching flesh of her sex, making Audrey moan out loud. Her arousal was unbearably intense. She had to have release.

Olivia's tongue flicked relentlessly over Audrey's clitoris, bringing her closer to orgasm with each second. Audrey's hips jerked spasmodically as her orgasm began, but Olivia didn't relent. Her tongue probed fast and hard, giving seemingly endless pleasure. Audrey felt her vagina clench powerfully as her orgasm seized her. Her legs kicked out just before her body grew limp.

She could see from Olivia's swollen breasts and erect nipples that she was very aroused.

'I know what you'd like,' Audrey whispered, kissing Olivia's shoulder blades.

She reached across Olivia to her bedside drawer, took out a large ivory dildo, and laughed softly at the look of delight on Olivia's face.

Audrey rubbed it against Olivia's wet flesh and rejoiced in the other woman's whimpers of pleasure. Lloyd – Audrey had forgotten all about him. She could only guess at his feelings as he watched his wife moaning for an ivory phallus. It was a large phallus though, and Audrey slowly pushed the smooth tip inside. Olivia was greedy, pushing on to the phallus and wanting more of it. Audrey knew that feeling well; she had enjoyed many hours of pleasure with the dildo. She pushed it deeper inside, watching the play of emotions on Olivia's face. Beads of sweat glistened on her brow and in the valley between her breasts.

Audrey wanted to receive as well as give pleasure so she removed the dildo and reached into her drawer for another of her toys. This dildo was smaller, but it could give them both pleasure – such pleasure.

Audrey inserted one end of the delicious phallus inside herself and leaned back as the pleasure rippled through her. With her eyes closed, she rubbed the other end against Olivia's wet flesh. Olivia wasn't standing for that, though. She grabbed the dildo and sank down on it, groaning with pleasure as it filled her. Audrey's eyes snapped open. They both thrust on to the phallus, their sexes inches apart, but feeling as if they were joined. Audrey could almost believe she had a cock of her own, a highly sensitive cock that was pounding into Olivia. Audrey gasped as she felt Olivia's index finger push inside with the dildo, and she quickly returned the favour. Their movements grew more frenzied as they both thrust against the dildo and used their fingers to give added pleasure. They both knew exactly how to please the other.

Audrey screamed as another orgasm shook her body. With a couple of quick thrusts, Olivia also climaxed.

They fell back on the bed, exhausted but sated, their arms entwined . . .

Lloyd couldn't sleep that night. The shock of seeing his wife enjoying the body of another woman had worn off; now he was simply angry. Olivia was sleeping soundly by his side and it was as much as he could do not to push her on to her back and screw her senseless. As tempting as that idea was, though, it simply wasn't Lloyd's style. He didn't want to force her; he wanted her to want him.

The physical side of their relationship had never been good. Lloyd had always put it down to a lack of interest in anything physical on Olivia's side, but now he knew different. It wasn't that she preferred women, either; according to Audrey, and he had no reason to doubt her, Olivia had been even more eager with Clive. He found it difficult to blame himself, though. He had always prided himself on being a good lover. He knew he'd had a good teacher and he liked to think he could bring out the best in his women. Willing to please, he could be gentle and tender, rough and demanding, dominant or submissive – whatever they wanted. The trouble was, he didn't have a damn clue what Olivia wanted. He never had. He'd believed her to be totally uninterested in sex, but that notion had been well and truly disproved today.

He thumped his pillow into shape and rolled on to his back to stare at the ceiling. Beneath the covers, his penis was stiff and hard. With a loud sigh that was pure frustration, he reached down and held himself.

Damn Olivia!

He'd been in a high state of arousal all evening. All he had done was watch Olivia move around the house, and remember the highly erotic scenes he had witnessed that afternoon. That was all it had taken.

It would be easy enough to jump in his car and find some woman who was willing to offer him relief but, for once, he wasn't interested. It was Olivia he wanted. Instinct told him that another woman could only offer a very temporary relief.

Too warm beneath the bedclothes, he pushed them away. There was no light in the room, the only form of illumination came from the streetlight outside but it was enough to let him see his rampant cock and the curve of Olivia's spine as she lay with her back to him.

He linked his hands beneath his head and tried to think of other things. It was no use, though. His body craved relief and it infuriated him to listen to the slow, even sound of Olivia's breathing. He thought of other couples in nearby houses and wondered if he was the only married man who was lying awake in such a state. He pictured other couples making love as he lay wide awake and longing for the touch of his wife's hand on his aching body.

As he rolled over, facing Olivia's back, the tip of his fully erect penis nudged the back of her thighs. Even that brief touch was pleasurable. He wriggled a little more, hoping she would wake, but she was oblivious to his agony. It was too much for him and he rolled on to his back again. He lay there, angry and frustrated, until the first light of dawn crept into their room.

Olivia awoke early and jumped straight out of bed.

'Where are you going?' he complained. 'It's early. I thought we could make love.'

'Sorry, Lloyd.' She was already on her way to the bathroom. 'I've a busy day ahead of me. I've got an appointment with the bank manager at nine, and a load of things to do before then.'

He couldn't argue, plead or complain. She had gone.

A few minutes later, he had the dubious pleasure of watching her dress. He was convinced she deliberately dressed in a manner that would arouse him. Whether she did or not, it worked. God, he wanted her.

'I'll get Dorothy to bring you breakfast,' she said as she strode out of their bedroom.

'There's no need,' he called after her testily. 'I may as well get up now.'

For all that, it was another hour before he finally got out of bed. He had heard her leave, and he had heard

Dorothy moving around the house, but now all was silent. Still angry, he strode to the shower and switched it on. The hot water did nothing to ease the ache in his body. As he soaped himself, he tried to imagine that it was Olivia's hands that touched him in such intimate places. As he washed his stiffening cock, he tried to imagine that it was her soap-covered hands sliding along its length. He leaned back against the cool tiles with his eyes closed and his hand still sliding along his cock. In his mind's eye, he saw her again, thrusting on to that huge ivory phallus Audrey had produced. He imagined her pushing down on his aching cock. It burned and throbbed for her, and his hand was a very poor substitute. He imagined her hot, wet flesh clenching around him. His eyes were tightly closed as he did all in his power to make his imagination seem as real as possible. All the while, his hand was busy. He cupped his balls with his free hand and stared down at the impressive width of his cock. His movements grew more frenzied, his breathing more laboured, as he desperately sought relief. In his mind, he could see her clearly, gazing in wonder at that ivory dildo as it slid in and out of her – and finally, with a groan that was a mixture of frustration and relief, he climaxed.

Chapter Twelve

Olivia gazed around the building and tried to see it objectively. It was massive and empty, like a warehouse on three floors, with huge if filthy windows that overlooked the Thames. The amount of work required to transform it into office and studio space was daunting, but not impossible. Unlike the other properties she had looked at, it didn't need walls knocking down or complicated structural alterations.

'Well?'

Jim and Darren broke off their discussion and turned at her question.

'It has possibilities,' Jim answered cautiously.

Both men were cautious, far too cautious for Olivia's liking, but they were experts and she needed them. More than anything, she wanted her own television production company. The dream was one thing; knowing how to achieve it was something else. She was eager and quick to learn, but there was such a lot to learn.

'When's the architect coming?' Darren asked and Olivia glanced at her watch.

'She should be here in half an hour or so.'

'Mmm.'

They resumed their low-voiced discussion, with Jim scribbling notes on a shorthand notepad every so often.

Olivia wandered over to the window and looked down to the car park below. Perhaps Tanya Robertson, the architect, would show more enthusiasm. Olivia hoped so. This was the fourth possible site they had looked at and she was growing frustrated. She had always been the same; when she had an idea, she wanted to turn it into a reality, not spend ages weighing up the pros and cons. And this place looked so perfect. True, it would need a lot of work, she knew that, but she'd had a chat with the bank manager and she couldn't see too many problems in that direction.

She tapped her fingers on the glass impatiently.

At least Jim and Darren wouldn't be distracted by Tanya's undeniable charms, she thought with amusement. The two men, both attractive thirty-somethings, had lived together for six years, something that struck Olivia as a waste. Jim especially could make any female's pulse race. He was tall, around the six feet mark, clean shaven, with a solid chest, strong-looking arms, and narrow waist and hips. In the past when Olivia had seen him he had been wearing a suit, usually conservative in taste, but today, because they were looking round an old building that had been empty for almost a year, he had sensibly chosen well-worn jeans and a shirt. A black leather belt rested on his hips and showed off a firm, flat stomach.

Away from Jim's particular assets, Darren would turn a few heads too. He was shorter than Jim, with a more casual attitude to his appearance and life in general. His hair was longer and much darker than Jim's, and it had a tendency to curl. Whereas Jim would have his cut regularly, so that it always looked the same, Darren was often seen with quite long hair and then very short hair. He wore a single earring, a hoop with a tiny gold cross hanging from it, and this, together with the most amazing blue eyes that seemed to penetrate your very soul, gave him something of a romantic gypsy air.

She had only known the two men for a month, and had only seen them on a dozen occasions in that time, but it was like spending time with a couple who had been married for twenty years.

Tanya's sleek white sports car pulled up outside and Olivia crossed the building to go and meet her.

'What a fabulous place,' Tanya enthused, not bothering with 'hello' or any of the social niceties.

'Isn't it!' Olivia was delighted. 'Come and see what you think. I think it's perfect!'

Olivia introduced Tanya to Jim and Darren and wasn't in the least surprised to see the gleam of interest in her eyes when Jim shook her hand.

'I don't think much of yours,' Tanya quipped as they walked up the stairs.

'I hate to disappoint,' Olivia retorted with a grin, 'but they're gay.'

'I might have known. Why is it that all the decent-looking blokes are either gay, married or dead?'

'I've no idea.' Olivia laughed.

A natural redhead, with a figure that curved deliciously in all the right places, Tanya was used to having the undivided attention of any men present. Olivia could see that Jim and Darren's lack of interest irked her.

The four of them threw ideas around for the rest of the morning. Olivia knew what she wanted to turn this building into her dream; Jim and Darren knew what she needed in terms of office and studio space, and Tanya came up with ideas that were both practical and appealing.

'It's going to cost a bomb,' she warned Olivia.

'I know.' Olivia chewed on her bottom lip. 'I'm in the

process of fixing up a loan with my bank, though, and I'm expecting substantial additional funding soon.'

Olivia hadn't mentioned her plans to Lloyd; she was waiting until the time was right. She needed him, though. She needed him as a business partner, both for his name, and for his financial input.

She was beginning to worry about him, though. He seemed to grow more stubborn every day and at every turn he was going against the government. He was about to submit a highly controversial report that would have everyone up in arms about the state of the health service again. If he was asked to resign, and the Lord knew he was pushing his luck, Olivia would have no hold over him whatsoever.

She consoled herself with the knowledge that every cloud had its silver lining. The more he stood up to the government, the more the public adored him, and that fact alone would be a huge bonus when they had their own production company.

It was *when*, not *if*, but time was running out. Olivia needed to persuade Lloyd to resign his seat before he was forced into it from other quarters. She had no doubt that she could persuade him. When he saw the video and the negatives, and when she had managed to convince him that she wouldn't hesitate to use them, he would have little choice but to go along with her wishes. It was a very satisfying thought.

When their meeting was over, Olivia said goodbye to Jim and Darren and took Tanya out to lunch so that they could discuss things in more depth.

'I've offered them twenty-five grand less than the asking price,' Olivia told her, 'and I should know within forty-eight hours whether my offer has been accepted. I'm fairly confident, though. The place has been empty for so long that I expect they'll be glad to see the back of it.'

'And if it's not accepted?'

'Then I suppose I'll make them a better offer,' Olivia replied with a shrug. 'I'm willing to pay the asking price but if I don't have to, it will ease the financial side of things. Oh, and Tanya, as yet this is confidential. Not even Lloyd knows about it.'

Tanya raised perfectly shaped eyebrows at that but didn't comment.

'My lips are sealed. Give me a call as soon as you know if your offer has been accepted. Meanwhile, I'll have a think about it and get some ideas down on paper.'

'Thanks, Tanya.'

For the rest of the meal, they caught up on the gossip. Olivia kept it brief; she had arranged to spend the afternoon with Audrey and was keen to leave.

Olivia was pleasantly surprised to see Henri's car on the drive when she arrived at Audrey's. She wished now that she hadn't spent so long with Tanya.

She had her own key these days and she quickly let herself in to go in search of Audrey. She was about to push open the door to the sitting room when it opened and she came face to face with Clive.

'I was coming to meet you,' he said.

'Where's Audrey?' She was slightly breathless.

'In here.' He opened the door wider and stood back to let her enter. 'We wondered where you'd got to.'

'Henri's just arrived,' Audrey greeted her, rising from the sofa. 'Would you like a massage, Livvy?'

'I would love one!' It was true. She hadn't realised until now just how tense the morning's meeting had made her. The prospect of fulfilling her dream was both exciting and frightening.

'You are looking very tense, Mrs Standish,' Henri remarked in his usual scolding fashion.

'Then you'll have to relax me, Henri,' she replied, laughing at him.

'We'll go into the drawing room,' Audrey said firmly. 'Clive, you'd better come too. We may need you.'

The four of them walked to the drawing room in a single file that made Olivia smile to herself. She knew why Audrey had chosen the drawing room. It had acres of floor space and she loved to enjoy her massages – and anything else she demanded of Henri – on the assortment of goatskin rugs that lay on top of the Persian rug.

Audrey wasted no time in lowering the zip at the back of her dress and letting it fall to the floor. She stepped out of it, picked it up and handed it to Clive.

'Come and join me, Livvy,' she said. 'I'm sure Henri can deal with us both.' She glanced at him. 'Can't you, Henri?'

'I shall do my best, Mrs Symington. Rest assured.' He knelt on the Persian rug and opened his black bag. 'I have plenty of the oils.'

Olivia undressed quickly. All she wanted right now was for Henri to remove the tension from her body.

As soon as she removed a garment, Clive took it from her, folded it neatly and put it on the chair.

Free from her clothes, she lay face down close to Audrey on two goatskin rugs.

'Plenty of oil, Henri,' she said, closing her eyes as she waited for his expert touch.

'Yes, madam.'

She didn't have long to wait. As always, Henri began rubbing oil into her feet. Almost at his first touch, she felt the tension ebb from her muscles. The oil smelled different this afternoon. It was pleasant, but much stronger than usual.

With her head resting on her arms, she looked across at Audrey and smiled.

'I needed this,' she murmured happily.

'Then enjoy.' Audrey reached out and stroked her arm. 'There's nothing to do this afternoon except enjoy life. What could be better than having two men at our disposal?'

'Life's pretty good,' Olivia agreed with a smile.

She sighed as Henri worked his magic on the backs of her thighs. It surprised her that Audrey, not noted for her patience, seemed happy enough to wait until it was her turn to enjoy his skills. After a while, it also made her feel a little guilty.

'Henri, don't forget Audrey,' she murmured.

'How could I do that?' he responded. 'You relax, Mrs Standish.'

Olivia tried to do just that as Henri began massaging his oils into Audrey's neck and shoulders. With Olivia, he always began with her feet. With Audrey, he was starting on her neck and shoulders. Fascinated, Olivia bent her elbow to prop up her head so that she could watch.

From the way Audrey wriggled on the goatskin, Olivia guessed she was already extremely aroused.

'Clive,' Audrey said, 'I'm sure you can help Livvy relax until Henri is ready for her again.'

Clive had been sitting on a chair by the window, but he quickly crossed the room and kneeled by Olivia's side. Olivia let her head drop on her hands as he began to rub her back. He stroked her ribcage and her waist and hips. His touch was very different to Henri's. Henri's was designed to relax the recipient; Clive's was designed to excite. It was successful, too. Olivia squirmed beneath his hands, seeking more pressure, more pleasure.

'Take your clothes off, Clive,' Audrey told him. 'I want to look at you.'

Olivia did too, but she wished Audrey wouldn't be quite so quick at giving orders. It irritated her. It was as if Audrey saw her as a young child who couldn't be expected, or trusted, to speak for herself. True, Olivia liked to take things more slowly than Audrey, but she was quite capable of calling the shots. More than capable. She enjoyed it.

Her irritation evaporated as Clive began to undress. His powerful-looking body never failed to please her.

When completely naked, he returned to her side and once more began to caress her body. Olivia's skin grew warm beneath his hands. She turned over so that she was lying on her back. Henri, she noticed, was watching her while he continued to rub oil into Audrey's back. Audrey, too, was watching her. Their interest aroused her still further.

Clive must have been aware of them but he paid them no attention. He was far too busy giving Olivia pleasure. He stroked and caressed her body with a firmness that made her ache for more. She parted her legs a little and thrust her hips towards him but he wouldn't be rushed.

Olivia felt Audrey's soft hands on her breasts and she moaned softly. Henri began to massage her arms while Clive stroked her thighs. At times, it was difficult to tell who was touching her. Only Audrey's softer skin gave her away. Feeling gentle lips teasing her stiff nipple, Olivia opened her eyes and saw Audrey's red head bent over her. Audrey's tongue flicked over one nipple while Henri made sure the other wasn't ignored. Clive's tongue touched the wet flesh of her sex, making her gasp.

Their tongues were hot and greedy, and Olivia felt her body open up like a flower for them. Soft moans of contentment escaped her. She could hardly believe such pleasure was possible.

A tongue probed her opening. She assumed at first that it was Clive's, but when she felt his lips on her neck, she knew that it was Henri. His tongue was hard as it pushed inside her, and her muscles clenched around it. She whimpered with pleasure as Audrey sought her mouth and pushed her tongue inside. The rhythm was thrilling. As Henri pushed his tongue into her eager sex, so Audrey probed her mouth. Every nerve ending felt as if it were on fire. Her skin tingled and burned.

For a few moments her sex was abandoned, but soon she felt something wonderfully hard and hot nudging her. Again, she assumed it was Clive, and again she was wrong. It was the first time she had seen Henri naked. The sight thrilled her. His body looked so strong and powerful; full of promise. The penis nudging her throbbing sex was shorter than Clive's, but it was very, very thick. As she felt it push its way inside her, she cried out.

Henri's movements were calm and unhurried. Audrey sucked on her swollen nipples. Clive kneeled behind her head and stroked her hair and forehead. Three pairs of hands, Audrey's mouth and tongue, and Henri's fat cock were all intent on pleasuring her. Clive lifted her head so that it rested on his thighs as he kneeled. Each time she moved her head, she felt his stiff cock and finally, she lifted her arms and reached for him. He must have guessed what she wanted because he moved slightly so that his gorgeous prick was within reach. While Henri slid in and out of her, his movements still unhurried, Olivia sucked on Clive's cock. And while Olivia sucked on Clive's cock, Audrey licked and suckled on her nipples. Six hands continued to worship her body. Pleasure rippled through her body as if she had been put on the earth solely to receive. She felt as if she was in a trance. It was difficult to separate the sensations, to say who was responsible for such joy.

Audrey lifted her head and joined Olivia in sliding her tongue along Clive's hard cock. They kissed; Olivia took Clive's cock in her mouth; Audrey licked his balls; Olivia licked his balls and Audrey flicked her tongue across his glans – such pleasure.

Henri's movements grew quicker just when Olivia wanted – needed – them to. He slid in and out of her exactly as she wanted him to. All the while, his hands caressed her waist and hips. She was close to orgasm and needed all of Clive's cock in her mouth. It excited her to take all of him, just as she was taking all of Henri. Audrey teased her aching nipples, licking them, biting them, sucking on them.

Olivia's orgasm began slowly, somewhere near her navel, then raced through her whole body. She screamed aloud, her legs drumming on the goatskin and her arms reaching out to the bodies that had taken her to such heights . . .

Lloyd didn't know what the devil Olivia was playing at, but he'd had enough. Correction – he'd had *more* than enough.

She was rarely at home; in fact she spent more time in Audrey's house than in her own, and Lloyd knew only too well what she did there. At the time, watching her in Audrey's arms, he had very much liked what he was seeing. Now, though, the images of that time haunted him. He seethed with anger and jealousy. The anger was directed at them both; Audrey for having the sheer bloody audacity to seduce his wife, and Olivia for parading the charms of her delectable body in front of him, night after torturous night, and then taking her pleasure in the arms of another woman while denying him any pleasure whatsoever. She had become a damn tease. As for the jealousy, that was directed purely at Audrey. He had experienced the delights of Audrey's body many times, but he had never made love to his wife as he should have. He had never had her begging him to take her, never heard her whimpering with pleasure, never heard her cry out as she climaxed.

She was sitting opposite him, a glass of wine cradled in her hands as she glanced through a book. Lloyd got up, poured himself another whisky and returned to his chair.

And that was another damn thing. She rarely even spoke to him these days, and when she did her words usually took the form of requests designed to annoy him like 'Pass me a towel, would you, darling?' or 'Could you do my zip, darling?' or 'Is this skirt too short, darling?' No more, he vowed. He wasn't old-fashioned enough to believe he could demand his conjugal rights, but surely to God he was entitled to something.

'How are things, Lloyd?'

The sound of her voice startled him.

'Sorry?'

'You never tell me what's going on these days,' she complained. 'Unless it makes news, I don't know what you're doing.'

'Everything I do seems to make news at the moment,' he pointed out with a wry smile. 'The public have taken to me, but – well, I'm not the most popular person in the House at the moment. I'm not the most popular person with your father, either.'

'He doesn't matter.' She waved a dismissive arm. 'They won't ask you to resign, will they?'

'No. Not yet, at least.' He found her concern strangely touching. 'They keep making threatening noises, but that's all they can do at the moment.'

'I hope so. You do seem to be pushing your luck a bit.'

Lloyd wasn't so sure if it *was* concern. She seemed annoyed with him rather than worried about his future.

'I'm just going along with what I believe in,' he defended himself.

'Is that really wise?'

'I think so. Yes.'

'Mmm.'

And that was that. Her head was buried in her book

once more, signifying that the conversation was over. They would soon see about that. The conversation would be over when Lloyd said it was, and not before.

'Does it worry you?'

She looked up from her book.

'Of course,' she replied irritably. 'It wouldn't reflect well on anyone if you had to resign, would it?'

'It would depend on the reasons behind it, surely. I have to do what I believe is right. I can't be a bloody Yes man for the rest of my life.'

She made no response.

'That's not what you want, is it?' he persisted.

'I suppose not.' She glanced at her watch and rose to her feet. 'We'd better think about getting ready.'

Talking to Olivia, he decided, was a damn sight more difficult than extracting blood from a stone.

He would have liked another drink but he decided against it. Driving wasn't a problem as he had booked a taxi to take them to the gallery but he felt sure he would need a few drinks to stave off the boredom of the evening. In a moment of rashness, he had promised Barry Blake, London's freshest up-and-coming photographer, that they would attend his exhibition. Lloyd had no interest in photography whatsoever and guessed the evening would be extremely tedious. They didn't have to stay long, though.

Barry Blake was a bit of an enigma. Lloyd had only met him three times – each time at some social function or other. That was a mystery in itself as Barry always seemed a little out of place at the functions Lloyd had to attend. The young photographer was making a name for himself, though, and was therefore high on people's guest lists. Because he always showed great interest in Lloyd's work, and because he seemed genuinely knowledgeable on Lloyd's views, Lloyd felt obliged to show an equal interest in his work. It had been easy to enthuse about his exhibition. Now, however, the thought of trying to appear interested at a dull cocktail reception was daunting.

He went to their bedroom and showered and dressed while trying not to notice Olivia dressing, brushing her hair, applying her make-up, posing in front of the mirror in her black dress, adjusting her stockings, trying on three pairs of high-heeled shoes before settling on the first pair, and all the other things he felt sure were done to frustrate him. If he had to spend the evening in such close proximity to her, he would rather not think about her body . . .

As soon as they arrived at the gallery, they accepted the obligatory drink and went to inspect the photographs on display. They were very good. Even Lloyd, who knew nothing about it, could vouch for that, and he suspected that before the evening was over he would feel obliged to buy one. Surprisingly, even Olivia seemed to find them interesting. There was one, a black and white picture of a country church, that she stood in front of for a long time, frowning as she gazed at it.

'Do you like it?' Lloyd asked, seeing nothing special in the picture.

'Not really.' Her reply was clipped and she quickly moved on to the next photograph.

Bemused, Lloyd followed her.

A few minutes later, they were crossing the room when Barry Blake came towards them. Olivia, walking in front of Lloyd, stopped so suddenly that Lloyd cannoned into her and spilled his drink over his hands. Cursing beneath his breath, he tried to dry himself off with his handkerchief before shaking hands with Barry and making the introductions.

'I believe I know your sister, Mr Blake,' Olivia said, taking Lloyd completely by surprise. 'Carmen?' she added.

Lloyd wondered if he also knew the girl. Barry Blake

reminded him of someone, but Lloyd hadn't been able to give that someone a name.

'Half-sister,' Barry replied and, to Lloyd at any rate, his reply sounded cagey. 'We share the same father.'

'Really? Well, what a coincidence. I saw Carmen a few weeks ago and I believe I saw some of your work then.'

'Quite possibly.'

Lloyd saw that Barry was looking uncomfortable. He couldn't blame the man. For some reason, Olivia was sounding distinctly unfriendly.

'Of course,' she went on, 'I didn't realise it was your work at the time. I was very impressed, though. You're very – er – versatile, Mr Blake.'

'I try to be,' he answered, forcing a smile. 'And please, call me Barry.'

'There are no portraits,' Olivia remarked, waving an arm that encompassed the gallery. 'Don't you think people make the most interesting subjects?'

'Sometimes.' He was looking even more uncomfortable. 'But I prefer landscape photography.'

'I'm sure portraits are more lucrative.'

'Possibly,' he agreed. 'Now, if you'll excuse me –'

'Of course. Nice to meet you. Oh, and do give my regards to your sister – sorry, your half-sister.'

'Er, yes. Yes, I will.'

They watched him hurry away.

'What on earth was all that about?' Lloyd asked in amazement.

'Oh, nothing.' Olivia sighed heavily. 'Have we done our duty? Can we leave yet?'

'Soon. I thought we ought to show willing and buy one of his photographs.'

'Must we?'

'Well – no. I suppose not.' Lloyd too was eager to leave. 'Come on. Let's sneak out . . .'

As soon as they were home, Olivia decided she wanted an early night. No surprise there.

'Fine. I'll join you,' Lloyd replied.

Olivia went straight to the bathroom and had a quick shower. She was out, her silk robe tied at her waist, before he had even undressed.

'I won't be long,' he said, heading for the bathroom.

He suspected she would be asleep by the time he joined her, in which case he would damn well wake her. He showered quickly, dried himself off, threw down the towel and strode back into their bedroom. She wasn't asleep, though. Surprisingly, she was sitting up in bed, almost as if she was waiting for him. If only.

'Do I know Barry Blake's sister?' he asked curiously. 'It's just that he reminds me of someone, and I'm damned if I can think who it is.'

'Does he, indeed?' She sounded petulant. 'Yes, I believe you do know her. She knows you at any rate. Intimately, I gather. You certainly don't know her through me, though. I've never introduced you.'

Intimately?

'Who is she?' he asked warily. 'A friend of yours? You've never mentioned her.'

'I was at school with her.'

He got into bed beside her, expecting her to elaborate. She didn't.

'Really? And you still keep in touch?' he asked.

'No.'

Lloyd knew when to take a hint so he dropped the subject. It was clear she didn't want to talk about it, and Lloyd had more pressing matters on his mind. She was still sitting up but Lloyd lay down on his side, facing her. He stroked her thigh, silently marvelling at the softness of her skin.

'I'm tired, Lloyd,' she remarked.

'I'm tired, too,' he retaliated, his patience breaking. 'Sick and bloody tired. We're married, Olivia. Surely to

God it would be considered natural to make love now and again!'

'Do you want to make love to me?'

'Of course I damn –'

'Or do you simply want to satisfy your own needs and then go to sleep as you usually do?'

'What? Oh, come on. That's bloody unfair!'

It *was* unfair. It still hurt, though. Lloyd had always – *always* – prided himself on being a considerate lover. He enjoyed giving pleasure just as much as he enjoyed receiving. Olivia's totally unjustified comment sounded as if it was a case of wham, bam, bloody thank you ma'am.

It was true, he supposed, that their sex life had been a little dull, but he couldn't see that it was his fault. He wasn't saying it was hers, either. He supposed, if he were honest, that he hadn't ever, or not in the early days of their marriage at least, been physically attracted to her. He hadn't wanted her as he wanted her now. But was that his fault?

'Do you want to give me pleasure?' she asked, sliding down beneath the sheet into a lying position.

At that precise moment, he wanted to tell her to go to hell. That would achieve nothing, though.

'Of course,' he replied.

'Then you may. But hands only.'

Hands only? Who the devil did she think she was?

'And mouth,' she added.

It was very tempting to jump out of bed, get in the car and drive somewhere to find a more willing partner. God, he doubted if he could find a *less* willing one. The trouble was, he only wanted Olivia. Despite the fact that she infuriated him beyond words, he wanted her like he had never wanted anything or anyone else.

He threw back the sheets and kneeled by her side. There was a look of total disinterest on her face as she lay back, her head on the pillows.

213

'Touch my breasts first,' she murmured.

Damn and blast her! Lloyd was powerless to do anything but obey. He stroked her breasts and then bent his head to take her nipple in his mouth. He felt it harden in his mouth. While he sucked on one nipple, he caressed the other with his thumb and forefinger. Her skin was warm and still slightly damp from her shower. He ran his tongue down to her navel, leaving a moist trail on her skin. As he stroked her thighs, his anger melted and he felt a familiar ache in his groin. She parted her legs slightly and he bent his head to kiss her inner thighs. When he flicked his tongue across the moist flesh of her sex, she made no sound at all, just squirmed beneath him. Very gently, he parted her folds of flesh with his fingers and pushed his tongue into her opening. Her soft sigh made his heart race, and he flicked rhythmically with his tongue, longing to hear her cry out. She pushed her sex on to his face, opening out, pulled on his hair as his tongue flicked against her clitoris and, with a few short gasps, she climaxed . . .

Chapter Thirteen

Olivia didn't know how she had stopped herself crying out as Lloyd's tongue brought her so skilfully to orgasm. She gazed at his body as he kneeled beside her. His cock was hard and straight, jutting from crinkly dark hair. His abdomen was perfectly flat, his thighs strongly muscled.

She pushed him and he lay back, his expression questioning. It was impossible to resist him. She climbed across him, straddled him and very slowly sank down on to his beautiful cock. He groaned with pleasure, and Olivia vowed to make sure that any pleasure was all hers. She bounced up and down on him, thrilling at the sensations that coursed through her body.

While he had been in the shower, she had put a certain video in the machine and put the television on standby. Now, without getting off him, she reached across to her bedside table for the remote control unit, hit the button for the television and then hit the button to play the video.

She said nothing; she didn't need to.

'Where the devil –'

'Do you remember the day you took the video to my father?'

'Yes.' He groaned at the memory. 'Your father told you to have it burned.' He frowned, puzzled. 'And it did burn. I was watching from the window and I saw Margaret throw it on the bonfire.'

'No. You saw her throw another video on the fire.' She wriggled on him, and leaned right back, taking his cock with her, her hands on her thighs. 'I rarely do as my father tells me, Lloyd. You should know that.'

Lloyd seemed harder than ever inside her. Still leaning back, Olivia reached for her sex and touched the base of his cock. He thrust up at her and she slapped his taut belly.

'Keep still!'

She sat upright on him, and lifted herself up before sinking down hard and taking all of him inside her. He remained perfectly still.

'I've watched this video many times,' she told him. 'The two girls are gorgeous. Who are they?'

'I've no idea. Just a couple of prostitutes.'

'You paid them?'

'Yes.'

She bounced up and down on him and he moaned aloud. For some reason that she didn't understand, it excited her to think of him paying the two girls.

'Do you often pay for sex?' she asked, intrigued.

'Sometimes,' he replied.

'You're not paying me,' she reminded him sharply as he thrust his hips upwards, 'so I call the shots. I've already told you to be still. You wanted to give *me* pleasure – remember?'

'I do!' He was breathing fast.

'Then lie still. It pleases me to have your body to do with as I choose.'

She moved up and down on him quickly, marvelling at the feel of him, then lifted herself off him, grasped his angry-looking cock in both hands and rubbed the moist tip back and forth over her wet sex. Still holding him, she pushed it a little way inside, then further inside, letting the muscles of her vagina clench and unclench on it.

'Oh, God. Olivia –'

'I have photographs, too,' she cut him off. 'Very high quality photographs. Very expensive high quality photographs.'

He frowned, confused, and Olivia knew he didn't have a clue what she was talking about. Why should he?

'I don't know who the woman is – another prostitute, perhaps. I know it's not Carmen Blake, and it's not Audrey.'

His dark eyebrows rose at the latter.

'Oh, I guessed some time ago that you and Audrey had been lovers,' she said. 'I'm not surprised. She has a marvellous body, hasn't she? She's a marvellous lover, too. So experienced and adventurous.'

She had expected to see shock and disbelief on his face, but his expression was blank. Her self-assured, self-confident husband was suddenly floundering in a world that made no sense to him. Olivia revelled in the knowledge. It gave her even more power.

She climbed off him to sit on the bed. His penis stood straight and upright, reaching up, drops of moisture on the purple tip. She smeared the glans with her thumb and he gasped before pushing his hips off the bed in an attempt to gain more from her. Laughing, Olivia got off the bed. She was having great fun and intended to toy with him for hours yet.

Her skin was warm; the thick pile carpet felt cool on her feet as she walked round the bed to her cupboard. She kneeled to take out the envelope that proved Lloyd's guilt. Apart from putting the collection of photographs together, she hadn't looked at them since that last visit to Steve's studio.

Leaving the negatives in the envelope, she pulled out the large black and white prints.

'At least you can boast that you were caught on film by a very talented photographer,' she muttered, tossing the prints down so that they landed on his chest.

One by one, he picked them up and looked at them.

'Barry Blake took these?' he demanded in amazement.

'Yes. Credit where it's due, they're very good, aren't they?'

'The bastard! The two-faced little shit!'

'Indeed.' Olivia took the photographs from him. 'His sister – sorry, his half-sister – is no better. I paid her ten thousand pounds for this little collection.'

'You did what?' he spluttered. 'You bloody fool, Olivia. Why in hell's name didn't you come to me? I could have sorted it out.'

'But I didn't want you to sort it out, Lloyd. I wanted to buy these. They are good, don't you think? It all looks very cramped though. Where were you?'

'On a boat.' He sighed, his anger changing to resignation. 'A narrow boat – a barge.'

'And who's the lucky lady?' She hoped her voice sounded as if she couldn't care less. She hoped there was no trace of the jealousy she felt every time she thought of the unknown lady in the photograph.

'Linda. An old friend from university.'

'Presumably you don't pay her?'

'Of course not.'

'And the other man?'

'Ivan. He owns the marina.' He shrugged. 'I guess he and Linda are an item.'

'I see.'

She looked at the photographs in turn, taunting him and tormenting herself. When she'd had enough, she returned them to the envelope and put them back in the cupboard.

The video was still playing, although she had muted the sound, but now she hit the remote control so that they could hear the sounds of the three lovers enjoying each other. The tape never failed to excite her and, with Lloyd lying naked on their bed, wanting her, she was more aroused than ever.

'You enjoyed watching those two prostitutes make love, didn't you?' she remarked, her skin tingling as she watched the girls pleasure each other.

'Yes,' he confessed.

He was enjoying watching them on film, she suspected, so she picked up the remote control and switched off the television. Tonight it was her turn for pleasure, not his.

Still his cock was hard and full of promise. Taking advantage, Olivia once again impaled herself on it. It felt wonderful to have him filling her. He fitted her perfectly. She began to bounce up and down on him.

'The question is,' she said, struggling to think of anything but the excitement coursing through her veins, 'what am I going to do with the video and photographs?'

'What do you mean?'

'If I expose you –'

'You wouldn't do that!' He laughed, but the laughter quickly died. 'You wouldn't. Would you? What in hell's name could you expect to gain from that? Apart from a highly embarrassing scandal?'

'Scandal has never bothered me, Lloyd,' she murmured.

It was no use; she couldn't think of plotting his downfall, planning their future, or any other thing. All that registered was the wonderful feeling that came from having his gorgeous body beneath hers, inside hers. She moved up and down on him slowly, delighting in each delicious sensation that accompanied her movements. It took great self-control, she could tell, but Lloyd remained perfectly still. For now, he was her plaything and Olivia was taking full advantage. She licked her fingers, then caressed her breasts with them. Lloyd reached for her –

'Keep still,' Olivia reminded him. 'When I want something from you, I'll tell you.'

A shudder ran through her body. It was the knowledge that she was in complete control that added so much to her excitement. She could feel his cock throbbing inside her. His breath came in short, deep bursts as she began to ride him more vigorously. She wanted to slow down, to tease him much longer, but it was too late. Her body craved satisfaction. Her muscles pulsed and throbbed their need until she was out of control. She shouted aloud and dug her fingernails into his waist as her orgasm exploded inside her. Wave after wave of sensation washed over her, leaving her sated, warm and lethargic. When she was finally still, she climbed off him. He reached for her, but Olivia dodged him.

'Getting back to the video and the photographs,' she murmured lazily.

'Let's forget them, for now.' Lloyd's voice was husky with desire. 'Let's enjoy each other.'

It was so tempting!

'But I've already enjoyed you, Lloyd,' she answered smoothly. 'Are you saying that now you've given me pleasure, you would appreciate some pleasure of your own?'

'I was thinking of pleasure for us both. God, Olivia, I want you.'

Olivia's heart skipped a beat at his words. For so long she had waited to hear those words. She had vowed that, one day, Lloyd would be begging her. And now that day had come.

'Do you, Lloyd?'

'Yes. So much. Come here –'

She dodged his embrace.

'How badly do you want me, Lloyd?'

'More than you'll know. I've wanted you for so long. You've been driving me crazy. Every night, every day – let me make love to you, Olivia. Please, sweetheart.'

It was so difficult to resist him that Olivia had to get off the bed. She stood at the foot of it, admiring his nakedness. Sweat glistened on his smooth chest.

'The video and the photos,' she reminded him, fixing her gaze on his pained face. 'If I were to use them against you, you would have to resign, wouldn't you?'

'Of course. I'd never work in politics again. What sort of damn fool question is that?' His expression changed. 'Come here. Let me hold you, Olivia.'

'That's what I'm going to do – if you don't go along with my plans.' She walked around the bed, flexing her toes on the thick carpet. 'I want you to resign, Lloyd.'

He said bolt upright.

'You want what?' he demanded in astonishment.

'You heard me. I want you to resign.'

'What the hell for? I mean, why? And what, pray, am I expected to do with the rest of my life?'

'I want us to start our own television production company.' She stretched out on the edge of the bed, one leg straight and the other bent. 'As you say yourself, Lloyd, you're becoming nothing more than a performing monkey. Everyone else is the same. Let's face it, no one in their right mind would trust today's MPs as far as they could throw them. The whole set-up is corrupt.'

'You're exaggerating –' His gaze lingered longingly on her breasts. 'Do we have to talk about this now? It hardly seems the right time.'

'No,' she said smoothly. 'I'm just giving you your

choices. Either you resign of your own free will, or you resign amid a great scandal. The choice is yours, Lloyd.'

'Yes, but –' He stroked her calf muscle and groaned softly as if even that small pleasure was too much to bear. 'I want you, Olivia. I want you so damn much.' He moved into a half-sitting, half-lying position and slid his hand along her inner thigh. 'Let me make love to you.' His voice was husky with pleading now. 'Let me show you how good we can be together. Let me show you, Olivia, for the very first time.'

'Oh, yes.'

Olivia was trembling with desire. She could offer no resistance. Now that she had Lloyd practically on his knees, there was no need to.

For all the urgency in his voice and the hunger in his eyes, his touch was surprising light. Kneeling on the bed in front of her, he seemed content to stroke her skin. He barely brushed her which, somehow, made the light touch of his fingertips, as they glided over her hardening nipples, all the more arousing. As if he could read her mind, he seemed to know exactly how and where to touch her. Because his caresses were so light, Olivia couldn't help moving beneath his hands. It was as much as she could do not to grab his hands and demand more pressure.

She gasped as his lips took hold of her left breast and slowly drew the stiff nipple into his mouth. He suckled so gently that she thought she wouldn't be able to stand it; then his tongue became more urgent. From his shallow breath, Olivia knew he was even more excited.

His arm went around her waist, pulling her close and again his mouth teased and suckled on her nipple. She seemed to stop breathing for a moment when his other hand went between her legs. He stroked her with maddeningly light caresses for what seemed like an age before seeking out her wanton flesh. He would know how wet she had become, would see from her swollen flesh how eager she was. It didn't matter. She wanted him desperately; she could no longer hide it from him.

His thumb took great delight in rubbing her hard clitoris and within a matter of seconds Olivia reached orgasm. She shook violently with his arm still tight around her, but he didn't relent. He continued stroking her so that her climax couldn't completely subside. She was dizzy, in a trance-like state, only knowing that she never wanted him to stop.

'God, I want you,' he breathed softly against her face.

'You can have me,' she whispered breathlessly, moving from under him.

She lay on top of him, and left a moist trail on his skin with her tongue. She teased his nipples with her mouth, just as he had teased hers. She sucked on them, pinched them between her lips and flicked them with her tongue. All the while she writhed on his hard, firm body. His cock was hard against her pelvis and she pushed against it, swaying from side to side. He grunted his hunger.

She moved down, and took his dick in her hands, caressing him in a way that was so natural. Her need made her breathless and dizzy.

Lloyd groaned aloud as she took his hard cock into her mouth. She sucked on him greedily, wanting all of him, until she felt him throb in her mouth. She pulled away, not wanting him to come yet, and grabbed his prick with one hand, stroking him up and down. She wanted to prolong everything, wanted him to remain at the same level of excitement without reaching the point of no return.

She knew though, at the exact moment that Lloyd pushed her on to her back, that she could hold off no longer.

She cried out as she felt him filling her. It seemed to Olivia that she had waited all her life for this moment. She hadn't, of course, but even if she had, it would have been worth the wait. She felt him twitch inside her. He pulled away until his prick almost abandoned her, then thrust deep inside her again.

When he was satisfied that she was as hungry for him as he was for her, he grabbed her ankles and brought them up to rest on his shoulders. Kneeling between her legs, he grabbed her hips and pulled her towards him.

Olivia cried out as he penetrated her. Her arms were above her head as she enjoyed his slow, powerful thrusts stretching her. She was his to do with as he pleased, and he delighted in it.

Her every sense seemed heightened. She could smell him and she inhaled deeply on the highly arousing masculine scent that mingled with her own. She could hear his breathing, and her own, and she could hear the delightful noise coming from her wet sex as he plunged into her. She could feel his swollen prick pushing deeper and deeper inside her. She could see the arousing mix of agony and ecstasy on his handsome face, and the beads of sweat on his brow and on his chest.

He increased his tempo and her body slid up the bed with each thrust. The sheets were a crumpled mess beneath her back but this seemed only to add to her enjoyment.

Her orgasm built up slowly, sweeping her along until she was overwhelmed by its intensity. It lasted longer than anything she had ever experienced and brought tears to her lashes.

Lloyd's thrusts were shallow but much faster so that her whole body shook with the force. Sweat was trickling down his chest. With a loud scream, he gave one strong thrust, and Olivia felt his cock jerk powerfully inside her.

When he collapsed next to her on the bed, tears were trickling down her cheeks. She was too exhausted to wipe them away. They lay in silence, motionless, as they recovered.

In a gesture that was pure tenderness, Lloyd lifted a finger to brush away her tears. He didn't question them, just accepted that they were there. Olivia didn't question them, either. Then he lay behind her and cradled her in his arms. The only sound in the room was that of their breathing as it slowly returned to normal.

Sunlight was streaming through the window when Olivia woke up. She blinked, adjusting her eyes to the brightness, then stretched luxuriously as she recalled the previous evening. She ran through it all in her mind, remembering every touch, every sensation, every single moment.

The smile was still on her lips when Lloyd walked into the room carrying a tray laden with coffee, croissants, orange juice, and newspapers. He was wearing his thick white robe and it showed off his powerful legs. Still holding the tray, he sat on the edge of the bed and leaned across to kiss her.

'Coffee?' he asked.

Feeling like a child who had been given all she wanted and more for her birthday, Olivia nodded. She sat up and hugged her knees to her chest. Was it possible for anyone to feel any happier than she did right now?

Lloyd put the tray on the bed between them and poured them each a coffee.

'Tell me,' he said, handing her the cup, 'what was all this nonsense about me resigning last night?' He laughed at the idea. 'You know it's out of the question. Why, it's ludicrous.'

Olivia felt her happiness begin to ebb away. She wasn't sure what she had expected exactly. If she had been a gambler, she would have bet on him going along with whatever she desired but it seemed as if last night was forgotten. He had enjoyed himself, taken what he wanted, and now it was back to normal.

'I hope it's not out of the question, Lloyd,' she answered crisply. 'As I said last night, the choice is yours. Either you resign of your own free will, or I make use of the video and the photographs. And don't think you can destroy them, because I have copies,' she lied.

He raised his eyes to the heavens as if he was dealing with a difficult, spoilt child.

'But why?' he asked with exaggerated patience. 'Why the hell do you want me to resign?'

'I told you. I want us to form our own television production company. I've found suitable premises, so that isn't a problem. I need your money, I need your contacts, and I need your name, Lloyd. We're going to make programmes that are honest. We'll show the public exactly what the government are doing for them – or not doing for them. We'll be in complete control, Lloyd. We won't have anyone telling us what we can do and what we can't . . .' Her voice trailed away. The subject had grown so close to her heart that she was getting carried away. 'I know what I'm doing, Lloyd. I've done a lot of television work recently –'

'Doing a five-minute interview is hardly the same,' he scoffed.

'I know that.' She bit back her anger. 'What I was going to say, before you interrupted me, was that I've asked a lot of questions and hunted out the people who know what they're doing. I'm going into this with the help of experts.'

'So you've got it all figured out? You've found premises, you've got your little team of experts – what the hell do you want me for?'

'I told you –'

'I realise you want my money,' he cut her off, his

voice like ice, 'but, apart from that, what do you want from me?'

'I want your contacts,' she said, trying not to turn this into a slanging match. 'I want your expertise. Above all else, though, I've always believed that you care about British politics.'

'Of course I do!'

'And I believe that just as much, if not more, good can be done through the medium of television.'

The croissants were ignored and Olivia struggled to even drink her coffee. She was hurt that he could seemingly dismiss the events of the previous night so easily, and she was angry with him.

'I'm going for a shower,' she announced, getting out of bed. 'It's the fifteenth today, Lloyd. I'll give you until the thirtieth to make up your mind. Then – well, you know what I'll do.'

'I don't believe you would,' he said levelly. 'I don't believe you could face the scandal any more than I could.'

Olivia turned away from him before he could see the colour that rose in her cheeks. Was he right? Would she be able to do it? If she were totally honest with herself, she wasn't so sure that she could.

'I wouldn't count on that if I were you, Lloyd,' she murmured, walking towards the shower.

The hot jet of water soothed her nerves. After last night, when she had fallen asleep in his arms, happier than she had ever been, she had expected them to wake up in the same blissful state. She had expected Lloyd to be loving. She had expected, and wanted, them to make love again.

She soaped her body, washing every last trace of him from her. Perhaps he thought that, after last night's impressive demonstration, she was his whenever he wanted her. He would soon realise that she wasn't.

She stepped out of the shower and padded through

to their bedroom leaving wet footprints on the carpet. She dried herself in a way that was deliberately provocative, then began to dress in the same seductive way.

'Why don't we discuss everything later?' Lloyd murmured, walking over to her.

She was wearing a white bra and skimpy briefs.

'But there's nothing to discuss, Lloyd. I thought I'd made it quite clear. You have until the thirtieth of this month to make up your mind. Now – if you'll excuse me.'

She went to her drawers and bent over in a way that was designed to arouse him as she pretended to hunt for just the right pair of stockings. Having found them, she sat on the chair and eased them, very slowly, up her legs.

'Didn't you enjoy last night?' he asked.

'God, Lloyd, do you want a medal or something?' she demanded scathingly. 'Yes, I enjoyed last night. Of course I did.'

'I want you,' he said simply.

She wanted him too. It was almost impossible to resist him. Almost.

'Not now, Lloyd. I've arranged to see Audrey.'

She saw his mouth tighten at the mention of Audrey's name.

'Can't you phone and cancel?' he asked.

'Why would I want to do that?' She forced a light little laugh.

'And what do you plan with Audrey?'

Olivia took a dress from its hanger and slipped it over her head.

'The same as you've done with Audrey – enjoy her.' She turned her back on him. 'Could you do my zip please, darling?'

Lloyd yanked the zip up her back with such force that Olivia was surprised he didn't tear the fabric.

'Do you object to me making love to another woman?' she asked him, then before he had the chance to reply, added, 'I don't suppose you can, really. Like me, Lloyd, you appreciate a little variety in your life. That's obvious from the video and the photographs.'

She slipped her feet into a pair of black high-heeled shoes.

'In fact,' she went on, 'I suppose you'd like to join us. Perhaps one day you will.'

'I don't want to join you, damn it,' he exploded. 'I want *us* to make love, Olivia. Now!'

'Ah, but you'd like to watch me with Audrey, wouldn't you? I know how much you enjoyed watching the girls in the video. I'm sure that watching me with Audrey – seeing two women that you've screwed enjoying each other – would appeal to you. Would it?'

'Possibly,' he admitted.

'Possibly? Oh, Lloyd, you know it would!'

'Can't you see Audrey later?' he asked, his voice soft and coaxing.

'No.'

Olivia could see from the way his white robe fell around his body that he was aroused. The knowledge excited her, but as much as she wanted him, she wasn't going to give in. She had no plans to see Audrey, but he wasn't to know that. In any case, she might call on her. She would go and see how work was progressing at what would soon be the site of their very own production company, and then – well, she might as well call on Audrey. If Audrey wasn't in, Clive might be.

'Perhaps I'll invite Audrey here for dinner one evening,' she mused. 'Clive would come too, of course, because Audrey can't bear to go anywhere without him. I can't say I blame her.'

'The wonderful Clive,' Lloyd muttered sarcastically. 'I've heard a lot about him one way and another.'

'He is pretty special,' Olivia agreed smoothly, refusing to respond to his anger. 'He has a gorgeous body, and he's tireless.'

'Good for him!' Lloyd snapped.

'So how does that appeal to you, Lloyd? How would you like to watch me with another man?'

She saw from the way a vein throbbed at his temple that the idea appealed to him a lot, just as she had known it would.

'I've enjoyed watching you with other women, albeit on film,' she admitted, 'so I'd like to return the favour. Yes, I'll invite them.'

'Fine.'

She reached up and dropped a kiss on his cheek.

'See you later, darling. Have fun. Oh, and don't forget to think about the future.'

'Ha! There's nothing to think about. I'm not resigning and that's final. I've worked bloody hard to get where I am today. I'm not giving it all up for some half-baked idea of making a few TV programmes.'

'As you like, Lloyd.'

With that, she skipped out of their bedroom. She was half-way down the stairs when she doubled back. When she pushed open the door, Lloyd was lying on the bed, his robe covering his stiff penis like a tent.

'I forgot something,' she told him.

How she wished she could push his robe aside and impale herself on his gorgeous dick. But she couldn't. There would be plenty of time for that in the future.

She went straight to her bedside cupboard and removed the photographs and the video. It was unlikely that he would destroy all the evidence, not when he believed there were copies, but she couldn't afford to take chances. She would deposit them at the bank. And, just to be on the safe side, she would have a copy made of the video.

'See you later, darling.'

As she left the room for the second time, her mind was filled with visions of him. She could picture him taking his shaft in his hand . . .

Chapter Fourteen

The following day, Olivia held a book-signing session in Newcastle-upon-Tyne. Her agent persuaded her to do such things, and Olivia usually set off filled with optimism but today she was bored to tears.

Earlier, there had been a queue in front of her table, but once she had worked her way through that, it was a matter of sitting at her table, surrounded by a pile of her books, and sending people who, for some reason, thought she was a member of the shop's staff, to the shop's cookery or computing section.

A book was slapped down in front of her and she automatically lifted her pen to sign it.

'The name's Steve,' said a very familiar voice.

Olivia's head flew up. He looked the same as ever. He was dressed as casually as ever in jeans, shirt and brown suede jacket. Even the smile was as appealing as ever.

'What on earth are you doing here?' Olivia asked in amazement.

'Ronan King was doing a book signing yesterday,' he replied easily, smiling at the memory. 'Of course, that was a very small affair in the local library where, I might add, it would have been more profitable to take the fees on overdue books.'

Olivia couldn't help smiling.

'All I'm doing is telling people where they'll find Delia Smith's latest offering,' she admitted. 'People are far more interested in whipping up omelettes than reading about dead politicians.'

He nodded at the truth of that.

'There's a coffee bar next door,' he said. 'I don't suppose I can persuade you to join me when you get a break? Just to show there are no hard feelings?'

Against her better judgement, Olivia nodded.

'OK. About one o'clock?'

'Great. I'll see you then.'

She bent her head and signed his book: *All best wishes from Jane and Olivia*.

He smiled at the inscription. 'Thanks.'

She watched him walk out of the shop, still finding pleasure in the way he moved.

She was glad to escape the shop and take a break. Surprisingly, the coffee bar was almost empty and they found a secluded table.

Even more surprisingly, Olivia was genuinely pleased to see him. Despite everything that had passed between them, she liked to think of him as a friend. For as long as she lived, she would never forget that magical train journey when he had made her feel like a very desirable woman for the first time in her life. It seemed a long time ago, and a lot had happened since then, but it was a memory she would always treasure.

'How's Carmen?' she asked.

'I don't know,' he admitted with a sheepish smile. 'I haven't seen anything of her. A starving writer didn't really appeal to her in a long-term way.'

'I guess it's not everyone's cup of tea,' she quipped, pleased that Carmen was no longer part of his life. He deserved better.

232

'Is she doing well at the shop?'

'I think so, yes. She bought me a new computer out of the money you paid her, and the rest was going to be ploughed into Carmen's Casuals. She's quite passionate about it.'

Olivia nodded.

'And how are you?' he asked.

'Fine, thanks.'

'What exactly did you plan to do with those photographs?' he asked curiously.

'Oh, I'm still working on that one.'

'I keep in touch with Barry,' he remarked. 'He said he'd seen you.'

'Yes. Lloyd and I attended his exhibition.'

'Don't think too badly of him,' Steve said quietly. 'Carmen can be very persuasive.'

'I'm sure she can,' Olivia replied, wondering how long it had taken her to persuade Lloyd into her bed. She didn't want to think about Carmen, though. 'And how is Ronan King's latest book doing?'

'Not bad actually. For some reason, it's attracted some good reviews. It's a shocking thought, but I think people might be starting to think of good old Ronan as a serious writer.'

'Heaven forbid!' She laughed.

'I know,' he said with a grin. 'That will never do, will it? I'll have to make sure the next one is extra trashy so that I can sink back into oblivion.'

'Oblivion doesn't pay well,' she pointed out.

'True. Oh, well. Fame and fortune, here I come.'

They spent a pleasant half hour together, then Olivia had to get back to signing books.

'I'm glad I've seen you,' she said truthfully. 'All the best with your new book.'

She kissed him on the cheek and walked smartly away from him.

* * *

'Time for another, Lloyd?' Jeremy asked.

Lloyd checked his watch. He had time for a quick one, he supposed. He might just as well sit in his club counting the minutes as sit at home.

'Just one,' he replied. 'We've got guests for dinner and it would be more than my life's worth to be late.'

It wouldn't. He very much doubted if Olivia would care one way or the other if he was there or not. He would, though. He had been unable to think of anything else all day, since Olivia had so casually announced during breakfast that she had invited Audrey and Clive to dinner.

It had been tempting to reveal Audrey's secret, to tell Olivia that he had already watched her making love to Audrey. But no. The idea of a repeat performance excited him too much. Also, there was a world of difference between being hidden behind a two-way mirror and being in the same room as the two women. No doubt they would enjoy each other, just as they had the last time, but he felt sure they would want a man. They would want him.

Clive would be there, of course, and that thought niggled. Lloyd was torn between wanting to watch another man take his wife, and a sense of outrageous indignation that he was expected to sit back and watch . . .

'I had a phone call,' Jeremy broke into his thoughts. 'Anonymous, of course. They always are, aren't they?'

'About what?' Lloyd asked with a frown. Thinking about it, Jeremy was drinking far more than usual today. He was having three drinks to Lloyd's one. 'Something wrong, Jeremy?'

'I accepted a gift – and it was only a gift –' He sighed loudly. 'I asked a question –'

'You didn't?' Lloyd groaned. 'Good God, Jeremy. You know the current climate. The blasted "Cash for Questions" problem is at the top of the list. Far better to be gay, or paying whores a vast fortune for some perversion, than to be caught asking questions for cash at the moment.'

'I know, I know. But you just don't think –'

'That you'll be found out,' Lloyd finished for him. Jeremy nodded.

'And have you been found out?' Lloyd asked.

'So it would appear. As I said, I had this anonymous phone call this morning. What the hell do I do, Lloyd?'

'Deny everything,' Lloyd replied immediately. 'And keep denying everything until they have a rock solid case against you. Where's the money?'

'It wasn't money.' Jeremy emptied his glass. 'It was property. I was given a house – cottage, really – in the Cotswolds.'

'Very nice,' Lloyd said dryly.

'I just didn't think anyone could possibly check up. I mean, property's different, isn't it? The company involved own a lot of property and they offered me this cottage.'

'Presumably the company involved won't want any whisper of this getting out,' Lloyd pointed out. 'Take out a mortgage on it. Get it backdated as far as you can. Can you do a mortgage through them? I don't know, Jeremy, but it sounds as if you need to act quickly.' Lloyd glanced at his watch again and finished his drink in one swallow. 'Sorry, Jeremy, but I really do have to make a move. I'll give the matter some thought. Let me know what develops.'

'I will.' Jeremy stared morosely into his glass. 'It makes you wonder, doesn't it, Lloyd? You do your best but –' He sighed heavily. 'It really makes you wonder.'

'It does,' Lloyd agreed. He suspected that Jeremy would be in a better state to 'wonder' when he had sobered up a little. 'We'll talk about it tomorrow. Good-night, Jeremy.'

Lloyd felt guilty about leaving Jeremy when the poor

chap was obviously in need of some moral support, but he had to get home. He couldn't help Jeremy when his mind refused to budge from the thought of the forthcoming entertainment. Besides, Jeremy would talk his way out of it. They all managed to talk their way out of things.

As soon as dinner was over, Olivia suggested the four of them took their coffee into the sitting room. There was a feeling of tension in the air. Audrey, outwardly her usual bubbly self, seemed a little self conscious. Even Clive, usually so laid back, seemed to sense the air of tension. Lloyd had been on edge all evening. Olivia had told Audrey and Clive exactly what she wanted, and had rehearsed this a million times in her mind, but her nerves were jangling. It was all well and good teasing Lloyd, but she had no idea how she would feel to have him watching her bring Audrey to orgasm, or writhing beneath Clive.

They chatted about the weather, Olivia's books, a new play that Audrey had seen – anything. Coffee cups rattled nervously against saucers.

Oh, to hell with it!

The lights had been dimmed, something Olivia was grateful for as she stood up and asked Audrey to deal with her zip. Audrey's fingers fumbled at the back of her neck but finally the zip slid smoothly down her spine. Olivia shrugged her shoulders out of the dress and let it fall to her feet. She bent to pick it up and threw it on the empty chair.

Her underwear had been chosen with great care. Bra, panties and suspender belt were in a deep shade of blue. The design was plain, except for two tiny bows at her hips, and the material was of the finest silk. She wore black stockings and very high-heeled black shoes that were a criss-cross of thin suede straps that fastened around her slim ankles. She knew she looked good.

Audrey expelled her breath which gave Olivia an extra boost of confidence.

'Stand up, Lloyd.'

He did as she asked, looked immensely pleased with himself.

Smiling seductively, she slipped the jacket of his suit off his shoulders. He took out his arms, eager to help her. His tie came next. She untied it with great care and pulled it from his collar. Refusing to be hurried, she carried jacket and tie across the room and laid them on the chair with her dress. Lloyd was already kicking off his shoes. Olivia smiled to herself; he had a shock coming to him. Audrey and Clive sat completely still, their gazes locked on Olivia as she took off Lloyd's trousers and then his underpants. She was delighted to see that he was already aroused. The evidence jutted out at the hem of his shirt. Ignoring his penis, she unfastened the buttons on his shirt, taking her time on each one, then slid that off him so that he stood before them completely naked. He looked magnificent.

'Clive, tie him up!'

'What? Oh, come on, Olivia,' Lloyd protested.

'You're here as a spectator,' Olivia reminded him sharply.

She watched as Clive took a reluctant Lloyd over to the chair that Olivia had brought into this room specially for the purpose. The chair usually sat in her study, but she never used it. It was too uncomfortable. It was an old-fashioned design that had been modernised by a sophisticated tilt and swivel mechanism, with wooden narrow slats at the back, thus making it ideal for her purpose. Clive, who had already received his instructions from Olivia, looked as if he took great pleasure in fastening Lloyd's hands behind his back and then fastening his ankles to the chair's legs.

It was impossible not to admire Lloyd in his nakedness. His back was ramrod straight against the chair, making his shoulders and chest look broader than ever. His thighs were parted and his penis flopped against his belly. The look he was giving Olivia was one of pure anger. He was furious.

Olivia smiled sweetly at him and, satisfied that he was securely tied, she turned to Audrey and smiled. In truth, she wanted no other's touch but Lloyd's, but she knew that Audrey would soon change that.

Audrey, still dressed, caressed Olivia's shoulders and the tops of her arms. Olivia shivered, despite the warmth of the room. Audrey's skin was so smooth that it glided like satin over her own. She gasped as Audrey put a hand behind her head and kissed her fully on the lips before leaving nibbling little kisses on her bottom lip. Her hands slid down Olivia's ribcage before they stroked the swell of her breasts.

With growing impatience, Olivia struggled with the row of tiny buttons on Audrey's dress that stretched from neck to mid-calf. She had reached the button at hip level when Audrey laughed softly, let the dress fall away and stepped out of it.

Unlike Olivia's understated garments, Audrey's underwear was a blaze of blood-red lace. And it looked very, very sexy. Olivia couldn't resist tracing a finger along the lacy edge of the red bra. It fastened at the front and, as delightful as it was, Olivia quickly unhooked it so that Audrey's full breasts sprang free. The hardening nipples hinted at her arousal and Olivia bent her head to take one into her mouth and suckle on it. They kissed and stroked each other's skin, pausing only to remove another flimsy undergarment.

Olivia's gaze wandered to where Lloyd was restrained in his chair. His face was flushed with colour and his breathing was shallow. From his mound of dark hair, his hard cock stood straight. He wriggled on his seat slightly.

It was immensely exciting to have him watching them. She felt her skin grow warm beneath his gaze.

Clive, who had seen it all before, looked only slightly more relaxed.

'Why don't you undress, Clive?' Olivia murmured. 'It will give us something to admire if we get bored.' She looked at Audrey and laughed softly. There was no chance of them getting bored. 'In any case, we may – just may – require your services later.'

Audrey dropped to her knees and left a trail of warm kisses on Olivia's inner thighs. With her hands in Audrey's hair, she guided Audrey's mouth to her sex. She longed to feel Audrey's tongue on her hot flesh, and she parted her legs to allow easier access. Audrey's hands were soft on her bottom as her tongue teased the folds of flesh. Her expert tongue darted inside and Olivia sighed with relief.

She looked across at Lloyd, just in time to see him moistening his own lips.

Her hands still in Audrey's hair, she thrust her sex in Audrey's face to obtain more pressure. Audrey's tongue flicked across her clitoris relentlessly and within moments, Olivia gave a short, sharp cry as she experienced her first orgasm.

Too weak to stand, she dropped to her knees so that her face was level with Audrey's. They kissed and caressed for a while, then lay back on the soft carpet. Olivia took great delight in suckling on Audrey's breasts while using her hand to caress Audrey's thighs and hips. Audrey began to moan softly and Olivia knew that she was highly aroused. She slipped her hand between Audrey's legs and felt Audrey's muscles tense briefly as she slipped a finger inside her hot, wet sex. She rubbed Audrey's stiff clitoris hard until Audrey climaxed.

'Poor Clive must be feeling left out,' Olivia said teasingly. From the carpet, she looked up to where he stood. 'Let's give him a little treat, Audrey. After all, he often treats us.'

They stood up, one either side of him, and began to use their hands and tongues to caress Clive's body.

'Oh, please –' Lloyd murmured, his voice so soft that Olivia almost didn't hear him.

'Did you say something, Lloyd?' she asked, running her hands across Clive's powerful chest.

'Do I have to be tied up?' he complained. 'If you'd just untie me –'

'Sorry. Maybe later. You wanted to watch, Lloyd.'

He groaned his frustration.

Olivia and Audrey ignored him. Olivia suspected they were both aware of every breath he took, she certainly was, but they were putting on this show for his benefit – as well as their own.

They kissed Clive's hard body, slid their hands across his torso, over his taut buttocks and down his firm thighs. Audrey kissed his neck, shoulders and chest while Olivia dropped to her knees before him and ran her tongue along his hot shaft. He spread his legs wider and she cupped his balls, enjoying the feel of their weight in her hand. She flicked her tongue across his glans, heard him groan, and turned her attention to his thighs, licking them and kissing them. When she felt she had teased him enough, she took his cock into her mouth and sucked on him. He groaned again and Olivia sucked harder. When she glanced up, she saw that he was kissing Audrey and flicking her nipples with his fingers. Olivia found the sight extremely arousing.

Moments later, Audrey too got on her knees. They kissed each other, they kissed Clive's swollen penis. While Audrey sucked on his cock, Olivia licked his testicles. Occasionally they broke off to caress each other.

Olivia knew she had achieved her objective; she was

driving Lloyd wild. She could see the naked hunger in his eyes and hear the longing in his moans.

She was driving herself wild, too. She was so aroused, she knew that if Clive's gorgeous cock so much as nudged her aching clitoris, she would climax immediately. She tried to calm her body by concentrating on his thighs but it was too late.

'Fuck me,' she begged him in a voice that was just loud enough for Lloyd to hear.

With an urgency that matched her own, he bent slightly, slid his hands beneath her buttocks, lifted her off the floor and pushed his cock inside her. Olivia cried out with delight. Her arms were tight around his neck and her legs crossed behind his back as he thrust inside her. How many times did he plunge inside her? Olivia had no idea. Not many. A powerful orgasm swept through her and she screamed out loud, drowning Lloyd's agonised pleas for release.

Still safely held, she flopped against Clive for a few moments.

'Enough,' she whispered in his ear. 'Put me down now.'

'Must I?'

'Yes.' She smiled. 'It's Audrey's turn.'

He set her down on the carpet and both he and Olivia turned their attention to the patient Audrey. They caressed her silky smooth skin until she could bear it no longer. She grabbed them both by the hand, pulled them down to the carpet with her, and embraced them.

It was almost possible to feel sorry for Lloyd, Olivia thought with an inner smile. She couldn't even begin to imagine what he must be going through, but she could tell it was sheer hell for him. The more he pleaded with them to set him free, the more they ignored him. He used all his strength to try and free himself but the straps used to hold him were too sturdy and he only succeeded in moving the chair a few inches.

Olivia delighted in watching Clive use his tongue to excite Audrey. She caressed Audrey's breasts, suckling on nipples that stood out hard and erect. Olivia was highly aroused, possibly due to the fact that Lloyd was watching her.

'Look at Clive's cock, Audrey,' she murmured. 'Isn't it gorgeous? Why don't you sit on it?'

It wasn't a suggestion; it was an order. It was one that Audrey was more than happy to obey. So was Clive. He lay on his back, his phallus looking so inviting that Olivia was already jealous of the pleasure Audrey was about to have.

Audrey sank down on to it slowly, giving short gasps as she did so.

'Olivia!' Lloyd pleaded.

She ignored him. It crossed her mind that they should have had him gagged as well as bound, but it pleased her to hear him begging. She felt she would never tire of the sound.

Without even glancing in his direction, she kneeled on the floor, facing Audrey who was happily moving up and down on Clive's dick. Olivia reached up to kiss Audrey, then began to tease Audrey's nipples with her teeth and tongue. As Audrey bounced up and down, her breasts jiggled provocatively in Olivia's face. Olivia was incredibly aroused. She straddled Clive so that her eager sex could gain pleasure from his tongue. He nibbled playfully on her folds of flesh before delving inside her with his hot tongue. Olivia wriggled back and forth, seeking more pressure.

The sight of his cock sliding in and out of Audrey's sex was incredibly beautiful and she bent forwards, her tongue outstretched, to lick his prick and Audrey's sex at the same time. Clearly enjoying this unexpected pleasure, Audrey slowed the tempo. Olivia sighed with pleasure – she could taste both of them. She lifted her head and kissed Audrey on the lips so that she, too, could enjoy the taste of their union.

It was heaven. They could both enjoy Clive's body while pleasuring each other. Clive was magnificent. He thrust his cock into Audrey's sex while forcing his tongue into Olivia's. All the while, Audrey and Olivia kissed, stroked and fondled each other.

Olivia felt her orgasm build slowly into something incredibly powerful. She groaned aloud and screamed out, grinding herself on Clive's tongue while sucking hard on Audrey's pouting nipple. Her orgasm left her feeling dazed and weak. Lloyd was shouting but she was in such a trance-like state that she couldn't take in the words. Exhausted, she flopped forwards, her head resting on Audrey's thigh.

When she thought she had recovered sufficiently, she got up and threw herself down in a chair. Audrey was still riding Clive joyfully.

'Perhaps it's time Lloyd had some fun,' she murmured playfully. What she really meant was perhaps it was time they had some fun with Lloyd.

She wanted him. She wanted him more than she ever had; more than she would have believed possible. She desperately needed to feel his vibrant tool inside her, filling her, stretching her, taking her to the pinnacles. For a short while though, she was willing to wait.

'Audrey, give Lloyd some pleasure. Not too much, though,' she added.

Audrey was more than willing. She left Clive without a second glance and moved to stand in front of Lloyd. She sat astride him and gradually lowered herself on to his upright shaft. Ignoring his pleas, she took it slowly, wanting to tease him. Olivia watched her edge down on him, taking in only the head of his cock. She watched her friend move up and then down again on her husband's phallus. Audrey's boobs bounced in front of his face and Olivia smiled as he tried, without success, to fasten his mouth around them. He was too tightly bound.

'That's enough,' Olivia said after a few minutes. She didn't want Lloyd to gain any pleasure at all – not yet.

Audrey climbed off him but stood in front of him and began to play with her wet pussy.

'My turn,' Olivia said, her throat dry with aching for him.

He was all hers. She could do exactly as she pleased with him. There was no need to consider his wishes; they didn't concern her. She idly swivelled his chair as she savoured this knowledge.

Just as Audrey had, Olivia sat astride Lloyd and lowered herself, very slowly, on to his stiff, upright cock and, just as Audrey had, she took it slowly. It wasn't that she wanted to tease him so much as she wanted to take the time to savour the slightest movement. How she longed to impale herself on him. But she didn't. She edged down on to his shaft, enjoying knowing that just the head was inside her. She rode him slowly, gently, up and down, and each time she went down, she took in a little more of his prick. He was holding his breath, she noticed, making his chest seem huge. Her muscles worked around his cock and she made slow progress until she had all of him inside her. Still she moved with calculated, slow movements. Still he held his breath. She leaned forwards, rubbing her full, aching breasts against his chest, and wrapped her arms around his neck. At last she was within reach and he seemed determined to take full advantage. He bit her shoulders and neck, and tried to lower his head far enough to reach her breasts. It was impossible, though. Olivia leaned back again, although she still kept her arms around his neck, and continued to ride him tantalisingly slowly. His eyes were closed, and his head thrown back. Apart from soft moans of pleasure as she slowly dropped down on his shaft, he was silent. Even his struggles had ceased.

Olivia was too dazed to even think about what Audrey and Clive were doing. From the sounds they were making, she knew they were enjoying themselves but she didn't care to look. She wasn't interested.

Without conscious thought, she began to move slightly more quickly up and down Lloyd's hot shaft. She had her hands behind her, resting on his knees for support. She swayed from side to side, making him groan. He had endured so much, had been tied in what had to be an uncomfortable position for so long, yet he too seemed willing to accept her slow pace.

She leaned forwards slightly, held her swollen breast in her hand and offered the stiff peak to his lips. He lunged, suckling on it greedily, making grunting noises that excited her almost as much as the sensation of feeling his tongue and teeth on her. She held the back of his head, allowing him no escape even had he wanted one.

She wanted it to last for ever, wanted to experience the slow movements for ever, but it couldn't. She wasn't in control of her body's needs. She made one final slow movement up his shaft until only the tip was inside her, then came down on him with great force. She rode him like a crazed wanton. Faster and faster.

'Untie him!' she managed to gasp. 'Clive, untie him!'

Clive was there in a second, quickly untying the straps that bound Lloyd's ankles.

'Quickly!' Olivia cried.

As soon as Lloyd was freed, Olivia used all her weight to pull them off the chair and down on to the carpet. The chair went crashing over.

'Fuck me, Lloyd. Fuck the living daylights out of me.' She clung to him, biting hard on his ear.

There had been no need to say the words. Olivia knew that he wouldn't have been able to stop himself if he tried. At last he could give vent to his raging hunger. He thrust into her like a man possessed and she matched him. His lips claimed hers in a long, hot, gasping kiss. They couldn't get enough of each other. Backwards and forwards they rode, their bodies in complete, rapturous union. They came together in an explosion so violent, so all-consuming that Olivia no longer knew if she was in this world or the next. They clung to each other, both shaking violently.

Lloyd held her close, his arms wrapped tightly around her, his lips against her neck, until she fell asleep . . .

When Olivia awoke, she didn't know where she was at first. Then, when she realised she was lying in their bed, and realised from the sunlight streaming through the window that it had to be almost midday, she lay for long moments trying to remember how she had arrived there. Had she walked to their bedroom? Had Lloyd carried her? Had she said goodnight to Audrey and Clive? Had they even left? It was no use. She remembered every crazy, passionate moment with Lloyd, but she could remember nothing after that.

She sat up, her brain slowly finding some grasp on the here and now, and realised what it was that had woken her.

'Lloyd?' He was sitting on the bottom of the bed with his back to her, wearing his dressing gown, staring at the television screen. 'Lloyd, what's wrong?'

He switched off the TV and spun round to face her.

'Jeremy's dead.'

Olivia stared at him. She saw the shock in his eyes but still she couldn't take it in. Her brain was still struggling to function normally.

'Dead?' she whispered.

'Yes. He left the club last night and was hit by a car. Died instantly.'

246

'Had he been drinking?' she asked, confused.

'I was probably the last person to speak to him,' he said as if he hadn't even heard her question. He seemed to shake himself mentally. 'Yes, he'd been drinking.'

'God, what a shock.' Olivia wasn't sure what to say. 'Poor Jeremy. Poor Sue and the kids, too. At least it will have been quick and painless, I suppose. He won't have known anything about it.'

Lloyd shook his head.

'He knew about it all right.' He ran his hands across his face in a weary gesture. 'It was no accident, Olivia. He deliberately walked straight in to the path of that car.'

'Oh, Lloyd, you can't say that!' Olivia was horrified.

'I can. I know it. The driver is being treated for shock. He said Jeremy just seemed to step out in front of him.' He sighed heavily. 'Jeremy accepted a gift – a cottage in the country, I gather. You know how edgy folk are about "Cash for Questions". He couldn't face the scandal.' He walked to the window and stared out for a few moments. 'God, what a bloody life!' He suddenly turned to face her, anger burning in his eyes. 'I suppose that's what you want to do with your bloody television programmes – expose people like Jeremy. Bring the bastards to their knees – yes?'

'No.' She spoke calmly. 'I want to expose the lies and corruption, yes, but Jeremy was one of the most honest people I know.'

'Ha! You wait until the tabloids get to work. Every skeleton will be aired for all the bloody world to see. They'll soon make him look like the biggest monster to walk the earth.'

'I don't want to end the careers of –'

'You want to end mine,' he snapped at her.

'No.' She knew he was upset and she made allowances for his anger. 'I want you to start a new one, a more honest one. God, Lloyd, I don't want you ending up like Jeremy, walking in front of a car because someone, somewhere, has discovered that you did something that the whole world will consider to be wrong. And they will. It could be screwing prostitutes, or fucking an old university friend senseless, or voting for something that benefits you financially – it could be anything, you know that.'

He said nothing, just paced the room a couple of times.

'I'd better get dressed,' he said flatly. 'The motions will have to be gone through with a bloody vengeance today.'

'Yes.' She wanted to persuade him to come back to bed. She was eager to enjoy his body again. The time was wrong, though; there would be plenty of time for that in the future. 'Lloyd, I'm so sorry about Jeremy.'

He nodded but didn't speak.

Olivia heard the muted roar of water as he had a shower. She closed her eyes and tried to picture him soaping his body. She remembered falling asleep in his arms last night. For the first time in her life she had felt completely at peace, her body finally satisfied. She wanted more, though.

When he came back to their bedroom he was naked. His skin shone damply and he rubbed at his hair with the towel.

He dressed quickly then stood with his hands in his trouser pockets, looking at her.

'I want that video and the photographs, Olivia. I refuse to be blackmailed by my own wife. I don't think you'd use them against me, but who knows? There's a little craziness in all of us, I suppose. When I get home this evening, I want you, the video and the photographs here.' His voice dropped. 'Either that, or I want none of it – and that includes you.'

Before Olivia could think of a response, let alone

voice it, he had left the bedroom and slammed the door behind him.

Half an hour later, she still didn't know what response she should have given him. To say she was shocked was an understatement. She wasn't entirely sure that she understood him, though. Did he mean he would resign and that he wanted to see for himself that all evidence had been destroyed? Or did he mean to call her bluff? Did he think she would meekly hand over the evidence? If he did, he was very much mistaken.

How, after all that had passed between them last night, could he turn on her like that? It had gone deeper than anything she had ever known. They had made love amid a bond of love and tenderness. Had it meant nothing to him? Surely not.

Chapter Fifteen

While Steve sat to eat his lunch, he switched on the television to catch the midday news. The heroine in the novel he had recently started wasn't just loosely based on Olivia; she *was* Olivia. As he typed up his first draft, he even called her Olivia. Before the manuscript was delivered to his publisher, he would do a search and replace on his computer and change her name to Kate or Sarah or something similar, but it was Olivia. She was on his mind constantly so it came as a shock to see her husband on his television screen. He listened to the news report with growing surprise.

'Well, well, well!' He couldn't believe it.

It was the excuse he needed. For weeks, ever since he had bumped into her in Newcastle, he had longed for some contact with her. Just to hear her voice would be something.

When he was back at his desk, staring at a blank computer screen, he tapped out her number. She answered immediately and he guessed she must be at her desk working.

'Hi, Olivia. It's Steve. I've just heard the news.'

'Hello, Steve. Yes – it's dreadful, isn't it? Jeremy was

such a nice man, too. I know it sounds terribly clichéd, but the country really has lost a good man.'

'Er – yes. Yes, he was.' He frowned, confused. Perhaps she hadn't heard the news, after all. 'So how are you?' he asked, deciding to change the subject.

'Fine, thanks. Busy, but that's nothing new. How about you, Steve? Hard at work on your latest book?'

Even the sound of her voice aroused him. 'Of course.'

He leaned back in his chair with his legs on the desk in front of him, unfastened the metal button on his jeans and lowered the zip. His dick was already stiff. It always was when he started to fantasise about Olivia.

'I'm truly sorry about that business with Carmen,' he said.

'Forget it.' She was abrupt.

'It's difficult to do that. What can I say? She's out of my life now. I just wish it hadn't spoiled our friendship, Olivia. Or has it? Will I see you again?'

There was a long pause before she answered.

'I expect so. Perhaps we'll be on book signings in the same town again.'

'That wasn't what I meant,' he said softly.

'Then what did you mean, Steve? Why do you want to see me?'

He gazed down at himself. Again, thoughts of Olivia had made him rock hard.

'If you could see me now,' he said provocatively, 'you wouldn't have to ask.'

There was yet another long silence and he rubbed his dick as he imagined her thinking about what he had said.

'But I can't see you now,' she said, her voice slightly husky. 'What would I see if I could? Where are you? Tell me. Describe it to me.'

'I'm at my studio,' he said, rubbing himself as he spoke. 'I'm sitting in front of my computer with my legs on the desk. My left hand's holding the phone and my right hand is where I wish yours was. Hang on a minute.' He kept the phone to his ear while he stood up and took his jeans off. 'That's better. I'm wearing just a shirt. What about you, Olivia? What are you wearing?'

'Just a towel,' she said slowly. 'I'm sitting on my bed. I've just had a shower. I was about to go out.'

'Are you in a hurry?'

'Not really.'

'Good.'

He closed his eyes and tried to imagine her. For a moment he wondered if she really was naked except for her towel. It didn't matter; she was naked in his imagination.

'Take the towel away,' he urged her, rubbing his cock hard. God, he was constantly horny these days.

'I have.' Her voice was little more than a whisper.

'Are you touching yourself?'

There was a pause.

'Yes.'

His breath escaped on a long sigh.

'Are your legs open wide?'

'They are now,' she answered shakily.

'Oh, God. I wish I could see you, Olivia. I wish my hand could be where yours is, and I so wish yours could be where mine is. Close your eyes,' he whispered. 'Imagine I'm kneeling between your legs.'

'I am.' Her breathing was fast.

'I wish you were here. A clenched fist is a very poor substitute.'

'I wish I was there too,' she answered immediately.

'What would you do?'

'I'd replace your clenched fist with my mouth –'

His heartbeat was racing. With his eyes tightly closed, he could imagine her mouth closing around his aching cock.

'But I'd like to watch you, too,' she went on, her

breathing shallow. 'I'd sit in front of you, with my pussy open wide, and watch your hand moving over your cock. Then I'd pull you inside me.'

'Oh – is your pussy open wide now?'

'Yes. The phone is cradled against my shoulder. My hands are spreading myself – I'm ready to take you right now.'

Steve cradled his own phone against his shoulder and used both hands on his throbbing penis. Moisture glistened on the head and he smeared it with his thumb.

'With my eyes closed,' she whispered, 'I can almost feel you entering me. Very, very slowly –'

Steve could hardly breathe. Both hands worked vigorously on his cock as he listened to her softly spoken words.

'Listen,' she said quietly.

Steve heard a muffled buzzing sound.

'A vibrator,' she explained. 'Can you hear it?'

'Yes,' he gasped. 'Is it inside you?'

'In and out,' she replied. 'At the moment it's caressing my folds. And now –' the sound changed '– it's inside me. Deep inside me. I'm holding it very tight, imagining it's you.'

'Dear God, I wish I could see you.'

'Just imagine.'

'I am. Believe me, I am. I wish you were standing over me, pushing it inside you. Is it still inside you?'

'Yes.'

He knew it was. He could hear the change in sound every time she pushed it inside herself. Now it was out. Now in. She didn't speak and Steve couldn't. His mind was filled with images as he pumped his swollen dick. He heard her movements become more rapid. He heard her soft moans of pleasure. The only other sounds were those of their rapid breathing.

'I'm going to come all over you,' Steve gasped. 'Are you ready for me?'

'Yes.' She let out a loud scream as she came. 'Yes, yes, yes!'

With a long groan, Steve came. In his mind, his hot semen had landed like tears between her breasts. It came as something of a surprise to find that his own stomach had been the sole recipient of his seed.

It was several moments before Olivia broke the silence.

'We'll meet up some time, Steve,' she said, her breathing still shaky. 'In fact,' she added, 'there are some friends I'd like you to meet. I think you'd like them.'

'Oh?'

'Yes. I'd better go, Steve. I have to get to the bank. I'll be in touch.'

God, he hoped so. Thinking back it was hard to imagine that, on their first meeting, he hadn't found her even slightly sexy. Attractive yes, but not particularly desirable. She had changed dramatically since then though. The day she had visited his studio to confront Carmen, it had taken all his willpower not to tear her clothes from her body and take her there and then. He had been incredibly aroused. Later, he had screwed Carmen instead. Even then he had used his imagination and pretended that it had been Olivia's soft, pliant body he had been plunging inside . . .

On her way to the bank, Olivia wondered what had come over her. It was all well and good having a fun telephone call with Steve, but meeting up with him was a different matter. As Audrey kept saying, she had to be careful. And as for telling him there were people she would like him to meet –

She *would* like him to meet Audrey, Clive and even Lloyd. Steve knew how to enjoy himself and they could have a lot of fun. Audrey would throw seventeen fits if she got to hear that Olivia had invited some two-bit novelist to meet her, but it seemed there was a rule for Audrey and another for the rest of the population. After all, what was Clive? He was simply Audrey's chauffeur. How the devil could Audrey know that he would be discreet? She couldn't.

She pushed the thought from her mind as she entered the bank and obtained the key for her deposit box. She still didn't know what Lloyd intended to do, and she didn't know what *she* intended to do, but she knew she had to do as he said and have the video and photographs ready.

From the bank, she drove out to what she had hoped would be hers and Lloyd's new offices to see how work was progressing.

She counted eight workmen, most of them carrying large sheets of plasterboard around or hammering those sheets to wooden uprights, so she supposed work was going to schedule. It was difficult to tell.

'It might look a mess at the moment,' one of the workers shouted over the noise of hammering to her, 'but you'll be surprised how it all comes together.'

It did look a mess. There were piles of timber lying everywhere, and loose cables dangling from every ceiling and wall. For all that, she still found it exciting to think that soon – hopefully – she would be looking at a fully functional studio.

'I'm sure,' she mouthed back at him.

She stood gazing at the view across the Thames for a while, and thinking about that telephone call from Steve. Right from the start of their friendship, something about him had excited her. Today, speaking to him on the phone and imagining what he had been doing, she had been extremely excited. Perhaps it was dangerous and foolhardy, but she was determined to see him again. She had to; it was that simple.

The noise around her began to grate on her nerves so she drove home. Lloyd wasn't there; she hadn't really expected him to be.

She was restless. Until she heard exactly what he had to say about their futures, there was little she could do. She couldn't plan her reaction until she knew exactly what it was she needed to react to. One thing was certain, she wouldn't give up without a fight. Although after last night, she hadn't expected to have to fight him.

Audrey phoned later that evening and Olivia still couldn't remember her and Clive leaving last night or whether she had said goodbye. Fortunately, Audrey didn't bother to mention it.

'Tony's just phoned me with the news,' she greeted Olivia. 'I've been too busy all day to hear anything.'

'I should have called you,' Olivia said apologetically. 'Poor Jeremy. I can hardly believe it.'

There was a long pause, a pause exactly like the one she had noticed when Steve rang to say he had heard the news. Thinking about it now, she couldn't understand why news of Jeremy's death had meant anything to him. He wasn't a friend of Jeremy's and he wouldn't necessarily know that she and Lloyd were.

'Yes. Yes, a great shame,' Audrey said. 'Is Lloyd there?'

'No, he hurried off when he heard about Jeremy and I haven't seen him since. He should be home soon, I imagine. Did you want him?'

'No. I'll speak to you tomorrow, Livvy. Bye.'

And that, thought Olivia, had to be the shortest conversation she had ever had with Audrey.

It was a little before ten when Lloyd came home. Olivia heard him speaking to Dorothy – he sounded cheerful enough – but she didn't rush to meet him. She would play it by the ear, as Henri would say, and keep quiet until he spoke.

He came into the sitting room, removing his tie and unfastening the top two buttons on his shirt as he did so.

'Hello, darling.' He bent to kiss the top of her head. 'Good day?'

'Fine, thanks.' She was wary. 'You?'

'Yes, fine.'

He poured himself a whisky and Olivia gained the impression he was waiting for her to speak.

'Has your father been in touch?' he asked.

'No. At least, I don't think so. I've been out most of the day.' She wasn't going to tell him she had been to the bank, or that she had been to visit the building around which all her dreams were hanging. 'Dorothy didn't say anything. Why? Are you expecting him to call?'

'Yes, I am. So – where have you been?'

'Shopping,' she lied.

'Did you buy anything?'

'No.'

They were both on edge. Olivia poured herself a glass of wine. She felt as if she was about to stumble her way through a minefield. Lloyd was clever, she wasn't going to forget that, but she could match him. She refused to meekly hand over the evidence.

He glanced at his watch and switched on the television to catch the news broadcast. As might be expected, the first five minutes were taken up with tributes to poor Jeremy. Then, immediately afterwards, a reporter was standing outside the House of Commons talking about 'the shock resignation of Lloyd Standish . . .'

'Lloyd?' Olivia frowned at him. 'What's he talking about?'

'Listen,' he said, smiling.

Olivia did as she was told. Her mind was racing as

Lloyd was interviewed. 'It's something I've been considering for some time,' he said, smiling at the cameras.

'Is it true that you're planning to start a new career in television?' the young reporter asked him.

'It's true that I'm thinking about it,' Lloyd said affably.

'Does your resignation have anything to do with today's tragic news?'

'Nothing at all,' Lloyd said. 'As everyone knows, Jeremy was a valued friend and colleague. He knew my plans.'

'Is your wife pleased, Mr Standish?'

'Of course,' Lloyd answered immediately. 'We both want the chance to spend more time together.'

The report ended. For a few moments Olivia stared at Lloyd.

'I had no idea,' she said, still reeling from the shock.

'I know.' He emptied his glass and rose to his feet to refill it. 'Don't think you've won, though, Olivia. I don't believe you would have used those photos against me.' He stood behind her chair, towering above her. 'Would you?'

'Yes, Lloyd, I would.' But she wasn't nearly as confident as she sounded.

He laughed softly.

'We'll never know,' he answered. 'Where are they?'

'I'll get them.'

She was pleased to have an excuse to leave the tension in the room behind her.

She went to their bedroom and took the video, photographs and negatives from her bedside cupboard. It was tempting to hold a negative or two back, just in case they proved useful in the future, but she didn't. She had what she wanted.

She sank down on the bed as she savoured the knowledge. It might not feel like a victory, but she had exactly what she wanted. She – they – would soon be running their own television production company. She wouldn't end up disliking her husband as intensely as she disliked her father. She wouldn't be married to another of the government's Yes men. She would be sharing her life, and her bed, with the man she loved, the man who desired her as much as she desired him. Never again would Lloyd refer to their marriage as 'a bloody inconvenient marriage of convenience'.

When she took the evidence into the sitting room, Lloyd was stretched out on the sofa looking completely at peace with the world.

'Here you are,' she said, dropping it on his lap.

Ignoring the video, he took the negatives and prints from the brown envelope. He studied them for a long time then swung his legs off the sofa, tore the photographs into tiny pieces and dropped them and the negatives in the large glass ashtray on the coffee table. He reached into his pocket, took out his lighter and set fire to them.

They didn't burn; they simply shrivelled and melted.

When the damage was complete, he yanked the tape from the video case and dropped the tangled mess into the ashtray to meet the same fate.

'That's a shame,' Olivia murmured. 'I enjoyed watching that video.'

'Did you?' Lloyd smiled.

'Yes.'

There was no point in telling him that she'd had a copy of the tape made and that it was safely locked away in her safe deposit box. She had no plans to use it against him; she simply thought it would be pleasurable to watch one day.

'We don't need celluloid, my love,' he murmured as they watched the tape burn. 'After last night, I think I can safely say that we both prefer the real thing. In fact, I would love to sample the real thing right now.' He reached for her hand and pulled her to feet. 'Oh, and I've bought you a present.'

'Oh?'

'Yes.'

It was in the hall, lying on the table next to the phone. Olivia couldn't begin to imagine what Dorothy had thought, assuming she had seen it, but Olivia was delighted. His gift was far better than the most expensive jewellery. It was a short, stiff riding crop.

'Lloyd!' She laughed delightedly. 'Oh, thank you. I can't wait to use it.'

'But not tonight,' he murmured huskily. He was pulling her up the stairs, but he stopped suddenly and pressed her against the wall. 'Everyone enjoyed your little games last night, Olivia, but tonight it's my turn.'

His words thrilled her, as did the way he pressed his body tight against hers. She could feel the power of his arousal hard against her. His breath was warm against her face. She would love to use the crop on him right now, but she could wait. She would love to use it on Steve, too. And Clive.

Yes, she could wait for that particular pleasure, but her body was growing more and more impatient.

'Take me now, Lloyd,' she whispered in his ear. 'Right now. Right here. On the stairs. Fuck me senseless!'

So he did . . .

BLACK LACE NEW BOOKS

Published in September

DEVIL'S FIRE
Melissa MacNeal
£5.99

Destitute but beautiful Mary visits handsome but lecherous mortician Hyde Fortune, in the hope he can help her out of her impoverished predicament. It isn't long before they're consummating their lust for each other and involving Fortune's exotic housekeeper and his young assistant Sebastian. When Mary gets a live-in position at the local abbey, she becomes an active participant in the curious erotic rites practised by the not-so-very pious monks. This marvellously entertaining story is set in 19th century America.

ISBN 0 352 33527 0

THE NAKED FLAME
Crystalle Valentino
£5.99

Venetia Halliday's a go-getting girl who is determined her Camden Town restaurant is going to win the prestigious Blue Ribbon award. Her new chef is the cheeky over-confident East End wide boy Mickey Quinn, who knows just what it takes to break down her cool exterior. He's hot, he's horny, and he's got his eyes on the prize – in her bed and her restaurant. Will Venetia pull herself together, or will her 'bit of rough' ride roughshod over everything?

ISBN 0 352 33528 9

CRASH COURSE
Juliet Hastings
£5.99

Kate is a successful management consultant. When she's asked to run a training course at an exclusive hotel at short notice, she thinks the stress will be too much. But three of the participants are young, attractive, powerful men, and Kate cannot resist the temptation to get to know them sexually as well as professionally. Her problem is that one of the women on the course is feeling left out. Jealousy and passion simmer beneath the surface as Kate tries to get the best performance out of all her clients. *Crash Course* is a Black Lace special reprint.

ISBN 0 352 33018 X

Published in October

LURED BY LUST
Tania Picarda
£5.99

Clara Fox works at an exclusive art gallery. One day she gets an email from someone calling himself Mr X, and very soon she's exploring the dark side of her sexuality with this enigmatic stranger. The attraction of bondage, fetish clothes and SM is becoming stronger with each communication, and Clara is encouraged to act out adventurous sex games. But can she juggle her secret involvement with Mr X along with her other, increasingly intense, relationships?

ISBN 0 352 33533 5

ON THE EDGE
Laura Hamilton
£5.99

Julie Gibson lands a job as a crime reporter for a newspaper. The English seaside town to which she's been assigned has seen better days, but she finds plenty of action hanging out with the macho cops at the local police station. She starts dating a detective inspector, but cannot resist the rough charms of biker Johnny Drew when she's asked to investigate the murder of his friend. Trying to juggle hot sex action with two very different but dominant men means things get wild and dangerous.

ISBN 0 352 33534 3

To be published in November

LEARNING TO LOVE IT
Alison Tyler
£5.99

Art historian Lissa and doctor Colin meet at the Frankfurt Book Fair, where they are both promoting their latest books. At the fair, and then through Europe, the two lovers embark on an exploration of their sexual fantasies, playing dirty games of bondage and dressing up. Lissa loves humiliation, and Colin is just the man to provide her with the pleasure she craves. Unbeknown to Lissa, their meeting was not accidental, but planned ahead by a mysterious patron of the erotic arts.

ISBN 0 352 33535 1

THE HOTTEST PLACE
Tabitha Flyte
£5.99

Abigail is having a great time relaxing on a hot and steamy tropical island in Thailand. She tries to stay faithful to her boyfriend back in England, but it isn't easy when a variety of attractive, fun-loving young people want to get into her pants. When Abby's boyfriend, Roger, finds out what's going on, he's on the first plane over there, determined to dish out some punishment.

And that's when the fun really starts hotting up.

ISBN 0 352 33536 X

If you would like a complete list of plot summaries of Black Lace titles, or would like to receive information on other publications available, please send a stamped addressed envelope to:

Black Lace, Thames Wharf Studios,
Rainville Road, London W6 9HA

BLACK
lace

BLACK LACE BOOKLIST

Information is correct at time of printing. To check availability go to www.blacklace-books.co.uk

All books are priced £5.99 unless another price is given.

Black Lace books with a contemporary setting

THE NAME OF AN ANGEL £6.99	Laura Thornton ISBN 0 352 33205 0	☐
FEMININE WILES £7.99	Karina Moore ISBN 0 352 33235 2	☐
DARK OBSESSION £7.99	Fredrica Alleyn ISBN 0 352 33281 6	☐
THE TOP OF HER GAME	Emma Holly ISBN 0 352 33337 5	☐
LIKE MOTHER, LIKE DAUGHTER	Georgina Brown ISBN 0 352 33422 3	☐
THE TIES THAT BIND	Tesni Morgan ISBN 0 352 33438 X	☐
VELVET GLOVE	Emma Holly ISBN 0 352 33448 7	☐
DOCTOR'S ORDERS	Deanna Ashford ISBN 0 352 33453 3	☐
SHAMELESS	Stella Black ISBN 0 352 33485 1	☐
TONGUE IN CHEEK	Tabitha Flyte ISBN 0 352 33484 3	☐
FIRE AND ICE	Laura Hamilton ISBN 0 352 33486 X	☐
SAUCE FOR THE GOOSE	Mary Rose Maxwell ISBN 0 352 33492 4	☐
HARD CORPS	Claire Thompson ISBN 0 352 33491 6	☐
INTENSE BLUE	Lyn Wood ISBN 0 352 33496 7	☐
THE NAKED TRUTH	Natasha Rostova ISBN 0 352 33497 5	☐
A SPORTING CHANCE	Susie Raymond ISBN 0 352 33501 7	☐

------ ✂ ------------------------

Please send me the books I have ticked above.

Name ....

Address ....

....

....

.... Post Code ....

Send to: **Cash Sales, Black Lace Books, Thames Wharf Studios, Rainville Road, London W6 9HA.**

US customers: for prices and details of how to order books for delivery by mail, call 1-800-805-1083.

Please enclose a cheque or postal order, made payable to **Virgin Publishing Ltd**, to the value of the books you have ordered plus postage and packing costs as follows:

UK and BFPO – £1.00 for the first book, 50p for each subsequent book.

Overseas (including Republic of Ireland) – £2.00 for the first book, £1.00 for each subsequent book.

If you would prefer to pay by VISA, ACCESS/MASTER-CARD, DINERS CLUB, AMEX or SWITCH, please write your card number and expiry date here:

....

Please allow up to 28 days for delivery.

Signature ....

------ ✂ ------------------------